Thursday's Child

Clare Revell

Thursday's Child

Contact Information: titleadmin@pelicanbookgroup.com

All scripture quotations, unless otherwise indicated, are taken from the Holy Bible, New International Version(R), NIV(R), Copyright 1973, 1978, 1984 by Biblica, Inc.™ Used by permission of Zondervan. All rights reserved worldwide. www.zondervan.com

Cover Art by *Nicola Martinez*

White Rose Publishing, a division of Pelican Ventures, LLC
www.pelicanbookgroup.com PO Box 1738 *Aztec, NM * 87410

White Rose Publishing Circle and Rosebud logo is a trademark of Pelican Ventures, LLC

Publishing History
First White Rose Edition, 2013
Print Edition ISBN 978-1-61116-245-5
Electronic Edition ISBN 978-1-61116-244-8
Published in the United States of America

Monday's Child must hide for protection,
Tuesday's Child tenders direction
Wednesday's Child grieves for his soul
Thursday's Child chases the whole
Friday's Child is a man obsessed
Saturday's Child might be possessed
And Sunday's Child on life's seas is tossed
Awaiting the Lifeboat that rescues the lost.

****

The Firefighter's Prayer

When I am called to duty, God, whenever flames may rage;
Give me strength to save some life, whatever be its age.
Help me embrace a little child before it is too late
Or save an older person from the horror of that fate.
Enable me to be alert and hear the weakest shout,
And quickly and efficiently to put the fire out.
I want to fill my calling and to give the best in me,
To guard my every neighbor and protect his property.
And if, according to my fate, I am to lose my life;
Please bless with Your protecting hand my children and my
wife. ~ Author Unknown

Dedication

To all the firefighters who put their lives on the line for us each and every day. You are all heroes.

Special thanks go to
Station Manager Tim Edwards of Norfolk Fire & Rescue for the technical edit of the fire and rescue scenes
Dora and Ernie Hiers for the firefighting advice
Nicole Targett of the Royal Berkshire Fire and Rescue Service
Natalja Paramonova of the London Fire Brigade
Jacqui Broadbridge and Gina McGee of the Reading CPS

Praise for Clare Revell

Monday's Child

Packed with action and laced with faith, this romance builds excitement for the next book in the series of seven romantic suspense novels based on a rewrite of the popular nursery rhyme, Monday's Child. ~ Author, Dora Hiers

Times Arrow

I stand in awe of Revell's ability to pack an entire novel's worth of action and emotion into so few pages. ~ Author, Delia Latham

After The Fire

What a wild ride in *After the Fire*! Ms. Revell created a sweet romance within a beautiful setting, but don't let that fool you. There's plenty of action in this book as Freddie and Jason work to uncover the truth. Just when you think you're near 'The End,' Ms. Revell pulls out a few more surprises. ~ Author, Dora Hiers

Other titles by Clare Revell

Novels
After the Fire
Monday's Child
Tuesday's Child
Wednesday's Child

Novellas
Season for Miracles
Cassie's Wedding Dress
Time's Arrow
An Aussie Christmas Angel

Dollar Downloads
Saving Christmas

Free Reads
Kisses from Heaven

Glossary of Terms Used

Niamh—The heroine's name; is pronounced Neeve.

CPS—Crown Prosecution Service.

Shout—Term UK firefighters give emergency response calls.

BA—Breathing apparatus or air canister firefighters wear in a fire

RTC—Road Traffic Collision or Crash

Dock—this a separate box at the back or to one side of the courtroom where the defendant and a police guard sit. The prosecution and defense barristers sit on either ends of a long bench/desk in front of the judge. Sometimes the dock is behind a glass partition depending on the age of the courtroom or what the defendant is accused of.

Skippy—"Skippy the Bush Kangaroo" was an Aussie TV program in the early 70's. Therefore, all Aussies are affectionately known as Skippy in the fire service.

ED—Emergency Department. Also known as A&E or casualty or the ER.

Resus—This is the large critical care room in the ED in which all patients with life-threatening injuries are taken. It gives the doctors and nurses more room to stabilize and treat patients before transferring them to surgery or ICU.

Ni—Pronounced Nigh; Niamh's nickname

Li—Pronounced Lie; Liam's nickname

Pi—Pronounced Pie; Patrick's nickname. (Hence Niamh calling him 3.14; a play on the math term.)

1

Thursday's Child chases the whole...

But those who hope in the Lord will renew their strength. They will soar on wings like eagles; they will run and not grow weary, they will walk and not be faint. ~ Isaiah 40:30-31

Dressed in her black gown and white wig, Niamh Harkin sat in Crown Court number three and sent up a prayer that she would do her best and that justice would be done.

As senior crown prosecutor for the Headley Cross Crown Prosecution Service, she hoped she was beyond pre-trial jitters by now, but this case could prove to be as long and messy as it was big. The preparation had been awful, with files disappearing, and witnesses vanishing or changing their stories, due to death threats. Having finally got the case to court, she owed it to the victims to ensure the defendant was put away for a long time.

The Jonathan Acre case had made the national news and the public gallery was full to the rafters with reporters, and everyday folk alike. All of them eager to catch a glimpse of the man accused of a string of mafia type murders. The TV and ordinary cameras, prohibited under the current legal system, remained outside the court building. Thus sketch artists drew furiously on their pads to record the images for the evening news and the morning papers.

Niamh was dead against the proposed changes to allow cameras inside the courtroom. The media circus needed to stay well away from criminals and victims alike. They needed to protect the anonymity of jurors who weren't permitted to speak to anyone about the cases they heard at all—even after the case was completed.

The jury was finally sworn in and seated. The introductory speeches concluded. Sitting under the Royal Coat of Arms at the bench, Judge Matheson looked from his papers to Niamh. The gold trimmings on the judge's red gown caught the sunlight streaming through the barred and frosted windows. His long white wig rested on his shoulders, and he regarded her over the top of his glasses for a long moment before pushing them up his nose.

"Mrs. Harkin, you may call your first witness." His gravelly, yet quiet voice resounded in the hushed courtroom.

Niamh stood and nodded. She tapped her papers on the desk in front of her. "My Lord, the crown would like to call Mrs. Gina Luckett."

"No." A shout of protest and shuffling footsteps came from the dock behind her as the defendant leapt to his feet. "You can't call her."

Niamh turned and glanced at him. She picked up the file and opened it.

"Silence in court!" The thunderous roar from the bench echoed in the courtroom. "Mr. Kingsman. If you can't keep the defendant quiet, I will have him removed and jailed for contempt, and the trial will continue in his absence until it is completed."

There was a nod from the defense counsel, and he twisted toward the dock for a moment, gesticulating at his client.

Niamh took her seat and waited apprehensively as Mrs. Luckett came in. The court usher escorted the woman to the witness box. She looked terrified, her shoulders shook, and she kept her gaze down on the floor. Niamh glanced over at the dock to catch the expression of utter panic on the defendant's face, as Mrs. Luckett placed a hand on the Bible and took the oath. Then Niamh rose to her feet and smiled at the witness.

Before she had chance to say anything there was another outburst from the dock. "You can't do this."

Judge Matheson cleared his throat. "Mr. Kingsman, your client has been warned already. I will not repeat myself in my own court room."

"Your Honor, might I have a word with my client?" Miles Kingsman got to his feet.

Judge Matheson nodded. "Two minutes. *If* that's all right with the prosecution?"

"Of course, Your Honor." Niamh sat and twisted her pencil in her right hand, watching the agitated conversation at the dock. The voices were kept low, but from Kingsman's stance, it wasn't what the defense barrister wanted to hear.

Kingsman turned to face the bench. "Your Honor, my client wishes to change his plea to guilty on all counts."

Surprise flitted across the judge's face for an instant before he regained his composure. "Really? He does understand the severity of his action? That it will mean a custodial life sentence? And one in a maximum security prison without the chance of parole for at least forty years?"

"He does, Your Honor."

Niamh was unable to suppress her smile as Judge Matheson promptly dismissed the jury and remanded the convicted man into custody until sentencing the following week. She gathered her papers.

Someone blocked the light in front of her. It could only be one person.

"Is something wrong, Miles?"

"That was a dirty trick, Niamh," Miles Kingsman hissed.

Niamh viewed the angry man before her. "What was a dirty trick? It's not my fault that your client changed his plea. Or are you referring to the fact that I managed to track down the witness someone tried to hide? When I did find her, the paperwork conveniently went missing. I had to hunt high and low for those files, and if I ever find out your office had something to do with their disappearance—"

"Then you'll what? Are you making an allegation here, Mrs. Harkin?"

"Of course not, Mr. Kingsman." Why had he gone all formal?

"If you have any kind of proof—"

"Oh, please. If I could prove it, do you think I'd be standing here having this conversation? I said *if* I ever find out. There is a difference."

"Are you threatening me, Mrs. Harkin?"

Niamh picked up her files and briefcase and got to her feet. "I don't do threats, Mr. Kingsman. I leave that sort of thing to your clientele. I deal in promises and the truth. Now if you'll excuse me, I have a pile of paperwork that needs attending to." She swept past him, wanting nothing more than to de-robe and head back to her office. She'd put the papers in her briefcase in the robing room.

She was almost to the door when a hand grabbed her and spun her around. She gasped, her files flying to the floor. A figure in black shoved her back hard against the wall. She'd have a bruise where her hip caught the edge of the bench. She stifled her instant reaction. "What are you playing at, Miles?"

"Don't start something you're not prepared to finish." Miles's low, deadly voice hissed in her ear. "Or you will regret it."

Niamh stared at the blond man holding her. His icy lavender eyes glinted at her, and his fingers dug painfully into her arm. She swallowed, refusing to show fear. "Now who's making threats?"

"To coin a phrase, that wasn't a threat, Niamh, that was a promise."

Ice slid down her spine. It wasn't the first time she'd been threatened in her career. In fact she'd also received a series of death threats over the few weeks she'd been preparing this case. It came with the job, but this? This was something different. Miles was a colleague, even if they were on opposite sides of the fence.

Judge Matheson's voice came from the other side of the courtroom. "Is everything all right over there?"

Miles nodded and dropped her arm as if it burned. He turned to face the judge, his voice a more normal level. "Everything's fine, Your Honor. Niamh tripped and dropped her papers. I was just making sure she was all right."

Niamh bent to retrieve her files, snatching them off him.

"Mrs. Harkin?" Concern filled the judge's voice.

"Everything's fine, Your Honor." Niamh took the last of the papers and shoved them into her briefcase.

"Very well. Good work by the way."

"Thank you." Niamh stood and looked at him, her fingers tightening on the briefcase. She forced her voice to remain calm. "I should be going."

The judge nodded. "I will see you soon no doubt."

Niamh left the court and headed swiftly down the corridor. Which part of her offhand comment had rattled Miles...unless he or someone he worked with really did have something to do with the files disappearing? He stood to gain much if he'd won the case. He'd only gone into pubic defending because she got the CPS job instead of him.

"Mrs. Harkin, please wait." Footsteps ran down the hallway behind her. A frightened voice called her name. "Mrs. Harkin, could you take a look at this? I received it this morning, and I don't know what to do. I was going to hand it to the police, but now the case is over I thought maybe you should have it instead."

Niamh turned. The last thing she wanted was a conversation with a witness, but she smiled and listened before taking the letter and, promising to read it and take the appropriate action when she got back to her office, hurried on her way. Once in the robing room, Niamh changed out of her robes and hung them back in her locker. She left the court via the back entrance to avoid the press. Taking a few deep breaths of the damp October air, she speed dialed the fire station, hoping Jared would be there.

Despite everything that was happening between them, her husband's voice always calmed her. Besides, she'd promised to tell him how she'd got on in court.

****

"Hey, Jared. Phone."

Jared looked up from the pile of equipment he was cleaning at Cedarwood Fire Station. "Be right there." He stood and brushed the dust from his uniform trousers. Tugging down his navy T-shirt, he ran to the office. "Who is it, Skippy?" he asked the firefighter sitting at the desk.

"Your wife. Make it quick." Pete Callaghan, the duty officer for Green Watch, known as Skippy due to his Australian accent, rose, moving to the side to give Jared some privacy.

Jared picked up the phone. Eight years married and still the sound of Niamh's voice sent a warmth down his spine. He just wished things were better between them. "Hey, Niamh. How did it go?"

"It went good. I won. The defendant changed his plea to guilty."

"I keep telling you that you're scary in those robes." Jared laughed. "Does this mean I can take you out to celebrate tonight? It is tradition after all. Maybe we could talk over dinner."

"Talking isn't going to change anything, but OK. Far be it for me to be the one to break with tradition." She sighed. "We'll go to that new Chinese place you wanted to try. I'll make a reservation for eight fifteen."

"That sounds great. Gives me time to shower and change when I get home."

"Yeah."

The alarm bells began their shrill call to duty ring. Jared wasn't sure if he was relieved or not. "Niamh, I got to run. See you tonight. I love you."

"Love you too, Jarrie Jace." Her voice sounded stilted as she gave him the standard answer. Did she mean it? He dismissed the thought. No matter how rough a patch they were going through, Niamh had never lied to him. She hated liars as much as he did.

Jared hung up, tore the message specifying the details of the fire from the printer, and ran out into the main section, shouting as he went. "Both pump and ladder, house fire at One Five Four Whitgate Road, persons reported." He handed the sheets to the drivers of both fire engines and pulled on his fireproof clothing.

The familiar surge of adrenaline filled him. He loved his job and the fact that what he did saved lives. Climbing in the fire engine, he leaned back in the seat and took a deep breath.

Lord, be with us on this shout. Protect us, help us do our jobs to the best of our abilities. Give us the strength to save lives, to be alert and hear the weakest of cries for help. Enable me to give my best. You alone know what awaits us on this shout. If I am to lose my life, Lord, be with Niamh, and protect and comfort her. Above all, grant me the courage to sacrifice my life in the line of duty without thinking twice about it.

A hand touched his leg. He opened his eyes and looked at Phil Rodgers, the watch manager. "Yes, Sub?" It was kind of funny how they all still called him by his old rank title. The new one of 'Watch Manager A' didn't have the same ring to it.

"The lads noticed you do that every time we go on a shout, but none of them wanted to ask. Tell them what you're doing."

"Praying." He held the gaze of the senior officer.

Phil smiled and gave a warning glance to the

young men. "Nobody's going to mock you for doing that, least of all me. I don't think there are many of us that don't say the Firefighter's Prayer every so often."

Jared nodded and addressed the newer firemen. "And I believe what I'm saying. It's not just words to me."

Skippy nudged him. "Well, let's just hope you don't find out if God really does exist today."

"I know He exists and meeting Him is something I am looking forward to doing. And if it's today, then so be it. If not, I go home to Niamh, and we celebrate being alive and loved by God and her winning another case."

The fire engine pulled to a stop outside a blazing house. "Here we go." Jared tugged his helmet on securely and jumped out.

***

Finishing dead on five, Niamh left the office and headed through the vaulted hallway to the main door. She smiled at the security guard as she signed out. "Goodnight, Duncan. You have a good evening."

"This came for you about half an hour ago. Young girl dropped it off."

"Thank you." Niamh took the envelope. Her name was printed on the front. She ripped it open. Making sure she showed no outward reaction, she smiled and nodded to Duncan. "Goodnight."

Duncan smiled back. "Goodnight, Mrs. Harkin. You take care out there, now. Rain's coming down real heavy."

"I will." Swallowing hard as bile rose in her throat, Niamh turned and headed over to the elevators. The one good thing about the underground car park was not getting wet on days like this. And it was secure, only accessible by CPS staff, another very good thing.

She pressed the down button, grateful she was the only one there. Why was she still getting these letters? OK, death threats went with the job, but this one was worse than the usual. The elevator came and she got in. Just before the doors closed, her boss, Alan Reynolds jumped in. She managed to smile at him, hoping it was enough to convince him she was fine. "You're leaving early tonight, boss."

He smiled, the familiar pain showing now they were alone. "I'm planning on visiting Morag before it gets too late."

"How's she doing?"

"Good days and bad days. She doesn't recognize me at all now." He sighed. "I wouldn't wish Alzheimer's on my worst enemy."

"Give her my best." Niamh screwed the note in her hand into a tight wad.

"I will." He paused, staring at the paper. "What's that?"

"Another one," she admitted reluctantly.

"What does it say?"

"It's just the usual charming threats with a new twist this time. 'Just because Jonathan Acre is banged up, doesn't mean you're safe' et cetera, et cetera, et cetera..."

Alan held his hand out for the note. "OK, that's enough. I'm getting you protection."

"I don't need protection, Alan. I'm a big girl. I can take care of myself."

"Yes, I'm sure you can look after yourself, but you do need protection. I'll organize it now. Was the note delivered here?"

"Yes. Duncan just gave it to me." She handed it to her boss.

Alan put his finger on the hold button as the doors opened. "I will deal with this, check the CCTV, and so on. I want you to go home. Someone will pick you up in the morning. Any more contact and you come straight to me."

Niamh opened her mouth to protest, but he cut her off.

"No debate. I'm not risking the life of the best prosecutor we have. Niamh, you're up for a judgeship and therefore have to take extra precautions and follow the rules. Just let us do our jobs as well as you do yours. Goodnight."

Niamh smiled. She'd learnt a long time ago, that when Alan was in that mood, you just nodded, said "Yes Sir", and left him to it. "Goodnight." She exited the elevator and crossed to her car. The lights flashed, the beep-beep echoing in the silent garage. She got in and shoved the CD into the player. A compilation of hymns from her computer at home, she'd picked ones that made good driving music. Whacking up the volume full blast, she started the car and headed to the exit, singing as she drove.

The windscreen wipers didn't make much impression on the torrential downpour as Niamh drove along the main road. The lights ahead of her were red, and she changed down a gear, water spraying high on each side of the car, as she went through a deep puddle. There was a squeal of brakes behind her. Niamh glanced in the mirror horrified as the black car behind swerved in an arc as it aquaplaned. It slammed into hers, pushing it towards the junction.

A scream escaped her lips as she frantically stamped on the brakes. The pedal went straight to the floor and nothing happened. Out of the corner of her eye she saw a huge lorry bearing down on her.

Her breath caught, heart pounding, stomach plummeting as she knew in an instant the driver wouldn't be able to stop in time. His horn filled the air, echoing, as the impact jolted her forwards, flipping the car into the air and over.

Niamh flung her hands in front of her face as the windscreen shattered. She wasn't quick enough to prevent the glass from flying into her cheeks and forehead. She screamed as red hot pain flooded her body, everything spinning as the car flipped twice more before landing on its side. It teetered back and forth for a moment before finally righting with a spine jerking thud. Then she fell headlong into the blackness of oblivion.

2

Jared sat in the fire engine as it raced along the wet roads, blue lights flashing and sirens blaring. *Forty minutes before the shift ends and we get called to a shout.* A car crash was hardly surprising in this weather. People drove like maniacs, ignoring road conditions and other vehicles and the fact they couldn't see out of the windscreen due to the driving rain. The traffic around them slowed as they got closer to the pile up.

The fire engine stopped and the firefighters jumped out. A police officer came over to them, his yellow reflective jacket pulled over his uniform. Water dripped off his hat. Phil looked at him. "Hey, Pete. What have we got?"

"Five cars and a lorry. From what we can tell, the black car aquaplaned into the red one sending it into the path of the lorry, and it escalated from there. Driver of the blue car is dead. The lorry driver is shaken, but unhurt. The lady in the red car is trapped. She's alive, but non-responsive. The other drivers are trapped, but talking. The paramedics haven't got here yet."

Phil nodded. "Jared, Steve, start unloading. We'll need cutting gear, combi-tools, and the trauma care kit. Jared, I want you to supervise Steve."

"Sure thing." Jared glanced over at the red car. Same model as Niamh's. He pulled open the side of the fire engine and grabbed the equipment. He glanced at Steve, the probationer. "Have you ever done one of these?"

Steve shook his head. "In training, yeah, but not for real."

"There's a first time for everything. Nothing to it. Just remember what they taught you. And if you forget, don't be afraid to ask. No such thing as a stupid question."

Steve smiled. "Thanks."

Jared shouldered the gear. "Don't mention it." He headed towards the smashed vehicles, the oil and petrol from shattered engines and tanks, mixing with the rain water. Other firefighters started running out hose having considered the high risk of fire. He could hear them talking and equipment buzzing, the normal sounds of a shout mixing with what he knew he had to do.

He got closer to the red car. The woman lay slumped over the steering wheel, black hair stained red with blood. He looked at Steve. "Did you bring the trauma care kit?"

"No."

"Go get it. That way we can start treating her until the paramedics arrive."

Steve nodded and ran back to the fire engine. Jared smiled and then moved closer to the car. Though the teeming rain he could make out the start of the number plate in the tangled wreckage. ROO. The rest of the plate was torn off.

It's the same as Niamh's. Don't be silly. There are probably a thousand red cars that start ROO, if not more than that.

He got closer and suddenly the Station Manager, Brad Peters was there, blocking his path. "Jared..."

Jared looked at him. The look on the Guv's face

said it all. *Oh, God, no, please…* "Guv?"

"I'm sorry. It's Niamh."

Nausea and sheer panic filled him. Dropping the equipment to the ground, Jared moved as if in fire or lime. Everything slowed down, voices and sounds echoing. He shook off the arm that held him, his whole being determined to get to her, his eyes fixed on the wreck. Somewhere in that tortured and twisted hunk of metal was his wife.

"N-n-n-i-i-a-a-m-m-h-h-h."

Two firefighters caught him as he neared the car. "No, no. Jared, don't."

"Is she dead?"

Please, God, don't let her be dead.

He looked at them desperate for them to say no.

"She's unconscious."

"I want to be with her." He tore away and strode to the car. People moved around him. More sirens echoed as paramedics and additional fire engines arrived. Reaching the car, he leaned in through the shattered window. "Niamh? Baby, can you hear me?" He touched her face, but there was no response.

An ice cold spear pierced his heart and soul. He couldn't lose her.

God, please, let her be all right.

He looked around. "There's no response. I'm going in." He slipped and slid his way around the car and pulled at the passenger door. It was unlocked and he started to haul it open.

"Wait," Brad said looking at him. "Phil, run a hose out here, just in case. Jared, you don't go in there until the chocks are in position to stabilize the car."

Jared bristled and opened his mouth to object.

Brad cut him off. "I mean it. If you can't do that,

then you sit this one out. Over there in the fire engine. You know the rules, Jared, and I'm not breaking them for anyone. That includes you."

"Yes, Guv." Jared grabbed one of the chocks, helping set it in position so that the car wouldn't move when he entered or when they began cutting into it. It seemed to take forever until the car was secured. He pulled at the passenger door until it opened. Knocking the glass from the seat to the floor, he slid sideways into the car, and somehow managed to squeeze his large frame into the tiny space between the seat and the crumpled dashboard. He pulled off his glove and tucked it inside his jacket. "OK."

He touched the side of her neck and looked at the Guv through the broken driver's window. "Pulse is weak." He ran his hands down her body. "The dashboard is pushing down on her and the steering column is crushed against her legs. It's going to be a 'mare getting her out." He pulled his hand up quickly as it got wet. He looked at it. Red blood dripped from his fingers. "She's bleeding out. I can't tell where it's coming from. I think she's time critical."

The Guv turned away, barking instructions.

Jared tuned him out and wiped his fingers on his fire kit. He knew she was unconscious, but also knew hearing was the last sense to go. "OK hon, I'm going to put my hands around your neck to keep it steady. I need you to stay still for me. Then we're going to cut the car to pieces so we can get you out."

Steve looked in at him through the window. "Guv says she's your wife. The lads want me to tell you they'll not rest until she's out and safe."

Jared looked at him. "There are other people trapped, too. I don't want any favors done on my account."

Skippy laughed from the other side as he put a thick fire retardant cloth over Jared and Niamh. "You ought to be grateful she's unconscious, mate. Otherwise she'd hit you for that comment. Like that will happen, anyway. She's one of us. We'll get her out. There are other crews working on the other cars. We're going to smash all the glass first, then cut off the windscreen, and then the roof so the paramedics can check her over and we can see where this steering column is at."

"OK, I got her." Jared held Niamh gently as his colleagues started working on the car. She still hadn't said a word, and her pulse slowed each time he took it.

God, please overrule in this situation. Guide the hands of those working to free the people trapped. Not just Niamh, but all of them.

He looked down at his wife. "Niamh, can you hear me?"

There was still no response. The car suddenly jerked, and a blast of cold air and rain flooded the too warm compartment as the roof came off and was lifted away. The roar and chugging of the spreaders stopped, the silence almost as deafening.

The cover pulled back and a man in a green fluorescent jacket stood there. "I'm Ray Harper, one of the doctors from Headley General ED. I came out with the paramedics."

Jared nodded. "Jared Harkin. I'm her husband, but here because I'm working. I wasn't expecting this when we got the shout."

"I'm sorry, mate. What's her name?"

"Niamh. She's thirty-six, not allergic to anything, perfectly healthy."

"Is she pregnant?"

Jared shook his head. Children weren't an option now, for either of them. After Dayna they'd both said no more. "No." He held Niamh's neck firmly as Dr. Harper started checking her over. He looked down at his wife. "Niamh, please wake up."

Phil tapped Jared on the shoulder. "I need to know how badly she's trapped. You up to doing that?"

Jared nodded. "Put a collar on her so I can move my hands."

Once that was done, he reached down feeling between the steering column and Niamh's legs. He closed his eyes for a moment, his stomach dropping. It wasn't good. No, make that it was worse than he'd first realized. He glanced up at the others. "The whole dash has moved. There's a centimeter, maybe two fingers width at the top. Nothing below mid-calf." He looked at his hand as he pulled it free. "Blood loss is increasing. We're just going to have to do it."

Dr. Harper finished setting up the IV. "You release that dashboard and steering column, and she may just bleed out. If you don't know where the blood's coming from she could crash almost instantly."

Despair flared within Jared, making him short tempered. "I know that! I'm no medic, but from what I can tell, it could be her femoral artery. We don't have an option as she'll bleed out anyway." He looked at Brad. "Tell them to do it, Guv. We delay and we lose her."

Brad held his gaze for a long moment, and then nodded. "OK. Maybe it's time for more of your prayers."

Jared looked at him. "I haven't stopped since we got here."

"Good. Out you get. Now."

"But, Guv—"

"Out. Skippy will sit with her."

Jared nodded and climbed out. He caught Skippy's arm. "Take care of her."

"Of course." Skippy clambered into the remains of the car.

Jared stood as close as he dared and kept praying while Dr. Harper made his final check. Rain dripped off his helmet, masking the tears in his eyes.

Dr. Harper turned back to the firefighters. "OK. If you're going to do this, start now. She's stable, but I can't say for how long, so move quickly."

Jared watched on tenterhooks as his colleagues worked to remove the steering column. With a crunch and shriek of twisted metal it finally moved.

Skippy raised his hand and yelled. "Doc! She's crashing…"

Jared's heart sank into his boots. He started to run, but strong arms held him back. Things slowed down. His hands waved and his voice echoed as he desperately tried to get to Niamh.

****

Voices permeated the thick fog surrounding her. Niamh struggled to wake despite the stabbing pain, and she moaned as she fought to open her eyes. It would be better to keep sleeping, and she closed her eyes again. She was drowning in a sea of pain and darkness.

Distorted images flooded her mind. A car spinning, a lorry, brakes squealing behind her. A thud as her brake pedal uselessly hit the floor over and over again. Children frolicked in a playground, laughing and calling to each other. A young child sat on a swing, her long blonde hair spreading out behind her as she flew through the air. "Faster Mummy. Make me go faster. I want to fly."

A small white coffin, bearing a gold plaque engraved with the name Dayna, and an unbearable ache filled her heart, then more pain and so much noise. A weight suddenly lifted. Someone shouted from a great distance. Was it her name? She didn't know. For a moment there was darkness, and then gentle arms surrounded her, bearing her towards a bright white light.

She'd never known such peace and stillness, yet at the same time there was a rustle and flapping like wings on a bird. Another voice spoke, a kind and gentle voice that filled her with peace and hope, cradling her in love. "It's not your time, go back to him. He needs you."

Darkness crept over her again and the pain returned. The voices echoed, something beeped in her ear. "We got her back. We need to move now."

"Niamh, Niamh just hang on, love. Don't leave me."

She tried to open her eyes, but they were just too heavy. She wanted to go home. Things swam again, and she was back in the park. Tall trees swayed in the wind, leaves rustled and cast dappled shadows on the ground. The little girl skipped at her side, holding her hand.

A male voice whispered in her ear. "Don't leave me, Niamh. I love you far too much to ever let you go."

Then she could smell burning and smoke, and images of a coffin draped in a Union Flag filled her mind. A voice echoed in the growing darkness.

I will wait for you. I will always wait for you. And if you don't remember me when you come back, then I will find you, and make you fall in love with me again and never let you go.

****

Jared paced outside the Resus room in the Emergency Department. He felt sick with worry and constant prayers wound their way to the One who was always listening. It hadn't worked before, but maybe this time it would be different.

Running footsteps came up behind him and someone called his name. "Jared."

He turned to find himself enveloped in a pair of arms. "Liam, you're here. But I didn't call you yet. How did you know?"

Liam Page, Niamh's twin brother, looked at him, his eyes red rimmed and full of pain and emotion. "I knew. I just knew. I was just picking Jacqui up from work and had the most awful pain in my chest, stomach and legs. She drove us back to my place. I was going to call you when the police arrived on my doorstep. How is she?"

"They won't tell me. She crashed once on the scene, and again in the ambulance on the way here. There's a whole team or two in there working on her, trying to stabilize her before surgery. I can't lose her, too, Liam, I just can't—"

He broke off, aware of how selfish that sounded. Liam of all people understood just how he felt, having seen Sally, his first wife murdered in front of him.

Liam just hugged him. "Do they know what

happened yet?"

"I don't know. The police would have told the Guv when we arrived, but I didn't pay much attention. Could be the weather or she hit a puddle and aquaplaned or someone else did, but somehow her car shot the lights and ended up in front of a lorry. There wasn't much left of it when we cut her out."

Liam looked at him closely. "*We* cut her out? Jared, you're in uniform. Were you on a shout when they rang?"

Jared looked at him, as tears slowly tracked down his cheeks. "We got the call. Mine was the first crew on the scene. The Guv let me sit with her, but she didn't wake up. There was so much blood. I think one of her legs is broken, not sure what other damage there is. It could be anything as the dash and steering column were crushing her. I have never felt so helpless on a shout before, ever. All my training just…All I could think of was her and losing her."

Liam hugged him tightly. "I'm so sorry. What happens now? Will there be an investigation?"

"Yeah. SOCO are going to look at all the cars involved." Jared looked at him. He didn't need to explain. The Scenes of Crime Officers only attended when foul play was suspected. "They would anyway, in light of who she is, but under the circumstances they can't take any chances."

Liam's expression darkened. "SOCO? I can understand the Road Traffic people, but *forensics*? They think someone tried to kill her?"

"It's a possibility they want to rule out. She's been getting death threats at work." Jared looked back at the door. "I just wish they'd let me in there. I hate all this waiting. I feel so useless."

"You're not. You did your part. Now let the docs do theirs."

"I should call Patrick and Mum and Dad." Jared realized with a sickening thud that he hadn't told Niamh's older brother or her parents. Or his parents.

Liam pulled out his phone. "Let me call them and Jacqui and then we'll sit somewhere quiet and pray. Ask God to put His healing hand on her and the medics in with her."

3

A loud beeping sound roused Niamh from the black pit which ensnared her. Before she could turn it off someone else did. Her eyes flickered open. A stark light, so bright it hurt, assailed her, and she screwed her eyes shut, flinging her left hand up to protect them. Pain shot down her arm. Cautiously she opened her eyes and looked at her hand. An IV needle protruded from the middle, the tubing snaking somewhere way above her head. Tape surrounded the base of her ring finger and what appeared to be a crocodile clip sat on her index finger. She wriggled her fingers. That caused another stab of pain, but at least they moved.

She wrinkled her nose at the tangy clinical smell filling her nostrils. Machines beeped and hissed. Taking a deep breath, she did a quick mental inventory of her body. Ribs hurt, there was something heavy on her left leg, most likely a cast. She ran her tongue over cracked and dry lips. There was a tube in her nose, but thankfully it didn't go down her throat. *What happened? Did someone pull me through a hedge backwards?*

Something was touching her right hand. Glancing down, she counted eight fingers. Four suntanned fingers laced firmly into her pale ones. Her gaze ran from the tips of the neat, clean nails along the long tanned fingers, up the arm and across the broad shoulder to the face of the hand's owner. Her breath caught.

Fast asleep and snoring softly beside her in a hospital chair, sat the most stunning man she'd ever set eyes on. Short, scruffy dark hair fell over his forehead and five o'clock shadow outlined his strong chin and cheek bones. A navy blue T-shirt with the fire service logo hugged his broad chest. Strong biceps protruded from the short sleeves. A phone and keys hung off the belt that looped through the top of his uniform trousers, and his fireproof coat slung over the arm of his chair. One leg crossed over the other showing his calf length boots.

As gorgeous as he was, she didn't know him from Adam and didn't want him holding her hand. She pulled it free, and raised her brows when he didn't stir. He was a sound sleeper. Tearing her eyes away from his handsome features, she glanced around the rest of the room. Not that she could see much from flat on her back. Women in uniform moved between the other beds, each with as much equipment as there was next to hers.

The man beside the bed stirred, and she turned to look at him, to find herself drowning in the most incredible pair of hazel eyes. A smile shot across his face, his eyes lighting, and a dimple showing on his left cheek. "Hon, you're awake." His deep voice sent shivers down her spine. His glance moved to the end of the bed. "Nurse, Niamh's awake."

Her eyes widened, and her heart stopped for an instant. *Hon?*

Who was this man calling her hon?

His hand took hers again and squeezed it. "I was so worried. I thought I'd lost you." He leaned forwards and kissed her cheek, his lips soft and his breath warm against her skin.

She shivered. This wasn't right. She wanted Liam. Her twin brother would protect her. Or her older brother, Patrick. She pulled her hand back and pushed into the bed as much as she could. The weight on her leg and pain in her abdomen prevented her from getting up and running, so instead she wrapped her arms protectively around her stomach. "Don't touch me. Where's Liam? Why isn't he here?"

Consternation filled his eyes and his eyebrows furrowed. "Niamh, baby? What's wrong?"

Another voice came from the other side of the bed and dark fingers closed on her wrist, taking her pulse. "Hello, Niamh. How are you feeling?"

Looking up past the blue uniform into the nurse's face, Niamh took a deep shuddering breath, and instantly regretted it as pain pulsed in her chest. "Everything hurts. Where am I?"

"You're in hospital. You're going to be OK."

"What happened?"

"Don't you remember?" The nurse smiled.

"No. I don't want to be rude, but if I knew, why would I ask?"

The nurse laughed lightly "That's a very good question. You were in a car crash yesterday. You've been sleeping for the best part of a day."

Niamh's stomach plummeted and panic filled her. *What car crash?* What was she going on about? *Why don't I remember?* Alarms blared as her breathing and heart rate spiked, sending the monitors into overdrive. The pinging from one of the machines sky rocketed until the nurse cancelled it.

"Just relax. Everything's going to be OK." Her voice oozed calmness, her soft touch pushing Niamh back onto the bed. "Let me go and fetch your doctor.

He'll explain everything to you. I'll be right back."

"Can you ring my brothers? I want Liam or Patrick here."

The nurse nodded and headed over to the desk, where she picked up the phone and spoke rapidly.

A hand touched Niamh's arm making her jump. She turned her head to look at the man sitting beside her. "Niamh, baby, what's wrong? You know I'm not going to hurt you." Concern filled his deep voice.

Pulling her arm away, she couldn't stop shaking. Once Liam got here everything would be all right. She tried hard to remember the name of the man sitting there, but she couldn't. He must know her if his insistence on touching and pet names were anything to go by.

Footsteps thudded over to the bed and she opened her eyes. A tall grey-haired man with glasses stood there. He wore a white coat, with stethoscope slung around his neck and dangling over the name badge which confirmed him as the promised doctor. "Hello, Niamh. I'm Dr. Anders. How are you feeling?"

She pushed a hand through her hair. "Sore. Why's this man here and not my brother?"

The firefighter next to her took a sharp breath. "Hon?"

She looked sideways at him. "Please don't call me that. I have no idea who you are."

Shock resonated in his eyes and his jaw dropped. "I'm sorry? You don't you know who I am?"

"No, I don't." She looked back at the doctor. "I don't remember him at all. The only thing I do know, is when I woke, he was holding my hand."

Dr. Anders looked at her, then across at the firefighter, concern showing in his steel grey eyes.

"Would you mind waiting outside while I examine your wife?"

Niamh swallowed and choked. *"Wife?"* She didn't know who this guy was. What other surprises waited for her? Maybe she was still asleep and in some kind of weird dream.

"Yes, Niamh. You're my wife. I'm Jared. We've been married for eight years." He tore his anguished eyes from her and looked at the doctor. "Why can't she remember? I want to stay while you check her over."

She shook her head. "No. I'd like you to leave. Please." He claimed to know her intimately, but she had no idea who he was and was most definitely not stripping off in front of him. It'd be embarrassing enough in front of a strange doctor.

Fortunately the doctor seemed to agree. "I think it would be best if you waited outside, Mr. Harkin. I'll come and speak with you when I'm done."

Jared scowled, sighing as he pushed up from the chair. He snatched up his coat and crossed the room with heavy steps, pausing only to wash his hands before leaving the ward.

The coat slung over his arm swayed as he left. Was she really married to him? Did the sticking plaster on her left hand hide a wedding ring? The ward door shut and she turned her full attention to the doctor. "I know my name is Niamh and my brothers are Liam and Patrick. Can you tell me a bit more before you start poking and prodding me?"

"Sure." Dr. Anders perched on the edge of the bed next to her, her notes in his hand. A nurse pulled the curtains around the bed. "The ID in your bag, your brother and husband all confirm you're Mrs. Niamh Frances Harkin. You're thirty-six and live here in

Headley Cross and work for the CPS. Your birthday is February the twenty-ninth. You're married, no children. Your husband is the man who just left, Jared Harkin."

"He's a firefighter. I know that from his uniform, but I don't know him. I don't understand. It's like there's a big hole in my mind." She frowned.

Thirty-six? That's not right. I'm sure it's not. I'm not that old, but then how can I be sure of anything?

"OK."

"What I don't understand is how do I know some things and not others? Like I know I have an IV in my hand and you're a doctor and what things are called. I know I have a twin called Liam and an older brother, Patrick, but not who that man is. And I'm sure I'm not thirty-six. Do you have any idea why?"

Dr. Anders smiled. "It's not unusual for there to be some memory loss after a head injury. You were in a very nasty traffic accident."

"See I don't remember that either." She lay there, studying his face and body language, trying to take everything in. "And the rest of my family?"

"All fine as far as I know. We'll give Liam a call and let him know you're awake." He took her wrist again as he gazed at the readouts on the monitors. "What's the last thing you remember?"

"Other than waking up a few minutes ago with a total stranger holding my hand?" She thought for a moment. She hadn't lost her sense of humor, which she guessed was a good thing—although Liam probably wouldn't agree. "A blue light, sirens, it was raining. There was a voice. I remember being cold and wet. Umm…Fireworks. Lots of fireworks. There was a child, a little girl on a swing and a funeral with a flag over the coffin, but I don't know. It could have been a dream. Everything is so foggy. That's it, I'm afraid."

"No worries. I need to check you over."

"Sure." She lay still as the doctor pulled back the covers and started examining her. "Was anyone else in this car crash? Or just me?"

"There were several cars and a lorry involved. The police want to speak to you, but that can wait until tomorrow."

"Not that I can remember anything to tell them. How badly hurt am I? And I want the truth, none of your doctor speak or soft coating it."

"You coded twice. Once at the scene, and again in the ambulance on the way here. But we've had you on a monitor ever since and your heart is perfectly normal and steady. You have a lot of bruises, especially to your chest and abdomen. As well as finger shaped bruises on your left arm. Someone must have held you quite firmly to have caused them. Those were probably pre-accident, but no one seems to know how they were caused. You have a compound fracture of your left leg, which we repaired surgically, along with the damage to your femoral artery. You also dislocated your left knee, so the cast is a full length one from your toes to the top of your thigh."

She scrunched up her nose. "That's going to make walking and bathing interesting. Do I have a metal plate in my leg?"

He smiled wryly. "Yes, so you'll have to warn the airports before you travel. We'll give you a note to put in your current passport and a letter for the passport agency. You'll be on crutches for between four and six weeks. Even with them, you can't put any weight on your leg until the physio clears you to do so. We had to remove your spleen, but most people manage pretty well without it."

"What about bathing? I can't avoid washing for weeks."

There was a wry smile on his face as he checked the stiches. "My wife asked the same thing when she dislocated her kneecap. Cover the cast in a black bin liner, to keep it dry when you shower. Or strip wash."

She winced as his gentle touch sent white hot pain shooting through her tortured body. "That hurts."

"It will for a while, but I'll get the nurse to give you some pain meds."

"Thanks." Her mind went back to the firefighter. Surely she'd remember if she were married to someone as drop dead gorgeous as Jared? Wouldn't she? It was like turning on the TV to find the film had already started, the hero in the middle of a heavy duty action scene, and she had no idea what was going on. "Why can't I remember?"

"You had a severe concussion. That bump to your head was enough to knock you out for a while. It's not uncommon to lose your short term memory."

"Yeah, but this isn't just what happened yesterday. If that firefighter is right and we've been married for eight years, then it's everything in the last eight years if not longer, isn't it?"

Dr. Anders nodded. "And because of that, I want you to see a neurologist in the morning."

"Wait a minute. I'm not crazy. Just because I don't remember a few things, doesn't mean I need a shrink."

He smiled. "A neurologist, not a psychiatrist. A neurologist is a brain specialist. It's standard procedure in cases like yours. He'll run a few tests, should be able to give you an idea of when you'll start remembering things again. Meanwhile, would you like your husband to come back in?"

She shook her head. "No. I want my brother. Not a total stranger."

"OK. Try to get some rest. If you have any worries get the nurse to give me a shout."

"OK, thank you." She leaned back as Dr. Anders pulled open the curtains, his swift long strides taking him to the nurse's station. He put the file on the desk and made a few notes before picking up the phone.

She turned her attention to the ceiling, trying to remember something concrete, anything at all about the last eight years and the tall man she was married to, but there was just a big black hole where her memory used to be. She rubbed a cautious hand over her stomach. It hurt more since he had poked and prodded and changed the dressing.

The nurse reappeared. "I'll bring you the pain meds and something to drink. Tea, coffee or water?"

"Tea please. Milk, two sugars." Niamh smiled. *Silly, I can remember that, but not important things.*

"Sure." The nurse left and she leaned back against the pillow. A noise from the door caught her attention and she twisted her head to see what was going on.

Dr. Anders appeared to be having a very heated discussion with Jared. He didn't like what the doctor told him, his facial expression and hand movements made that all too clear, before he turned and walked away, his shoulders down and his head hanging.

For a moment she felt guilty for not letting him back in, then pushed it aside. Her fingers went to the base of her throat, in what seemed to be an automatic movement, but there was nothing there. It felt empty, as if there was something missing there too.

"Are you looking for your necklace? It's right here." The nurse put the cup down on the side. "Let's sit you up a little so you can drink your tea, then I'll get it for you."

Pain flooded her as the nurse gently began helping her sit up. Her skin grew cold and clammy, stars flashed in front of her eyes and she screwed them tight. She pushed back into the pillows, the pain easing a little, only to be replaced by wave after wave of dizziness.

The monitor chimed and the nurse cancelled it, her cool fingers taking Niamh's wrist. "You OK, Niamh? You're not going to pass out on me now, are you?"

"I'm really dizzy." She opened her eyes. "But, no, I don't think I'm going to faint."

White teeth shone in the nurse's dark face as she smiled. "Good, glad to hear it. Here's your necklace." She reached over to the drawer and pulled something out, before placing a gold cross on a delicate gold chain, adorned with a single diamond into Niamh's hand.

Turning it over Niamh ran her fingers over the initials engraved on it. "NFH..." A warm feeling of belonging and love and something else flooded her.

The cross lay in a red box, soft white cotton wool surrounding it. A card sat to one side, a verse on it. 'Whilst we were yet sinners, Christ died for us...'

"Romans five verse eight." She looked back down at the cross, trying to bring back the memory or whatever it was. "Could you put it on for me, please?"

"Sure." The nurse fastened it around Niamh's neck. "Your husband says you never take it off. It looks really pretty. OK, your tea and pain meds are on the side. I'm right here if you need anything."

"Thank you." She picked up the cup and took a sip. Letting the hot liquid slide down her throat, she finished it in several long swallows, taking the meds at the same time. She put the cup down and leaned back against the pillows. It was raining, huge drops pounded against the window. She closed her eyes, listening to them, the sound mixing with the beeping and hissing of the machines.

How long will it be before my memory comes back? Right now I'm here in this moment of time. No past, no future, just a present.

Her fingers went to the cross around her neck, playing with it. That had triggered something, but it wasn't enough. She needed more.

4

Jared paced the hallway while the doctor was in with Niamh, as he had done countless times over the past day. He knew there were risks of brain damage with every head injury, he saw way too much of that in his line of work to doubt it, but he'd hoped and prayed she'd wake and be fine. But she hadn't.

Lord, she looked at me in horror, pulled back from me scared. Why is she so frightened of me? We've known each other nine years, been married for eight, happily for the first six of those eight. I'd never hurt her, she knows that, yet she looks at me if I'm a total stranger. I don't understand why.

He turned and caught sight of Dr. Anders coming out of the ward. He moved over to him. "Doctor? How is she? What's wrong with her?"

The doctor's calm voice did nothing to reassure him. "I'm recommending she sees a neurologist first thing in the morning. Right now she remembers nothing recent to waking up here. She's forgotten at least eight years. That could be temporary or it could be longer lasting."

No…That's why she doesn't know me.

Jared took a deep breath, his heart sank into his stomach, and his gut twisted around it, squeezing it to the point of breaking. He struggled to get the words out. "Are you saying she might never remember me?"

"It's still too early to tell, but it's a possibility. We'll know more once she's seen Dr. Coleridge in the morning."

"Is it all right if I go and sit with her?"

"She doesn't want you in there right now. She's asked for her parents and brothers."

"What?" Jared clenched his hands tightly. A hot stab filled his soul as if a sword plunged into it. His voice rose. "She's my wife. I have every right to sit in there with her."

"Mr. Harkin, I know you're upset, but raising your voice isn't going to change things. She doesn't know who you are. I suggest you go home and get a good night's sleep yourself. She's out of danger now."

"I don't want to go home. I want to sit with my wife."

"She's my patient and right now she needs peace and quiet and rest. Go home, and come back tomorrow."

Jared's hands fell to his sides and his shoulders slumped, the fight leaving him. He turned and left. It was better to go voluntarily than have them call security and be thrown out. Besides, he was in uniform and didn't want to bring disrespect on the department. His heart pounded miserable and heavy, and felt like it was breaking. Slow footsteps took him from the building, into a world covered by a heavy, leaden sky and over to a bench.

Heavy rain drops fell. He slid his jacket on, pulling up the collar.

Sinking onto the bench, Jared closed his eyes. Tears welled up, but he refused to let them fall. He was stronger than this. His shoulders shook and for a moment he was afraid he was going to lose the battle waging within him as he struggled with the force of emotion bearing down on him.

Not here, not now. I need to keep a clear head, let the others know she's awake. God, please overrule here. Why give her back, just to take her away again? I'll ring Liam, then go to work. They're not expecting me, but I'll go in anyway.

Jared pulled his phone from his belt and then jumped as a hand fell on his shoulder. He looked up at the tall, dark haired, bearded man standing under an umbrella and smiled wryly. "Hey, Liam. Sometimes I wish I had your sixth sense. I was just about to call you. Niamh woke about an hour ago."

Liam sat beside him. "The hospital rang and told me. They asked me to come in. It's great."

"I guess so." Jared studied his finger nails. "She doesn't remember anything. Oh, she remembers you, Patrick, Mum and Dad, but that's it. She doesn't know who I am. She even pulled away from me, told me to go away." He twisted his wedding ring viciously "Do you have any idea how that feels? To have your wife shy away from your touch, look at you with wide, terrified eyes and have her beg you not to touch her?"

Jared paused, trying to regain control. This wasn't Liam's fault. "The doctor doesn't know if this is a short term thing or a long term thing. She may never remember me."

Liam's smile faded. "No, they didn't say anything about that. Are they running tests to find out why?"

Jared shrugged his shoulders. "She's seeing a neurologist in the morning. They want her to rest for now."

"Then let's go back to your place and have coffee."

Jared scoffed. "Coffee? I'd rather something stronger." He rubbed his hands over his face. "That shows how stressed I am. I haven't touched the booze since I met Niamh and God. Not even socially over dinner. I'm sorry. I wouldn't drink in front of you anyway. That wouldn't be right. How long have you been on the wagon now?"

"One hundred days." Liam smiled wryly. "So we'll have coffee. Actually the way you make it, I'm surprised you don't get hung over on it."

Rolling his eyes, Jared shook his head. "Thanks, but I'm going to work. The shift starts in a little over an hour. It was you she was asking for."

"You're in no condition to work a night shift." Liam looked at him sternly.

"You're not my boss. Besides, it might be a quiet night and we just sleep 'til morning."

"And if it isn't?"

"I'll manage." Jared stood. "I should leave. Go up and see her, she was asking for you. She kicked me out. They said they wanted her to rest. Or maybe she just doesn't want to see me again. Either way I'm outta here."

Liam caught his arm. "Before you go, bro, let's turn this over to God. He knows how this will work out even though we don't."

"OK." Jared flopped down and listened as Liam prayed. When he finished, Jared hugged him. "I'll ring you tomorrow when I wake. Let the nurses know I'll be at work. They can reach me there if need be."

****

Niamh lay on the bed looking at the rings on her finger. She'd pulled off the tape after the doctor left and hadn't taken her eyes off them since. Why didn't she remember Jared?

The nurse came over and smiled. "Your brother is here. Want to see him?"

"Yes, I most definitely do." She glanced over at the man the nurse beckoned across. He wore a dark suit with a blue shirt and tie. He smiled as he crossed the room. His dark brown hair and beard were short and tidy.

Beard? Since when did Liam wear a beard? He hated them. Something wasn't right. He looked older and careworn, but it was still him. Finally, someone she knew.

He held a bunch of flowers in one hand and offered her the other. "Hi, Niamh. I'm—"

"Liam!" Niamh exclaimed. She held out her arms and grabbed him, pulling him into as tight a hug as her broken body would allow. "I'm so glad you're here."

Liam hugged her back gently. "How are you, sis?"

"Pretty banged up according to the doctors. I've broken my leg, got a few cuts and so on. They said I crashed my car on the way home from work, but I don't remember." She pulled him to sit next to her. "It's so good to see you. You've no idea how scary it is, not knowing anyone."

"I'm here now." He set the flowers on the side.

"I'm so glad you are. Liam, there was a man here. A firefighter. He…" she broke off, her cheeks burning. "He claims to be my husband. He said we'd been married for eight years, but I don't know who he is."

"I just saw Jared outside. He said you didn't remember him. I have some photos in my wallet if you'd like to see them."

Niamh nodded, taking a closer look at him. Was that grey hair around his temples? "OK, but answer me one question. The doctor said I was thirty-six, but that doesn't sound right. We're not that old surely."

Liam smiled as he pulled his wallet from his inside jacket pocket. "You never were happy with your age, but yes, you are thirty-six. So am I." He handed her the photos.

Niamh took them, her gaze still fixed on his hair. "When did you start to go grey?"

Liam pushed his fingers through his close cropped hair. "The grey came through a couple of years ago. It's called teaching, amongst a couple of other things."

Niamh looked at the pictures. *This is infuriating. Remembering some things, but not others. Remembering trivial stuff, but important stuff just isn't there anymore. I hate it.* "We all got old. That's Patrick, you and me."

Liam nodded. "And despite being twins we were born on different days."

"I know when my birthday is," she huffed. "But we celebrate on your birthday, February twenty-eighth, as I only get a birthday once every four years. So there's no way I'm thirty-six." She glanced up at him. "Because even if you're right and I lost several years, it still only makes me nine, Li."

He laughed. "Nothing changes, Ni."

She reached up, rubbing her fingers along his chin. "You have. What's this? Since when did you grow a beard?"

"A while ago now. It hides a multitude of things I'd rather people not see."

She glanced down at the last photo of an older couple, both with grey hair and glasses. They were smiling at the camera, holding each other's hands tightly. "Mum and Dad look happy. But they're old, Li. What's happened to me?"

Liam looked at her. "The doctor said the amnesia

is caused by the head injury. What's the last thing you really remember? Doesn't matter when or what it is."

Niamh took a deep breath and closed her eyes. "Before I woke up here? Ummm…" She smiled. "Bonfire night. We'd all gone to the church bonfire. There were the most amazing fireworks and we ran out of petrol on the way home. Dad had to walk miles to a garage for some petrol while we sat in the car and sang stupid songs. And because you had the Walkman, you did air guitar so we'd know when to come in with the next verse."

Liam's face fell slightly and Niamh gripped his hand. Maybe she'd said something wrong. Liam managed a slight smile. "I remember that. But sis, that was ten years ago."

Niamh's stomach dropped. "Ten years? It can't be. What's the date?"

"October tenth."

"So the bonfire hasn't happened yet this year?"

"No. Niamh, it's been ten years."

She looked at him, tears in her eyes. "Ten years," she repeated. "Liam, I don't understand. How can I lose ten years of my life like that?"

"I don't know. Come here." Liam wrapped his arms around her.

She buried her face in her brother's chest, sobbing hard. After a few moments, she looked up. "You got a tissue?"

"Yeah." He felt in his pocket then pressed one into her hand. "Here."

"Thanks. What do I do? Am I still with the CPS?"

"You are senior prosecutor for Headley Cross now. Apparently, criminals panic when you're prosecuting them. Take the case yesterday. According to the paper, the defendant almost got sent down charged with contempt of court as soon as you stood up to start your case against him. Then he changed his plea to guilty."

"Am I that scary?"

"More like you're that good at your job, sis." He handed her another photo. "This one was taken on Mum and Dad's fortieth wedding anniversary in January."

"Forty years...wow." She ran her fingers over it. Jared was standing next to her, his arms around her. "Is anyone else married?"

Liam caught his breath and hesitated.

"Li?"

"It's a long story, which can wait for another time. The short version is I'm widowed. Sally died two years ago. But now I'm engaged. Her name's Jacqui. You really like her. You both get on like a house on fire. I'll bring her in to see you tomorrow. I should go. The nurse said I could only have ten minutes and it's been way over that."

"For a teacher you're a lousy time keeper. I bet the kids hate having you for detention. Or are you a headmaster now?"

He chuckled. "No way, I hate admin. I am head of the English department, though." He hugged her tightly. "I'll come back and see you tomorrow. Get some sleep."

Niamh hugged him back. "No chance of that. Might forget my name if I fall asleep. Or forget you." She shook as she held him, her fragile grip on the situation beginning to falter.

"Niamh?"

"I'm scared, Liam, really scared. I hate not

knowing this Jared. I mean he could tell me anything. Not that I'm saying he's lying or anything, I wouldn't know anything about that. I just don't like not remembering anything. What if I never do?"

His warm lips pressed against her forehead. "Just give it time."

"You sound like the doctor. Can you ask Mum and Dad to come in? And Three-Point-One-Four, if he's not working?"

Liam laughed. "We haven't called Patrick Three-Point-One-Four for several years. He never did work it out. We just call him Pi now. I'll see you tomorrow. Night, sis."

"Night." She closed her eyes as he headed across the ward to the door.

Both Liam and Jared said she'd known Jared nine years. If she had no memory of the last ten, that's why she didn't know him. So where did that leave her? Still married?

She stared down at the rings. Jared's rings. Should she even wear them if she didn't remember him at all? Yes, marriage was a commitment, and she knew that, but at the same time, how could she promise fidelity to a total stranger?

Pulling off the rings, she laid the engagement ring on the table next to the bed. Maybe he would look after it until her memory came back. The wedding band she put on the chain around her neck.

She was so tired and wanted to sleep, but all the noise meant slumber eluded her. She had had her eyes closed for what seemed like a grand total of thirty-five seconds before someone else came over.

"Mrs. Harkin?"

"That's what everyone tells me." She opened her

eyes tiredly.

"I'm Dr. Coleridge. One of the staff neurologists."

"I don't need a shrink," Niamh muttered. "I want to sleep. I thought you weren't coming until morning."

"I'm not a shrink," he said gently, sitting down on the bed next to her. "And it's a little after nine a.m."

Huh? Niamh glanced at the daylight streaming through the window and then back at the doctor. "Oh… it didn't seem like I slept at all."

"How are you feeling this morning?"

"Like I got hit by a bus," Niamh said. She reeled off the list of injuries they had told her she had. "I'm sorry if I snapped, I'm just so tired."

"That's quite all right. Dr. Anders asked me to come and see you. He tells me you can't remember anything."

"Well, nothing recent. The last thing I remember is a bonfire party, but my brother tells me that's ten years ago. I remember nothing since then."

"I'd like to run a few tests, starting with an EEG. It's pretty boring and most people sleep through it. I'd also like to do a CT scan this morning and possibly an MRI too, just to rule out a few more things."

Niamh looked at him, trying to read his expression. Were all doctors as good at hiding things or was it something he'd perfected over the years? Mind you, she needed the poker face in her job. "Why can I remember some things and not others?"

"There is still a lot about the brain that we don't understand, although we are learning more each day. But, assuming the tests show no significant damage, your memories are still there; you just can't access them. I can't give you a time scale on remembering anything I'm afraid."

"Will I ever be able to?"

"We hope so."

"But you don't know for sure?"

He shook her head. "No, I'm sorry."

"OK, just do what you have to do to help me." She glanced at the ring on the side. "Before you start, do you have an envelope or piece of paper, please?"

Dr. Coleridge nodded. "Sure." He pulled an envelope from the back of her notes and offered it and a pen to her.

"Thanks." Niamh wrote on the envelope and placed the ring into it. She sealed it and looked at it. "Could you see that Jared—Mr. Harkin gets this next time he comes in, please?"

"I can't hold on to it personally, but I'll take it over to the nurse's station for you."

"Thank you." Niamh closed her eyes as he started attaching the leads to her head.

****

Jared stood at the nurse's station and sighed. "I know it's not visiting time. But I've just got off the night shift. I'm due back tonight and I need to sleep. Please, I only want five minutes."

"I'm sorry. The doctors are with her right now."

He sighed. "OK." He turned to go, pausing when the nurse spoke again. He turned back and took the envelope she held out to him. "Thanks." Glancing down he read Niamh's writing. *Jared Harkin. Please keep this safe for now.*

His skin grew cold and his heart turned to ice. His hands shook as he tore open the envelope and tipped his wife's engagement ring into his other hand. He turned and stumbled from the ward, his breathing coming in gasps and tears blinding his vision. Searing pain filled him, and he was aware of nothing else as he strode down the hallway, the ring clutched tightly in his hand.

He started running, pushing doors aside, letting them thud into the walls, no idea where he was going. Finding himself outside a final set of doors, Jared realized he'd found the chapel. He went inside and sat on one of the pews.

Tears fell like rain as the gold dug into the palm of his hand. He didn't even have the words to pray, the only thing coming to mind was the phrase *Oh, God. First Dayna and now Niamh. Why?* Over and over again, like a mantra. Sliding off the pew onto his knees, he sobbed, his heart breaking, as he leaned upon the only One he had left.

5

Half an hour after Dr. Coleridge finished all his tests, and Dr. Anders had done his ward round with half a dozen medical students, Niamh looked up as another man came over. He wore a short white tunic over grey slacks and looked like a dentist. She hoped he wasn't. She hated dentists. She was also tired of the constant parade of doctors wanting to see the 'freak who'd lost all her memories'.

He pulled the curtains around the bed, before he turned to her and held out a hand. "Hello, Niamh. I'm Gray Williams the physiotherapist. I know you don't remember me, but I'm in the same home group from church as you and Jared."

"Hello," Niamh said. "Are we good friends? Is it still Headley Baptist?"

"Yes. And yes, I like to think we're good friends."

"OK. Am I a church member? I remember applying, but I don't remember if it got accepted or not."

He pulled her notes from the bottom of the bed and flicked through the charts. "You are. How about I get Pastor Jack to pop in? He'd be better placed to answer any church questions you may have."

She furrowed her brows in thought. "I don't know him. Is he Pastor now?"

"He has been for about eight years or so."

"OK. That would be good. Maybe when I go home

or…" She broke off. "I have no idea where home is. Or what it is. It could be a tent or a shed."

Gray laughed as he made a note on the chart. "It's neither of those. I'll give him a call. Chances are Jared already has, but I'll do so anyway. OK, now if my treating you is going to make you uncomfortable in any way, since I know you from church, I can send someone else."

She shook her head. "It makes no difference to me. Don't take it personally, but I don't know you. So, why do I need a physiotherapist?"

He smiled. "It's my job to get you up and walking again."

She shot him a droll look and pointed to her leg. "Yeah, right. How am I meant to accomplish walking like this?"

"Crutches," he told her. "First step though is learning how to stand and sit down again."

Niamh looked at him. "I can't do that."

He looked at her. "Am I right in assuming the nurse removed the catheter?"

She winced slightly at the thought of discussing something like that with a man, especially one she supposedly knew. "Yes."

"So we need to teach you how to stand and sit so you can get to the bathroom," Gray said.

She nodded grudgingly. He did have a point. She didn't want to be a burden to the nurses, and the bathroom was something she would rather do alone. Not that she'd let him know that.

She watched as he sat on the edge of the bed and showed her how to push up into the crutches. "OK, your turn."

Niamh slid her legs off the bed, aware of his hand

on her back and arm steadying her. Niamh gasped as she shifted forward slightly, leaning into the crutches.

Gray looked at her. "OK, stop. Where does it hurt?"

"Where *doesn't* it hurt?" she whispered. She pressed a hand to her stomach. "Here most of all."

"OK, rest for a minute then we start again."

She scowled at him and deepened it as he grinned. "What's that smirk for?"

"Don't let pain defeat you, take it and make it work in your favor," he said. "Right on three, I want you to slide off the bed and stand."

Niamh took a deep breath and did what he asked, though it was more a cry of pain than of triumph. Her arms trembled as she stood, her broken leg barely touching the floor.

"Well done," he said smiling at her. "That was really good."

"Don't patronize me," she gasped.

"Oh believe me I'm not. If I think you can do better I'll tell you so in no uncertain terms."

She nodded slowly. "Now what?"

"Now you sit down and then we start over. Do that a couple more times, and I'll teach you how to walk."

She raised an eyebrow. "*We*?"

Gray winked at her, pushing his hand through his hair. "We."

Niamh thought for a moment. "OK, though from where I'm standing it's more *me* than *we*. But it hurts."

"It will," he said. "That doesn't mean you can't do it."

Taking a deep breath Niamh slowly followed his instructions and did what he wanted. She smiled as she managed a few steps. It wasn't as hard as she thought it would be.

"Brilliant. Right, I'll see you tomorrow. Say hi to Jared for me when he comes in."

"Can you leave the curtains closed, please?" Niamh sat in the chair next to the bed exhausted. She closed her eyes for a moment, and then opened them again. The pressure in her bladder wasn't helping the stitches.

Taking a deep breath, she gripped the crutches firmly. She could do this. Her hands shook as she pulled upright and swung herself slowly to the curtain. She reached out for it with one hand, trying to balance on the other. Somehow the crutches slipped and she fell, landing hard on the floor, crying out in pain.

Niamh lay on her side on the tiled floor, pain flooding her. What was she thinking? How could she have been so stupid as to try opening the curtains on her own? She tried to pull herself up to a sitting position, but the cast was too heavy, and her chest and stomach hurt too much for her to bend or roll over. She stretched for the alarm, but even that was out of her reach.

She cried out in frustration. "Help," she managed. Even breathing hurt. She must have jarred her ribs again when she fell.

The curtain moved to one side and she saw a pair of black boots and navy blue trousers by her face. "Niamh," Jared said and then yelled, "I need some help in here!" A hand touched her face. "Don't move, hon, it's going to be OK."

She looked up at him. "What are you doing here?"

"Visiting you, now don't move," Jared repeated. "What happened?"

"I was trying to—" She broke off as running footsteps echoed across the ward, and Dr. Anders face suddenly appeared by hers.

"What happened?" he asked. He turned her over, his hands expertly moving over her body.

"I was trying to open the curtain and balance on the crutches at the same time. It didn't work. I fell," she said feeling completely stupid. "Agh!" she cried as he checked her over. "That hurts."

Jared helped Dr. Anders lift her onto the bed. "Where were you going?"

"Bathroom."

"Why didn't you ring for help?" Dr. Anders chided. "That's what the nurses are here for."

Niamh glowered at the doctor, the pain making her temper worse. "I'm not a child that needs to first ask permission and then be taken to the toilet!" She shifted on the bed. "Speaking of which…" She tried to push up again, ignoring the pain shooting through her.

Dr. Anders looked at her. "I suggest you stop acting like a child, if you don't want to be treated like one. You can't go anywhere until I've had this chest x-rayed."

"This can't wait," she whispered. "Please, don't make me beg, this is hard enough as it is. And I don't want one of those bed pan things either. Look, if my rib is broken, then two minutes won't make any difference, will it?"

Dr. Anders held her gaze, but she didn't flinch. Surprisingly support came from Jared.

"I learnt years ago you can't argue with her when her mind is set on something."

Dr. Anders nodded. He vanished for a moment and came back with a wheel chair. He lifted her into it.

"I'll get a nurse to take you and then you go to x-ray." He turned to Jared. "Thank you."

Jared nodded. "Welcome. Niamh, are you OK? How are you feeling? If that's not a really stupid question."

"Other than sore, I'm confused. It's like I've woken up in the middle of a film or a story and don't have the faintest idea what's going on when everyone else does. And I hate it."

"Well, I can tell you about me. If you'd like me too, that is."

"Yeah, I would." She'd thrown him out, but he kept coming back and was offering to fill in the gaps. Maybe between him and Li she could piece things together again.

His eyes lit up as he smiled. "Then I will. I'll come back tomorrow. I've just got off the night shift and am due back at six tonight. I thought I'd come see you first."

Niamh smiled back, grateful he had turned up when he did. "Thank you." Was he going to say anything about the rings? He hadn't mentioned the fact she wasn't wearing them, but maybe he'd got the engagement ring and seen the other one around her neck.

He paused for a moment, then leaned in and kissed her cheek. Her skin burned where his lips touched it and butterflies raced in her belly. "Bye."

"Bye."

****

Jared watched her go. He very nearly hadn't come back, but something had told him not to leave without saying goodbye. His heart had almost stopped when he got on the ward in time to hear Niamh cry out and then pulled the curtain back to find her collapsed on the floor. He'd feared the worst for a moment and still did. He eyed the doctor carefully. "What do you think she's done?"

Dr. Anders looked at him. "Without the x-rays we won't know for certain. Her ribs are more painful than I'd like, but that could just be bruising."

"Can you ring and let me know?" He paused. "I know she doesn't know me, but I'm still her next of kin until she says otherwise. And Liam will only tell me anyway."

Dr. Anders nodded. "Of course, but I can only do that until she specifies otherwise. After that, I'm afraid I can't tell you anything."

Jared nodded. "That's fine, thanks Doctor. Any idea when she can come home?"

"Probably in the next day or two. Maybe even tomorrow, but that does depend a lot on these x-rays."

"Thank you. If you need me I'll be at home until about five thirty, and then I'll be at work from six p.m. until nine tomorrow morning." Jared left the ward and headed for the car park. He sat in the car for a moment, and pinched the bridge of his nose before he started the engine.

Nine years of history wiped out in the blink of an eye. He took a deep breath.

I will wait for you. I will always wait for you. And if you don't remember me when you come back, then I will find you, and make you fall in love with me again and never let you go. Niamh had told him that once years ago, right after a huge fire which left several Firefighters from his station dead and one suffering severe brain damage resulting in total memory loss.

How do I deal with this? Oh, Lord, help me because I can't do this alone. I look at her and see the woman I love, the one I spent the past nine years loving and caring for and protecting. Yet she looks at me like I'm a stranger. But perhaps the stranger is her. The stranger with her face. Is this Your will? That I do for her what she promised me all those years ago, should I be severely injured? To find her and bring her back and help her remember? Then that's what I'll do. Help her remember, woo her and make her fall in love with me all over again.

****

The x-rays having come back clear, Niamh had a stream of visitors that afternoon and was exhausted. Patrick and her parents had been in, as had Liam's fiancée, Jacqui. Aside from the fact they'd all gotten old, nothing had changed. And Jacqui was sweet. Niamh had a feeling they'd be great friends.

She'd asked if she could stay at Liam's, but everyone had insisted she'd be better off at home. In familiar territory. Yeah, right. Nothing was familiar. Her parents' house would be, but that wasn't an option either. She had to go back to the house she allegedly shared with Jared. She just hoped he hadn't given her the bruises on her arm. They were definitely finger marks.

She looked up as footsteps crossed the ward and smiled as Dr. Anders came over. "What's up, Doc?" she asked, grinning as he rolled his eyes.

"Oh, aren't we funny," he said drolly. "I've heard that fifteen times so far today." He perched on the bed next to her. "How are you feeling?"

"Tired. When can I go home?"

"Depending on the remaining test results, tomorrow. So long as there is someone there to look after you. You were lucky earlier when you fell. You didn't break or sprain anything."

"I'll be fine. Just because I don't remember the last ten years, doesn't mean I can't cook beans on toast and make tea. And I can always sleep on the couch if the house has stairs." She smiled at him.

"OK. But I don't want you going back to work for six weeks."

Niamh nodded. "OK. Not that I remember my job. At least not the current one."

"I'll get the nurses to ring your husband in the morning once we know if you're going home."

Niamh looked at him. "I'd rather you rang my brother. If that's OK. He might not be able to come, but I know who he is." She broke off, yawning.

Dr. Anders stood. "I'll let you get some sleep, and we'll worry about that in the morning."

"OK." Niamh lay back on the pillows. She stared up at the ceiling, her mind full of images of the handsome firefighter who claimed to be married to her. But there was another face. Blond hair, piercing lavender eyes and a scent of some kind, something she couldn't put her finger on, but she knew it was important. Who was he? And why did his image cause something to stir inside her when her 'husband' meant nothing to her.

6

In the end, Jared picked her up just after eleven. Niamh spent the journey in silence looking out the car window. The town hadn't changed, some of the buildings looked a little more run down in places, and the trees seemed taller, but other than that, she was the one who had changed.

The car stopped, and she looked at the two-story house. The garden was neat and tidy and late autumn flowers nestled in a rainbow of colors in the window boxes and along the path. Net curtains hung at the windows and pinned back, old fashioned shutters gave the house an almost country look.

Jared smiled. "You like it?"

"It's amazing. When you said home, I never imagined anything like this. It looks like it should have a thatched roof."

Jared got out and opened the door for her. "I can't take credit for all of it. And yes, originally it did. We changed that about seventeen months ago. We needed planning permission, mind you, but we got it."

She swung her legs from the car and winced as she stood. Taking a minute to balance on her crutches, she glanced at him. "Why was that?"

"Thatched roofs are a fire risk." His voice was abrupt and stilted.

She'd obviously touched a raw nerve. "OK." She pulled herself slowly up the path. A beautiful mix of late yellow and blue roses bloomed on the bush growing up the trellis by the front door. Leaning over she took a deep breath, the delicious heady scent filling her nostrils and wrapping her in a warm fuzzy feeling. "They're lovely."

Jared smiled. "You planted them. The garden is your domain. No one else is allowed to touch it."

"Did I? I never planted anything before. Dad always did it."

"Then you must have gotten your green thumb from him, and your ability to pack a car. I have never known anyone as good at packing as you."

Her stomach twisted. Again, he knew things about her and their life together that she didn't. It was the most uncomfortable feeling and one she didn't particularly care for in the slightest. "Another one of Dad's many talents."

He unlocked the front door and held it open for her. "After you."

She eased over the front step and glanced around the hallway. Pale yellow and smelling new, the paintwork and dado rail glistened. Pictures hung on the walls, opposite a full length mirror and coat rack. "Pretty color."

"That was you, too. I went to work the night shift, came home, and thought I'd walked into the wrong house at first."

"I did all of this? The border, too?"

Jared nodded. "Yup. Usually you paint and I paper, but you did the whole thing this time."

"The paint smells new."

"Yeah, you did it the end of last week. Just head down that way to the kitchen." There was an edge to his voice. She must have said the wrong thing again.

Talk about walking on egg shells. Would she have to watch every single thing she said around him?

"OK." She swung slowly down the hall in the direction he indicated.

Jared pointed out the different rooms as they passed and she was pleased to note the downstairs bathroom. It'd save going up and down the stairs. "I'll put your bag in our room, Niamh."

Her stomach twisted and a sword plunged into her heart. "Our room?" Surely he didn't mean what she thought he did?

Jared smiled almost apologetically. "I've moved my things into the spare room," he said gently. "I'm not asking any more of you than you're prepared to give. Right now, we're strangers. I know that, so I figured, housemates. Shared bathroom, kitchen, cooking and so on, but separate bedrooms."

Relief flooded her. "Thank you." She paused. "You're not happy about it though, are you?"

"Can't say I am, but it's the way things need to be, right now." He smiled. "So let me take this upstairs and I'll let you settle in and find your way around. I need to sleep, as I'm due back at work at six. Can I make you some tea or something first?"

"No, it's OK. I can manage. Thanks anyway."

"OK, if you're sure. I'll see you around four thirty."

Niamh nodded and watched him head up the stairs. She turned again and slowly made her way into the kitchen. It was spotless, not a thing out of place or a crumb on the work top. Why didn't she remember any of this?

Flicking on the kettle, she then pulled a mug off the mug tree and set it on the counter top. Now where would the tea bags be? She pulled open cupboards one at a time, marveling at how neat they were too. Was this him? Because she wasn't so neat, assuming she hadn't changed over the past ten years and turned into a neat freak like her brother—when he wasn't drinking that is.

Finding some tea bags, Niamh tossed one into the cup. She turned and swung slowly across the kitchen, wanting to explore the rest of the downstairs. Upstairs could wait until Jared was at work.

Will he settle for just house sharing? Still I guess I can always go live with Mum and Dad or Liam if need be.

Leaning on one crutch, she pushed open a door. A huge airy lounge ran from the front of the house to the back. The front half was a living room, with an archway dividing the rest into a dining room. Patio doors beyond that led to a conservatory. A door next to the table led back into the kitchen. That was worth remembering. She opened the patio door and stumbled a little as she went into the conservatory.

Note to self, door frames and crutches are not a good combination.

Cane furniture with pale yellow cushions lined the walls. A huge garden lay beyond the glass walls.

"Wow." The autumn colors on the trees glistened and blew in the wind. White table and chairs with an umbrella stand stood on the patio. Flowers and trees lined the six-foot high wooden fence that surrounded them. The grass was neat and tidy.

The kettle whistled, and Niamh returned to the kitchen. She made the tea and somehow managed to put the cup on the table without spilling it. She slowly lowered herself into the chair and rested the crutches next to her. Picking up the cup, she sipped the hot liquid. Today's paper sat on the side and she opened it, glancing down at the news. The date on the front page seemed to bear out Jared and Liam's story about her having lost ten years.

"Why?" she whispered.

The one thing she was sure about was her faith. That hadn't changed, and as sure as she was that God had a reason for this, she just had no idea what it was. Perhaps it was temporary thing. Was Jared really the man she loved, or could it be this other man she saw in her dreams?

She finished the tea, and made her way into the lounge. She sat on the sofa and carefully put her leg up. Then she grabbed the remote, and put the TV on. She let out a deep breath. This other bloke...there were definite feelings associated with him, she just wasn't sure what. And she had no idea why her 'husband' didn't elicit the same response.

****

Peeping through the windows, Niamh saw the snow lying thick and pristine across the dark garden. She smiled and slid on her coat, hat, gloves, and boots and went outside. She made slow, deep tracks all around the garden, and then built the tallest snowman she could manage. She gave it twigs for arms, stones for eyes and buttons and another twig for a mouth. She ran indoors and picked up a carrot for a nose and Jared's spare cap for a hat. Surveying her handiwork, she smiled.

A tapping on the window made her look up. Jared stood silhouetted against the window. He shook his head at her.

She waved him to come down and join her, but he shook his head and mimed it being too cold. She pulled a face and turned away lowering her shoulders to make it look as if she were sad.

Less than a minute later the back door opened and Jared came out. "You are one crazy mad woman," he told her moving over to her. "Have you any idea what time it is?"

Niamh spun around and tossed a handful of snow at him and grinned. "Snowball time."

Jared yelped quietly as her shot hit right on target. He scooped up some snow and tossed it back, hitting her hard. "Oh really? And there I was thinking it was getting on for five forty-five in the morning. When all sensible people are still tucked up in bed."

Niamh threw another snowball at him. "That's why you're not then."

"No, because some crazy mad woman woke me up by traipsing around out here in the snow." He tossed three snowballs in quick succession. "What would the judge say if he could see you now, Mrs. Senior Prosecutor?"

She dodged and sent several snowballs flying towards him watching them miss as he moved fast. "He'd want to join in. We're not staid and boring all the time, you know."

His next several hit right on target. "So what's the snowman called?" He moved over to look at it.

Niamh ran up behind him and dumped a whole load of snow over him, making sure it went down the inside of his coat. "Jarrie Jace," she giggled.

Gasping with shock, he turned and grabbed her. "You brat!"

She laughed softly. "And what are you going to do about it?"

"This." Jared swiftly kicked her feet out from under her, laying her down in the snow. Holding her with one hand, he grabbed a handful of snow and shoved it down her neck, kissing her to stop her crying out. "Now you're a snow *woman," he grinned.*

She looked at him and winked. "I'm also wet." She tugged him to the snow beside her and grinned. "Snow angel time as we're both wet anyway."

He laughed and they both made snow angels. Then he reached over and kissed her again before pulling her to her feet. "Then we'd better go change before we have to leave for work." He looked at the snowman. "Think we'll call it H'main."

She shook her head. "Deraj sounds better."

Jared laughed, leading her back inside. "Then Deraj it is."

Niamh whimpered, twisting in the chair as the scene changed.

...A warehouse exploded and burned out of control before, unable to bear its own weight any longer, it crashed to the ground, vanishing from sight into a huge fiery lake of rubble and flame. A car door slammed and footsteps echoed up the path. She looked into the sad faces of two officers in firefighter uniform. A flag at half mast, coffins draped in the Union Flag carried on the back of fire engines with a sea of men in uniform following it. A burned face, bandages, a figure in a bed, trumpet music playing...

The images flowed from one into the other, incoherent jigsaw pieces trying to make a whole.

She was in a car, frantically stamping on the brakes as something inexorably hurtled towards her. She flung her arms up and screamed. Then it was dark and there were more footsteps, this time chasing her. She ran, ran as fast as she could, but he was quicker and gained. She turned; a knife glinted in the darkness and plunged towards her. She screamed...

A child's voice echoed with hers. "Mummmmyyyyyy."

****

Niamh sat bolt upright, screaming, tears streaming down her face, rocking back and forth. Someone spoke and touched her arm, but she pulled away, struggling for breath. A hand gently touched her cheek and guided her to look into a pair of hazel eyes.

Jared?

"Hey." His tone was gentle and soft. "It's OK."

Niamh tried to draw breath, unable to tear her gaze from his. Her whole body shook, and she grew light headed from lack of oxygen. Jared ran to the kitchen, returned with a paper bag and guided her hands to hold it. "Breathe into this. It'll help."

How is a paper bag going to stop me from suffocating?

Her head spun and her eyes wanted to close. Jared scrunched the bag up and placed it over her mouth and nose. "Breathe into the bag."

She did as he asked, grateful he was holding the bag as her hands wouldn't grip anything. This mad idea of his seemed to work, and as it got easier to breathe, Niamh realized he had his hand resting on her back, rubbing it. The touch felt strange, but at the same time familiar. She didn't shy away, but leaned into it. The scent of his aftershave filled her senses. Pushing the bag away, she looked at him. "I'm sorry, did I wake you?"

Jared smiled. "It's OK. I woke a while ago and was just finishing dinner when I heard you scream. Are you feeling better?"

Niamh nodded. "Yes, just a stupid nightmare."

He looked at her, brushing the hair from her eyes. "Want to tell me about it while we eat?"

"Sure. It doesn't make any sense though."

"Nightmares seldom do." He helped her to her feet, his sleep tousled hair giving him a childlike air. It was kind of cute. "What was it this time? Freddie or the fog monster?"

She leaned heavily on the crutches and walked slowly across the room. "Fog monster?"

"Hey, don't mock. I usually have to save you from him once a week."

"Oh, no, it wasn't a monster made of fog, and I wasn't being chased down a long dark hallway by a burned madman with knives for fingernails either. Though the guy in my dream did have a knife, and he was chasing me, right before I woke up. I was running, trying to get away, but he grabbed me and hit me and brought the knife down. Before that, I was in a car and the brakes didn't work, and I think I crashed, but I'm not sure because at that point the knife man appeared. Before that there was fire and flags at half-mast and coffins on fire engines."

Jared touched her shoulder for a moment then let go again. "You're safe now. Did you see his face?"

"The bloke in my dream? No, I didn't. Why?"

"No reason."

"OK." She took a deep breath. "Are you wearing Fascination?"

His voice caught as he replied. "Yes. You always buy it for me because you like it."

Niamh gazed at him. "What's my favorite perfume?"

"Eighteen fourteen."

She shook her head. It didn't sound right. "Oh."

"Why?"

"Half thought you'd say something else."

He smiled. "Well, strictly speaking that's your

current favorite. It seems to change each year or so. Why? What were you expecting me to say?"

"Blue Moon." She caught her breath as his eyes glistened and looked down at her hands. "Did I say something wrong?"

"No, no, you didn't. You wore that the day we got married. You had the whole range of stuff from body lotion, and bath oil, to hand cream…"

"That I do remember. It was all I ever wanted for Christmas and birthdays. I couldn't justify spending that much money on myself."

"That doesn't sound like you. You love shopping and buying yourself new stuff." He paused, changing the subject. "It's warm tonight, despite being October, so I figured we'd eat outside, if that's all right. Mind the step."

"I got it." She made her way outside and lowered herself onto the patio furniture. She hadn't told him about the voice crying Mummy because that bit made no sense, even to her. She needed to think it through first.

Niamh took the lap tray he offered and smiled. "Thank you." As the sun began to set, casting a purple hue over the clouds, she looked down at the plate and her smile widened. "I haven't had chicken chow mien in ages. Did you vanish down the take away?"

Jared smiled, a faint blush touching his cheeks. "No. I have to admit I was tempted as you love the food from the local Chinese place, but this I made all by myself."

Surprise filled her. "Wow, that's so clever. I wouldn't even know where to start. Did you make the fortune cookies, too?" She pointed to the bowl of cookies on the table.

"Ah, no. They came from this box." He laughed and reaching down beside his chair, picked up and then jiggled a cardboard container. "But yes, the noodles and chicken chow mien are mine. This was the first thing I ever cooked for you."

Niamh took a bite, and her eyes widened in delight as she chewed and swallowed. "It's delicious. Did I marry you for your cooking skills?"

Jared laughed. "Quite possibly. We shared the cooking. You cooked when I worked, and I cooked on my days off."

Niamh ate, enjoying the food. Then she reached for a fortune cookie. *"Do not sleep in a eucalyptus tree tonight,"* she read.

Jared laughed. "Don't think we have one of those even if I wanted to try." He broke his. *"Indomitable in retreat; invincible in advance; insufferable in victory."*

She grabbed a few more and kept two and tossed two to Jared. *"When you make your mark in the world, watch out for guys with erasers."*

"You will experience a strong urge to do good, but it will pass."

"Love thy neighbor. Tune thy piano."

Jared looked up at the clouds as he read the last one. *"It is said that no one regards what is before his feet; we all gaze at the stars.* Well, clouds in this case." He pointed upwards. "That one looks like a dragon."

She followed his finger but couldn't see which one he was pointing to. "Where? I don't see it."

"There," he said. "Second cloud to the right and straight on 'til morning."

"That's stars, not clouds. Dragon, huh?"

"Yeah, a big fire breathing dragon, that has chicken chow mien for dinner, and will have ice cream and fortune cookies for dessert."

She smiled, letting slide the fact he was implying she was a fire breathing dragon. "What kind of ice cream?"

Jared grinned at her "Your favorite of course. Neapolitan, with chocolate sauce and sugar strand sprinkles. So, this here dragon. Do you see it now?"

She looked at the cloud critically for a moment. "It needs a name. Call it Deraj. Unless it's a female dragon."

He fixed his eyes on her, a gaunt look in them. "We'll call it H'main."

"No. Deraj sounds much better. And if it gets cold, it can sleep in your room. Not going to let it melt all over my carpet." Niamh watched in surprise as Jared hurried inside with the plates. She sat there, really not sure what she had said, but was suddenly sure Deraj and H'main were snowmen and not clouds.

After a several minutes he came back out. His eyes were red rimmed. Had he been crying? "I need to get going. I'll see you tomorrow. I should be home around nine thirty or so in the morning. Assuming we don't get called out just before hand over. Can I get you anything before I leave?"

Niamh shook her head. He hadn't brought the ice cream, but she no longer fancied it. "I'll be fine."

"Let me help you upstairs and put the TV on in the bedroom. I put a patio chair in the shower for you, and a bin liner to put the cast in. Your towels are the navy blue ones hanging in the upstairs bathroom." His strong arms surrounded her as he picked her up and carried her.

She slid an arm around his neck. She knew he wouldn't drop her; he did this for a living.

The bedroom was bigger than she'd imagined, and the bed itself was soft as he settled her onto it. "Thank you."

"You're welcome. If you need anything, call me. Or Liam said you could call him. All the numbers are programmed into your mobile phone. Your laptop is here, you never log out of anything, so you don't need to worry about passwords for your email, social media pages and so on." For a moment it looked as if he was going to kiss her, then he straightened. "Goodnight."

"Goodnight. I hope work goes OK." She watched him leave, picked up the remote and turned on the television. Assuming she really had lost ten years, she shouldn't have a problem finding something to watch.

She glanced at the laptop. Email? Social media pages? It was as if he was talking a foreign language. She hadn't much cared for the new fad of electronic mail. A handwritten letter was far more personal than something typed and sent over this new internet malarkey. That was one thing she hoped didn't catch on. The personal phones, however, would be a good idea. Especially in her line of work.

****

Jared sat at the table in the canteen, his hand curled around a mug of tea and a plate of cold spaghetti bolognaise on the table in front of him.

Skippy looked over at him. "Hey, if you're not hungry, can I have that?"

"Go for it." Jared pushed the plate over to him, shaking his head as Skippy attacked it with gusto. "Doesn't your wife feed you?"

Skippy laughed. "She does, but I hate to see good

food go to waste. So what's up, mate? Is Niamh still in hospital?"

"No, she came home this morning." He took a deep breath. "But, she doesn't know who I am. She remembers nothing of the last ten years. If she were dead, at least I could mourn her, but this? That car crash took my wife and left me with a total stranger. How am I meant to just turn off my feelings and stop loving her now?"

"You don't, you daft drongo." Skippy's Australian accent came through sharply. "You give her time. Date the sheila all over again. Charm her, make her fall in love with you and maybe as she does, she'll remember you and all you've done together the past nine years."

Jared looked up, his cup dropping to the table. He closed his eyes and buried his head in his hands. *Dayna*. What if she remembered Dayna or found the photos? Losing their daughter had almost killed her.

It had killed their marriage.

Could she survive reliving that night again? Could either of them?

7

Jared let himself into the house just after nine thirty. It had been a quiet night, although he'd have preferred a busy one. Then he wouldn't have worried about Niamh. He wrinkled his nose. *Toast?* Had Niamh gotten up and made her own breakfast?

"Hello?" He hung his jacket on the coat hooks and took a deep breath. It was definitely toast and coffee.

"I'm in the kitchen." She sounded cheerful, something she hadn't been around him for a long time now. She smiled as he came in. "I made you breakfast. It's not much, but it'll fill a hole. And I worked out the coffee machine. Kind of impressive, don't you think?"

"Very impressive." Surprise filled him, and something touched his soul—a part of him Niamh hadn't reached in a long time. "And thank you. But should you be standing?"

"I'm not weight bearing which is what they told me not to do. Besides, I can't sit down all day long. I also discovered that I don't like coffee. It smells great but tastes nasty, so I'm sticking to tea."

"How did you sleep?" Jared sat at the table. It may only be beans on toast, but it was a sight for sore eyes and a feast for his empty stomach. "Thank you."

"You're welcome. And I didn't sleep that great, but I never do, first night in a strange bed." She lowered herself into the chair opposite, setting crutches against the edge of the table. "Can you say grace, please?"

"Sure." Jared obliged and then picked up his knife and fork. "I'm sorry you didn't sleep well. Hopefully you will tonight."

"Well, it can't be much worse. Do we have any photos? There don't seem to be any around. I can't find any apart from the ones on the mantelpiece of you in uniform and me in robes."

Jared paused, the cutlery hovering over the food. "No, we don't have many. Just the few copies I got from your family and mine. We lost everything in a house fire two years ago."

"Hence the no thatched roof on the house."

"Yeah." He concentrated on his food, hoping she'd drop the subject. But she didn't.

"Only I was thinking, perhaps they'd jog my memory a little. Would Liam have some?"

"Yeah, he would."

"Can we go see him? It's the weekend, so he's not working."

"I'll give him a call, and make sure he's going to be in."

"OK, thanks." She twisted her hair around a finger. "You said the house was destroyed in a fire. Could you take me over to where the house was? I want to see it."

Jared nodded, his stomach threatening to eject his breakfast. He didn't want to tell her about Dayna. Not while she was being civil to him. The old Niamh was almost there, just below the surface of the woman before him. If she remembered or got told about Dayna and exactly what happened the night of the fire, then the shutters would come down and the ice maiden would return. "There isn't much left now, or there wasn't last time I was over there. I'll take you, but I do need to sleep a bit first."

"Of course. Sorry, I forgot you were up all night."

"No worries. Let me sleep until about one and then we'll go." He finished his breakfast and stood. "Thank you. Want me to do the dishes?"

"I found the dishwasher. I'll do them. Sleep well."

"Thanks." Jared headed upstairs to his room. He shut the door and pulled out his mobile phone. "Hey, Liam, it's Jared."

"Hey, how are things?"

"She still doesn't remember anything. She's asking about photos and wants to come over and look at yours this afternoon."

"Sure."

"One other thing, please don't bring out any photos of Dayna. Niamh knows about the fire, as I had to tell her why we had no photos, but doesn't know about our daughter."

"She needs to know, Jared. Are you sure that lying to her is a good idea? You shouldn't do anything to impede her recovery."

"I'm not lying, just not telling her the whole truth, yet. Niamh's got enough to cope with right now. Without having to mourn Dayna all over again."

"If you're sure."

"Yes, I am. Some memories are best forgotten. For once, ignorance is bliss."

****

The morning rain had eased off by noon. After lunch, Niamh made her way down the front path, taking care over each step. Jared walked next to her, his hand just by her elbow in case she fell or slipped on the wet stones. He unlocked the car and held the door for her as she got in.

"Thanks, Jared." She set the crutches by her legs and wrestled with the belt as he went around the car and got in the other side.

He put the key in the ignition and turned it. Nothing happened. He tried again. Same result. "Oh come on," he muttered. He tried a third time. The engine turned once then stopped. Shaking his head, he popped the bonnet and got out of the car.

She watched him move around and open the bonnet. She could visualize him bending over the engine looking at it, pulling at the wires. She'd been here before.

Trying to get the car to move again, she sighed. She really didn't have time for this today. She was due in court in less than an hour and had a meeting beforehand. The car had stalled on a roundabout half way to work and although the engine restarted, the wretched thing refused to move. And in her 'delicate condition' as Jarrie and Liam laughingly called it, pushing a car anywhere was not going to happen.

Shaking her head, she reached down and pulled her phone from her bag. Maybe Jared could fix the car, or better yet, pick her up and then come back and sort out this mess. Fortunately, he started his four days off today.

He answered the phone on the third ring. "Hello?"

"Jarrie, it's me. The car's being stupid. It stalled and restarted, but it won't move. I don't suppose you could be an angel and come and pick me up could you, please? I'm due in court soon and can't be late."

"Sure, hon. I'll be there as soon as I can."

"Thanks, love." She hung up and then rang the office to warn them she may be in late. She tried to get the car to

move again several times but still nothing. Finally, she saw Jared pull up and park behind her. She yanked the keys from the ignition and got out of the car to greet him. "I don't know what's wrong with the wretched thing. The engine starts fine, the car just won't move. But if you could drive me in—"

"Let me have a look first in case it's something obvious. Pop the bonnet for me and start her up."

She got back in the car doing as he asked.

Jared checked the engine over, trying different things. "Hmmm." He moved over to the window. "Show me exactly what you did."

Niamh did so then glared up at him as he laughed. "What?"

"Try putting it in gear, hon." Jared had a huge grin on his face. "Cars work better in gear than in neutral."

Niamh rolled down the window. "Jared?"

He stuck his head around the bonnet. "Yeah?"

"Silly question, but you did have the car in gear just now, didn't you?"

He looked at her strangely for a moment, and then nodded. "Yeah." He turned back to the engine and fiddled a bit more. Then he got back into the car and turned it over. The engine clicked once then roared into life. He got out and closed the bonnet. "Just going to go wash my hands. Will you be OK?"

Niamh nodded as he went back inside, leaving the engine running. He wasn't gone more than a minute before he was back and they set off. She looked down at her hands. She'd remembered she was pregnant at some point over the past few years, but wasn't about to tell him. He hadn't mentioned it at all. Perhaps she'd lost the baby and it was a sore point. Because there was definitely no trace of a child anywhere in the house.

But it would explain the voice in her mind calling her Mummy.

****

Jared glanced at her as they pulled into the road they used to live on. Not even a spark of recognition. On the way here, he'd pointed out the park he'd courted her in, the church, the shopping center. All those she remembered, but not being in any of them with him. He tried hard not to let his frustration show. She was convinced she was twenty-six and single. The whole situation must be just as bad for her. If not more so.

His stomach knotted as he parked the car on the roadside. For a moment he saw the house as it was that winter's night two years ago. Flames leapt from every window and the thatched roof. Cracking timbers and shattering glass mixed with roaring flames and blistering heat. Thick black smoke leapt high into the sky, as inside the inferno, his daughter burned because he couldn't get her out.

Niamh sat there poker faced. "Are we here?"

He nodded. "Yeah, you want to get out?"

"No." She looked at him. "There's no sign of any fire."

"Looks like the house was rebuilt. No thatched roof this time, though."

"How long did we live here?"

"Just over five and a half years. I moved in just after we exchanged contracts six months before we married. We spent almost every evening here decorating."

She inclined her head. "Don't remember."

He took a deep breath, exhaling as slow as he could. "Your memories are still there, locked away in your mind somewhere. All we need to do is find the key and unlock them."

"What if I can't find the key?" she whispered. "What if they never come back?"

"Then you make new memories." He laid his hand on top of hers, his wedding ring catching the light. "Either way, nothing will change the way I feel about you."

She looked at him. "Even though I can't reciprocate those feelings?"

A knife twisted in his heart, sending shards of pain radiating out through every fiber of his being. Perhaps nothing had changed. "Even then. I'll be your friend."

"Are you all right with just being friends?"

Jared looked at her, unable to reply for a moment. "Yes."

"Are you sure?"

Jared nodded slowly. "Friends are just fine, hon." He started the car and pulled away. *And let's face it. Being friends is a lot more than we were this time last week.*

****

Houses and streets passed outside the car, and Niamh wished she could remember something of the man sitting next to her, but her memory was a big block of Swiss cheese. Not even being here at the house helped. It was like someone took an eraser and rubbed him out.

The image of the blond man filled her mind again. "Jared, can I ask something?"

He glanced at her. "Sure."

"I keep seeing this man in my mind. He's tall, around six foot maybe, thick shaggy blond hair, lavender eyes. He always wears a suit, I think. Or black. Something dark at any rate. I just don't know who he is, except the fact I know him. I don't suppose you have any idea who he might be?"

Jared shook his head. "Someone from work perhaps?"

"Maybe. Guess I'll find out when I go back next week."

"I'm sorry?"

She heard the catch in his voice. "Just a visit, if you can drive me. I thought it might jog my memory. I know I can't go back until the doctors say so, but a visit won't hurt."

"Sure I'll take you. I'm off until Wednesday. We only have the one car now, not that you can drive anyway, but we'll figure something out for when you do go back."

Niamh nodded. "OK, thank you." She drummed her fingers on the door handle. "I just get the feeling he's important somehow." She caught the anguished look he shot her and turned away.

Now would probably be a good time to shut up. Having an affair would be wrong. Oh, don't let that be true, Lord. Don't let me be the kind of woman who'd cheat on her husband. Not even one I don't remember ever having.

Jared pulled up at the lights. "Let's just go over to Liam's. He said he'd get his photos out. See what you remember."

****

Niamh sat with a pile of photos on her lap. She

laughed. "Pi was so unimpressed. He wouldn't let me make him coffee for a long time after that."

Liam grinned. "He never let his guard down around you again. Not that I blame him. But that was the last time you got one over on him." He winked at Jared. "Now a-days, Patrick is far too sensible for anything like practical jokes. I think Niamh cured him of it."

"Shame it didn't work for her." Jared sipped his coffee and put the cup down. "For someone as staid and boring as a barrister…"

Niamh threw a cushion at him, smiling as he caught it. "That's senior prosecutor, apparently, and we're not staid and boring, not even the judges."

He laughed and tossed it back. "No? Hmmm, that's not what you said last week. I'm sure you said you were."

Niamh rolled her eyes, hugging the cushion as she caught it. "I could have won a gold medal in wrestling last week for all I remember."

Jared smirked. "You won a wrestling medal last week? Why didn't you tell me? I'd have been there with bells on."

"Now that I have to see."

"OK, you're on. You wrestle and I'll wear bells. Liam can take the photos."

Liam shook his head. "You two are incorrigible."

Niamh put the photos down on the table and picked up her tea. "That's a good thing, right?"

Jared nodded. "It'd better be, or Liam's in trouble, no matter if he is your twin."

Liam laughed. "That a promise or a threat, Jared? Actually, neither of you have been this relaxed around each other since the fire."

"Why not?" Niamh glanced at him, puzzled. *Were we having problems? Is that why I don't remember anything?*

Jared cleared his throat and picked up his cup.

She twisted her head from one to the other, catching the anguished look that passed between the two men. "Will someone please tell me what I'm missing here?"

Jared finally spoke. "Every marriage goes through a rough patch, which is what we were doing. Actually you spent a couple of nights here, until Liam convinced you to come home and try to work things out."

"Had we worked things out?"

Jared stared at his cup. "Kind of. I'll be right back." He stood and hurried from the room.

Niamh sat there dumbstruck. She'd done it again. She said the tiniest thing and sent Jared bolting from the room. Almost as if she'd pulled the pin on a grenade and stood holding it. Did his reaction have anything to do with this other man she kept seeing in her dreams? Perhaps her brother knew.

"Li, was I seeing someone else?"

Liam choked on his coffee, spraying it over his lap. "What?" He pulled a tissue from the box on the table and blotted up the mess. "What makes you ask that?"

"No reason. I'm just asking."

He shook his head. "You and Jared were having problems, yes, but neither of you would ever consider cheating on the other."

"Only I keep dreaming about this other man and…" She broke off as Jared came back into the room. "Are you OK?"

He nodded. "Yeah. The timer's just gone on the

oven."

"And there's Jacqui," Liam added, rising as the doorbell rang. "Come through to the kitchen in a few."

"Can I take the photos home? I'd like to finish looking at them."

Liam smiled. "Sure. I'll go let Jacqui in and dish up."

Niamh waited until he'd left before saying anything. "Whatever happened between us, Jared, I don't remember any more than I remember you. Can we, I mean, is there a way to fix it?"

"It's all right. We'll work it out."

She held his gaze for a moment and then nodded. *What other secrets is he hiding? What caused the problems between us and had we really worked them out?*

8

Sunday morning dawned bright and sunny, but cold. Jared sat next to Niamh in church, in their usual seats. She appeared comfortable here, albeit seemed overwhelmed by the number of people who knew things about her, which she didn't remember. Her fingers constantly moved over the cross she wore—the one he'd bought her as a wedding present. Not that she'd asked where it came from.

Her wedding ring hung next to it. At least she was still wearing it. That was some consolation. He'd tucked the engagement ring away in his cufflink box until she wanted it back. *If* she wanted it back.

As the service finished, Niamh picked up her crutches and turned to him. "It really hasn't changed much. Aside from the addition of the drums and two new pastors."

Jared smiled. "Pastor Jack has been here about eight years now. Pastor Bruce about seven and a half. We were married by the previous minister, Steve Austin."

Niamh giggled. "I remember him. The bionic pastor we used to call him."

Jared looked at her, barely able to contain his own grin. "Yes, the church as a whole referred to him like that—but never to his face. Although I'm sure he knew. Let me go and catch Daphne, one of the registrars, and see if we can see the marriage register."

"Sure."

He rose and headed down the aisle, catching Daphne just as she left her seat. He glanced behind to make sure Niamh was following. It wasn't simply that she thought their marriage was fake; he wanted to show her that they were married in a church. She was making slow progress along the crowded aisle on her crutches. He shot her a smile and then turned to Daphne. "Hi, I was wondering if you could do us a favor."

Daphne nodded. "Sure. Hey, Niamh, how are you doing?"

"OK."

"That's good. We've all been praying hard for you. That was some car crash."

"I don't remember it."

"Sometimes that can be a blessing in disguise." Daphne smiled and looked at Jared. "What can I do for you?"

"Could we see the marriage register? Assuming you have a copy of it here?"

"To see your entry? Of course. We have all the books going back years." She headed towards the vestry at the front of the church.

Jared waited for Niamh and walked with her. By the time they reached the vestry, Daphne had taken the book from the safe and opened it to the right place.

Niamh stood there and looked down at it. "It's my signature," she said quietly.

Jared nodded. "Your dad and my best man, Danny, witnessed it. Liam and Patrick were ushers and you had your friends Tina and Vanessa as bridesmaids."

"What happened to them? Do they still live

around here?"

"No. Tina lives in Scotland and Vanessa married a soldier and they currently live in Italy where he's stationed."

"Was the wedding filmed?"

Jared caught his breath. "Yes, but we lost that in the fire, too. I think your parents have a copy." He saw the look on her face. "I know what you're thinking "

Niamh adopted the lawyer face he knew so well. "What am I thinking?"

"That all this is very convenient. Why would I lie about something like this?"

"I don't know. Maybe it's because I have to take everything with a pinch of salt right now, or because as a lawyer I'm used to having evidence to back things up with. I wish I could remember this, but I don't. I'm sorry. This isn't easy, you know. Having everyone else tell me stuff I've no recollection of at all. You could be making it all up for all I know. Perhaps I'm part of some huge conspiracy—like that film years ago where the woman lost her memory and this bloke decided to cash in on it and claimed her as his wife."

"Well I'm not like him. Are you painting Liam and the rest of your family with the same brush?"

"I—I don't know."

He reached out and put a hand on her arm, her broken tone stabbing at his heart. "I'm sorry. I shouldn't have said that. It was thoughtless and unkind."

"Yeah, it was."

"I promise you that record isn't false. That's a crime. You know that."

Niamh nodded slowly.

Jared looked at Daphne. "Thank you."

"You're welcome. If you need anything else, let me know."

"We will. Come on; best not keep your parents waiting. They even persuaded Patrick to come for lunch, too."

She followed him into the chapel. "Sounds like that's impossible."

"Patrick is married to his job. He works twenty-four hours a day, seven days a week, three hundred and sixty-five days a year."

"I see. A bit like me then."

"He's way worse than you are. Sure, at times you can get a little preoccupied with work. Especially the big cases, but it's what you do and you're good at it. Which is why you're in line for a judgeship."

Niamh stopped, a look of amazement on her face. "Seriously? But I'm only twenty-six."

"Thirty-six," Jared corrected as he opened the car door for her. "And even that's early, but you're good at what you do. You always have been." He smiled. "And I don't know about you, but I'm starved."

"Mum's roasts are always more than enough," Niamh said smiling. "She usually does ten different types of veggies."

"Oh yeah. Plus she always does cauliflower cheese, too."

"Yes. Dad loves that with his roast."

Jared grinned. "He's not the only one," he said as he shut the car door. For a brief moment, the old Niamh was there. He just hoped she'd stay once the whole truth came out.

****

After dinner, more stuffed than the turkey had been, Niamh stood in front of the sideboard looking at the silver gilt photo frames. There were a couple of Liam—one with Jacqui. Another one of him with a blonde woman she didn't recognize, but assumed from the conversation over lunch was Sally, his first wife. There was one of Jared, his arms wrapped tightly around her. One of Patrick standing under a tree and a really silly one of him she remembered being taken. He was standing on a plinth with an ice cream cone in one hand and a book in the other pretending to be the Statue of Liberty.

Other pictures had them all together. There were graduation photos, wedding photos. Photos of them all when they were kids. Kids…

Maybe this was a way to find out about this pregnancy she remembered.

Niamh turned around. "Mum? Where are the photos of the grandchildren?"

The babbling conversation behind her stopped dead, and her mother looked distinctly flustered before she answered. "We don't have any grandchildren. Sally died before she and Liam had any."

"Oh. And I guess with Patrick not married…"

"Other than to his job," Liam interrupted.

Patrick grinned. "Some of us have to be. We've got to keep the country safe. This is what Niamh does, in her own way."

"Used to do."

"You will again. Just don't go soft on them."

Niamh nodded slightly. She looked at Jared, pushing the issue. "So were we just too busy to have kids or unable to have them? Eight years is a long time to be married without any."

"You were concentrating on work for now," he replied. "You had a lot of cases running at the same time." He didn't look at her and from the way he shifted on the chair, Niamh knew he was avoiding telling her the whole truth. She'd been pregnant, she remembered that. Both he and Liam knew and by default, the rest of them would have done as well.

"Too much work to have kids?" she asked. "That doesn't sound like me. I made a list of names years ago. I wanted six."

"People change, circumstances change." He put his cup on the side table with an audible chink.

"I don't believe you." She looked back at the photos, then turned back to him. "There's no way I'd put my career before having children. Nothing is that important. Family matters."

"I don't want to fight," Jared said quietly. "Let's just accept there are no grandchildren and move on." He looked at her father. "Did you go to the match yesterday?"

Her father nodded. Was that relief in his eyes at the change of topic? "Yes I did. I don't think it should have been a penalty though."

She sat down, deflated as the conversation turned to the injustices of football. Why were Jared and everyone else lying to her? She took the cup Liam offered her and breathed in the heady scent of the cinnamon mixing with the cocoa. She'd just have to find out herself.

****

Once Jared had left for church that evening, Niamh eased up from the couch and moved over to where he'd set her laptop. Whilst that was booting up, she wanted to scour the house. Although why it was called 'booting up' she had no idea. Perhaps it had a tendency to break down and therefore needed a kick start.

She wasn't sure what she was looking for, but there must be something. First, she wanted to go and check the rooms upstairs. There was something bothering her about the one she was sleeping in.

Jared had said he'd moved some of his things out, but it was more than that. Ten minutes later, her suspicions confirmed, she headed slowly back down to the lounge. All of Jared's things were in the spare room. Every last shirt, tie, jumper, hanky and so on. He'd moved out completely and it didn't look recent either. There was dust around the cufflink box on the dresser in his room.

Sitting at the table, Niamh pulled the laptop towards her. She was supposedly logged in, which had to be a good thing as she had no idea what the password would be. She pulled up the email program and watched as her inbox began to fill.

A fair amount seemed to be from someone called Alan Reynolds. Opening one she worked out it was from the CPS and therefore work related. From his tone he seemed to be her boss. Strange. The only Alan she remembered was a new guy just transferred in from another county. She fired off a quick reply, grateful for the huge send button which made this whole newfangled way of communicating so much easier.

One entitled divorce query caught her eye. The sender was listed as Jack Chambers. Pastor Jack? What would he want with a divorce query? The CPS didn't handle those. And why would he want a divorce anyway? She opened it.

"*Niamh, as regards your query, I'd ask you to read First Corinthians chapter seven.*

I know you and Jared are having problems, but I would urge the two of you to pray long and hard before you divorce each other. My offer of counseling remains. Or, if either of you are uncomfortable coming to see me, I can suggest a good marriage guidance counselor. Either way I will keep you both in my prayers. God bless. Jack."

The words almost threw her from her seat. She had to read them several times before the pounding in her ears subsided.

Shock resonated through her. She read the words again.

"I don't understand. Why would we be living in the same house if things were bad enough for me to start thinking divorce?" Niamh pushed up and moved over to the mantelpiece, picking up the photos, one by one. There was one of her in a black gown and a wig, must have been taken in court at some point. There was one of Jared in his fireproof clothing and another of him in his dress uniform.

But there were none of the two of them together. *This is so frustrating. The doctors said there was nothing wrong, but there must be. OK, think. Where would I put something to keep it safe?*

Slowly she sat on the floor in front of the sideboard, her plastered leg outstretched in front of her and her other leg curled underneath. She set the crutches against the sideboard and pulled open the cupboards. Piles of dishes met her gaze.

Niamh ducked her head and ran her fingers along the back of the shelf. She pulled out a shoe box full of photos in frames. Jared stood in his dress uniform with his arms around her. She was wearing a white wedding gown, veil, and lifting her skirts to show off a blue garter. She looked so happy. She recognized Liam in a frock coat and Patrick next to him. She had no idea who the man standing next to Jared was. He was also a firefighter judging by the uniform.

In the other picture she and Jared stood kissing under an arch made of firefighter's axes. "Why don't I remember this? Ten years of my life just gone in the blink of an eye. And why did he tell me there weren't any photos, when there quite obviously are."

Niamh set those down and pulled out a triptych, tucked at the bottom of the box. The gilt frame contained three pictures. The first one was of her, obviously very pregnant, with Jared standing behind her. His arms lay protectively over her belly. The second was a picture of her holding a very tiny baby, Jared on the bed next to her. The baby looked newborn and she was in what looked like a hospital bed. The third showed a little girl probably about two or three. Bright blue eyes and a wide smile showing a missing tooth, flyaway hair pulled into bunches on either side of her head.

Tears sprung to her eyes and an overwhelming sense of loss filled her. Who was she? Where was she? If she hadn't lost the baby and had given birth to a child, why hadn't Jared or Liam said anything? And why the insistence this afternoon that there were no grandchildren—although they'd changed the subject quickly enough. She couldn't ring Jared at church, but he'd be home soon enough. She'd ask him then. And she wanted answers.

She looked down at the photo again, seeing the

child in her mind, playing on a swing. *"Higher Mummy, I want to fly with the birds and the angels."*

****

Jared unlocked the door and let himself in. The house was quiet and in darkness. "Niamh?" he called. He hung his coat in the hallway and tossed his keys onto the tray. His footsteps echoed down the hallway and he pushed doors open checking for her. "Niamh, are you still up?"

Reaching the kitchen, he pushed open the door. Niamh was sat at the table, her back rigid. He smiled at her. "Hey, how are you?"

Niamh looked at him, a mixture of anger and incredible sadness in her eyes. "Fine." Anger filled her stilted voice.

The smiled died on his lips. *Whoa, what have I done?*

"How was your evening?" he tried again. "What did you do?"

Niamh shrugged. "Read my email. Explored the house some. Found nothing of yours in what is meant to be 'our' room." She took a deep breath. "Maybe some things are best forgotten."

A double edged sword pierced his heart and soul. "Not everything, Niamh. Some things are too painful to deal with sometimes, but we can't forget. I'll fill in any of the gaps you want."

"OK, fine." She reached under the table and brought out the triptych and held it out to him. "You can start by telling me about her. She's obviously my daughter. Where is she? Why haven't you mentioned her before? Why are there no toys or any sign of her anywhere? And why was everyone lying to me this afternoon and saying there were no grandchildren, when I've had a child and these photos prove it?"

9

Niamh set the triptych down on the table where he could see it. She glanced at Jared to see the color drain from his face. His tongue moved over his lips nervously and his hands shook as he clenched them.

Lord, help me here. Don't let me say the wrong thing and upset him more, she whispered. *Although how could I possibly make this bad situation any worse?*

He looked awful. The grief radiating from him almost palpable as he slumped in the chair opposite her, his hands twisted in front of him. His eyes glistened. "Her name was Dayna. She was three when that photo was taken. She looked just like you, had the same mannerisms. She'd sing all the time, play dress-up and dolls. Her favorite game was putting on a long black dress and saying she was going to work to lock up the bad guys so they wouldn't hurt anyone anymore. She wanted to be a barrister like you."

"What happened?" She could see the child on the swing again and a small white coffin.

"The fire was almost two years ago. Twenty two months to be precise. It was Christmas Eve. We'd had a busy day, what with food shopping and visiting your parents for dinner. Dayna was over excited and hadn't gone to bed very early or easily. Eventually you convinced her that Father Christmas wouldn't come if she wasn't in bed and asleep. We'd gone to bed soon after she did, and left the fire in the lounge to go out by itself. Something we'd done a hundred times if not more. The fireguard was up and nothing should have happened. But it was a very windy night and the chimney caught fire. Something must have dislodged and fallen into the fireplace, knocking over the fireguard. It was an old house and burned quickly."

Tears spilled from his eyes and down his cheeks as he spoke. "The smoke alarm woke me. I could hear her screaming. I woke you and told you to get out while I went to get her."

Niamh's hand covered her mouth, tears filling her own eyes.

"I took you to the top of the stairs and you went down them and outside to call for help. Dayna's room was next to the chimney, further along the landing. It was a scene from hell. There were flames everywhere, the air full of thick choking smoke. Dayna stood in the middle of the room, screaming my name and begging me to come and get her. I called to her, but she was too scared to move. As I went into the room to get her, the floor she was standing on gave way."

Niamh whimpered, seeing it happen in her mind's eye as he spoke. Rivers of tears ran down her cheeks, huge sobs welled up within her and spilled from her uncontrollably.

"There was nothing I could do. I ran downstairs and into the lounge wanting to find her, but the place was an inferno. The blokes had to drag me out when they arrived. They didn't find her body until the fire was out." He looked over at her and stretched out a hand. "I'm so sorry."

Niamh ignored him, pushing up from the table. Balancing on the crutches, she left the room as quickly as possible, heading for the bathroom. Barely making it in time, she leant over the sink, heaving and retching.

****

Jared sat in the kitchen, not bothering to stop the tears from falling onto the triptych in his hands. Dayna's screams and the way she looked at him was something he'd remember until the day he died. He'd refused to let Niamh see her charred body.

Losing his only daughter had made him a little more, not exactly reckless, but more likely to take that extra risk in a fire if someone were trapped. He put his life and soul into his job. No other parent should ever have to go through what he and Niamh had.

He reached for the phone, and then shook his head. He'd try to comfort her first and if she didn't want it, if she blamed him like she had done every single day since the fire, then he'd call Liam. He stood and headed into the hall. The door to the downstairs bathroom opened and he looked at Niamh as she came out. The same hollow, gaunt look that he knew so well was back. "Hon…" he whispered.

"I don't…" She broke off in another sea of tears.

"Niamh, I really tried to get to her. I promise." Tears streaked his face. "If I could have died in her place I would have."

He moved closer to her and wrapped his arms around her. She stiffened and he pulled back. "Sorry. I'm sorry."

"You lied to me. You all lied to me. You, Mum, Patrick, Liam. You all sat there and told me I didn't have children. But I did and she's gone and I don't even remember her."

His heart broke again. He'd made the wrong

decision and things had just gotten worse. "I'm sorry. Do you want me to tell you about her?"

"No! I want you to leave." Sparks flew from her eyes, her distraught voice tinged with anger. "Just get out."

"OK. I'll go pack a bag, stay with Liam. Do you want me to send him over?"

"No. He's as bad as you are. I'm going to bed. I don't want you here when I get up." She turned and headed up the stairs as fast as the crutches would let her.

He sank to his knees, tears pouring down his face, his soul in turmoil.

How many times do I have to tell her I'm sorry before she'll forgive me? But why should she when I can't forgive myself? I killed our baby — oh, God, I'm sorry...

The storm of tears passed, he pushed up and went to pack his things. He grabbed the landline phone from the hall on his way to the stairs. "Hey, Liam, it's Jared."

"What's up? You sound terrible."

"Niamh found out about Dayna. She must have gone searching the sideboard whilst I was out because the pictures were buried."

"I did tell you that lying to her was a bad idea, but did you listen to me?"

"I know. Next time make sure I do. She doesn't want me here right now. Don't suppose I can sleep at yours on the sofa, can I? Just for tonight. Hopefully she'll calm down and we can talk about this tomorrow."

"Of course you can stay. I'll make up the couch for you. Want me to come over and speak to her?"

"I suggested that. She doesn't want to see you either. In her eyes, everyone lied to her this afternoon."

"That's because we did."

"No. Strictly speaking, we don't have children. We did, but now…" Jared's voice caught. "I'm packing as we speak. I'll be with you in a bit."

"OK. Look, do me a favor. Take the phone to Niamh. Tell her I have to speak to her."

"OK. But if she refuses, don't blame me."

****

Niamh glared at the shut door as the persistent knock came again. "I told you to go away," she called.

"I'm just leaving, but there's a phone call for you."

"Tell them I'm asleep."

"That's a lie."

"Hah!" she snorted. "That's rich coming from you."

"Niamh, they can hear you yelling, they know you're in. The phone is on the banister, please take it."

Niamh waited until the front door had slammed shut before she went to answer the phone. "Hello."

"Niamh, it's me."

"What do you want, Liam?"

"To explain and apologize."

"There is no explanation. You lied. You all did. I've no idea if Jared is a habitual liar, but I know you're not. I asked outright, Liam, and was told no kids."

"Jared had his reasons for not wanting you told about Dayna just yet."

"I bet he did." Anger spilled from every pore, filling her voice with bitterness and grief.

"Listen to me. You asked me if you and Jared were having problems, remember?"

Niamh snorted. "I remember this afternoon and

the last few days just fine. It's the preceding ten years I don't remember. I know we no longer share a room as there is nothing of Jared's in the master bedroom and I found an email talking about a divorce."

"*You* kicked him out. You never forgave him for Dayna's death. You put the blame solely on him."

She sat on the bed. Her heart hammered and she struggled to form the words. "I—I did what?"

"You blamed him. Said he should have made sure the fire was out before he went to sleep. That he should have saved her. He saves people for a living and was unable to save *your* daughter." Liam's voice cracked. "*Your* daughter, not his."

"Oh." The knife in her gut twisted further.

"Yes, oh." Anger tinged Liam's voice and she wondered how long he'd kept this bottled up. "You forgot he was grieving, too. The firefighters had to drag him out of the inferno your home had become. He got burned trying to save her and you didn't even go and visit him in the hospital. The only reason you are both living in the same house is because you insisted on him paying the mortgage and you couldn't afford a mortgage and rent on another place."

"I don't remember any of this." Her stomach churned and guilt riddled her. Was she really that horrible? He'd gotten so upset telling her about Dayna. Surely he wouldn't have stood there and watched a child die? Watched his child die and not tried to save her. But that didn't excuse the fact he'd lied to her.

"I never knew you had such a vindictive streak in you. He never stopped loving you. But you? You turned your love for him off at the mains and never looked back. Not once did you refer to Dayna as Jared's daughter or take his grief into consideration."

"I'm not the person I was then. She went to work one morning and just didn't come back."

"Oh, she's still there, Niamh. One slight mistake on Jared's part and you throw him out. Just like before."

Niamh closed her eyes. There was no listening to or reasoning with him when he was like this. "Jared lied to me. I'm going to bed. Night."

She cut off the call and tossed the phone onto the bed beside her. Leaning backwards, she pushed into the pillows. Why would she blame Jared? Would she really have just shoved him aside and looked into getting a divorce?

What kind of a horrid person was she? Bile rose around the heavy rock in the pit of her stomach. She shouldn't have spoken to either Liam or Jared like that. *Forgive me.* She picked up the phone and redialed. The phone answered on the fourth ring. "Liam, it's me. I'm sorry."

"Apology accepted." He was still mad at her, his voice taut and curt.

"Is Jared there yet?"

There was a long pause. "He's just got here." A muffled conversation took place before Liam spoke again. "He says he's going to shower and go to bed. He doesn't want to talk to you."

"Oh." Tears burned her eyes and the lump in her throat threatened to choke her. "What have I done? I'm sorry."

"It's not me you need to apologize to."

"I said horrible things to him. What if he won't forgive me?" She let the tears fall. She deserved to feel this way. Maybe they would have been better off if she had died in the crash.

Liam paused again. "Let me come and get you and you can sleep here. I'll kip on the other couch in the lounge with Jared, and you can have my room."

"I can't kick you out of your room. We shared a bedroom until we were what sixteen, seventeen? And if you sleep in with Jared, he's going to want to know why."

"Fine, you have the bed and I'll have the floor. That way you can talk with Jared in the morning and decide what you both want to do. I'll be here until eight, then I have to leave for school."

"And if he won't or can't forgive me?"

"Then I guess you just have to move on. One of you can stay at mine for the time being. Pack an overnight bag, sis. I'll be there in ten minutes."

The phone cut off and Niamh looked at it. Numb and cold, his words echoed in her mind. *You just have to move on?* "What have I done?"

****

Niamh looked up from the mug of tea as Jared walked into the kitchen just after seven thirty a.m. Shirtless, he pushed a hand through sleep tousled hair. Bare feet peeked beneath track suit bottoms. She knew she was staring, but couldn't help it. Across the muscled shoulders, puckered scarred skin stretched. The telltale marks of having been caught in a severe fire. Was it in the line of duty or...?

"He got burned trying to save her, and you didn't even go and visit him in the hospital."

Liam held out a mug of coffee. "Morning, Jared. How did you sleep?"

Jared took the cup. "I didn't really. Well, I dozed a

little. Dreamt about the fire and losing Dayna again." His voice tailed off, his gaze falling on Niamh. "What's she doing here?"

"I picked her up after you went to bed. She had my bed, I had the floor, and we shared a room just like when we were kids. You two need to talk."

Jared set the cup down forcefully, spilling coffee onto the table. "There's nothing to say."

The ice in his voice froze the blood in her veins. This was a stupid idea. She needed to get out of here.

Pulling the crutches towards her, Niamh stood. "I'm sorry. I should never have come. I'll get my bag and call a cab. I'll wait out the front for it."

"You'll do no such thing. Sit down the pair of you."

Stunned by the authority in Liam's voice, she sat, noting Jared did the same thing.

"Right," Liam continued, setting a series of photographs on the table between them. "You've both avoided this since she died, but no more. This is Dayna, your daughter, Niamh. Yours and Jared's very much loved and wanted daughter. She was three when she died. We were wrong to keep it from you. It was Jared's decision, but he assured us he had your best interests at heart. For what it's worth, I told him it would come back and bite him, but he's like you. Once he gets an idea in his head, he doesn't listen to anyone."

"Why lie to me?" She fixed her gaze on Jared.

"Because you didn't remember her, or me come to that." His voice was still icy.

"Still don't."

"Exactly. I'm a stranger you had a child with. A child you don't remember. A child who died in a fire you don't remember either. You're recovering from a major RTC, several injuries, as well as memory loss. You don't need to grieve for Dayna again on top of that." He looked down at the cup in his hand. "Besides, you were being civil to me."

"Why wouldn't I be? I don't understand. I know you've been sleeping in the spare room for a lot longer than you made out."

Jared nodded. "Yeah, for almost a year."

"Liam said I blamed you for Dayna's death."

"Yeah, you did."

"Why?" She wrinkled her nose in consternation. "Did you set the fire?"

"No. I. Did. Not." Jared shoved his cup across the table, his face red and his tone angry and indignant. His eyes glistened, and he shot her a pain filled stare. "The chimney caught fire, I told you that. If, and I mean *if*, I wanted to burn something down, it wouldn't have been our house with us inside it. I'm a fire *fighter*. Not a fire starter."

"It was a simple question," she whispered.

She turned her attention to her hands. She was beginning to hate the person she was before the car crash. Slowly she glanced up again. "If you didn't set the fire, then it wasn't your fault."

Jared sucked in a deep breath. "I didn't put the fire out before we went to bed. I'm a firefighter and should have known better. I should have saved her. You threw a dozen reasons at me since the fire. Including I didn't love her enough."

I said what? How could I blame him for an accident? Nothing he said so far makes it his fault.

She held his gaze. "The chimney could have caught without the fire still burning. You know that, as well as I do, if not better. You told me the floor collapsed before you could get to her. You tried, you did your best. No one can ask any more than that. It wasn't your fault."

"I'm sorry?" Jared sounded strangled, as if he could barely get the words out.

"It wasn't your fault," she repeated.

Jared pushed to his feet and left the room in a hurry.

Niamh turned from his retreating figure to her brother. "What? Did I say something wrong?"

Liam shook his head slightly. "You spent the last two years blaming Jared for all of it. Having an open fireplace. Not getting the chimney swept often enough. Having a thatched roof. You even accused him outright of killing Dayna by hesitating too long before going to get her."

Niamh's stomach plummeted and her heart twisted. Physical pain shot through her as her hand rose to cover her mouth. No wonder he'd looked at her the way he had. "Oh…"

"That's why he didn't tell you. For the first time in two years you were speaking to him without hatred. OK, you don't know who he is, but he'd lived with hatred for so long that he was prepared to do anything not to impede your recovery and probably keep the 'nicer you' around for a little longer."

"What kind of a person was I?" She managed, sobs welling up from her broken heart. She leaned into her brother as he hugged her. "It's no wonder he hates me. I hate myself."

"Shh…" Liam whispered, rocking her. "He doesn't hate you. No one does."

"He should. If I could take back every hateful

thought and word, even though I don't remember them, I would. But it's too late."

"It's not too late to put any of this right, I promise."

"Did you mean what you said?" Jared spoke from the doorway.

Niamh raised her head. He looked as bad as she felt. "Yes, I did. It wasn't your fault, and if I said it was before, then I am really, really sorry. You're a firefighter. You knew what to do and how to do it. But more than that, you were her father. You wouldn't want anything to happen to her. Or stand by and watch her die without trying to prevent it."

Jared didn't move. "That didn't stop you saying all kinds of hateful things. You wanted me dead."

She looked at him, overwhelmed with shock and horror. "Is that really what I said?" she whispered. "That you should have died instead of her because you didn't save her?" His silence spoke volumes. Niamh's stomach knotted further. "Please tell me I didn't say that."

"Yeah, you did," he whispered. "That's why I moved into the spare room."

"I'm so sorry." She held out a hand to him. "I'm not asking for forgiveness, because I don't deserve it."

"No, you don't," Jared said. He took her hand. "But I do forgive you."

"Thank you."

"I'll stay here for a few days, if that's OK. Liam wants to redecorate before he puts the place on the market and moves in with Jacqui after the wedding. And I'm on downtime the next few days."

Niamh shivered. He didn't want to come back to the house. She didn't blame him. She didn't sound like a very nice person at all. Perhaps she'd pushed him too far, and he really had given up on her. "Sure, it makes sense and you'd be quicker with the decorating if you were staying here."

Something flashed in his eyes for a moment. It could have been relief, but she hoped it wasn't. A faint smiled crossed his lips. "I'll drive you back to the house. Unless, you'd like to help me choose the paint first. You know Liam better than I do."

"Sure, I can do that." She looked at Liam. "If you trust me."

Liam smiled. "Of course I do. You have wonderful taste in color and interior design. Just look at your place."

"Maybe it was Jared."

Liam snorted. "Jared thinks navy blue and bright pink are cool. I want to sell this place, not give it away."

Jared sent Liam a hurt expression. "Can I help being color challenged?"

"No, but you tend to abuse it a fair bit."

"Niamh, don't let him be mean to me."

"You're a big boy, Jared and quite capable of defending yourself. But, I will help you choose the paint."

Relief filled her as he smiled at her. Perhaps they could work through this. The thought of him not being around and being mad at her, made her feel more than uncomfortable. It was as if part of her was missing, but for the life of her, she couldn't figure out why.

Help us work through this, Lord, she prayed as they walked to the car. *And please, curb this tongue of mine. Let me think before I speak. And, Lord, help Jared see that what happened to Dayna wasn't his fault. I was wrong to blame him for so long. Forgive me.*

She sat in the car, her fingers tracing the wedding ring on the chain around her neck.

Jared glanced at her. "I'm glad you're still wearing it," he said quietly. "Even if it isn't on your left hand."

"It just doesn't feel right. I don't want to lead you on. Does that make sense?"

"Yeah, it does. I'm just happy you're wearing it." His smile gave him a wistful childlike look. "You wore it like that towards the end of your pregnancy."

"Did I?"

"I offered to get it enlarged, but you refused. You put it on the chain until you'd had Dayna and could wear it again."

"I was going to ask you about the necklace."

"I gave it to you as a wedding present. The first night in the hotel. You still had your wedding dress on and we were jumping on the bed…"

Niamh laughed. "Jumping on the bed? Did we break it?"

"No, fortunately. And, yes, it was your idea. Anyway, we were jumping on the bed and finally flopped exhausted onto it. You rolled onto your side and then gave me the most beautiful pair of cufflinks I've seen. They were eighteen carat gold, with a tiny diamond and my initials on them. I gave you the necklace and you've never taken it off since." His voice faltered. "I lost the cufflinks in the fire. I didn't see the point in replacing them."

"I'm sorry."

"Not your fault." He parked the car and locked out of the window at the huge DIY store. "It's in the past. Now we just need to move on. If you want to, that is?"

"I'd like that. Now, let's go get this paint. Sooner you start the sooner it's done."

10

Niamh made her way to the front door, balancing on one crutch to open it. She'd been home about an hour and just settled on the sofa with a movie she hadn't seen on the TV and a large mug of tea in her hand. The man standing on her doorstep looked familiar. If it was who she was thinking of, he'd aged and looked sick. "Hello?"

The tall, stocky greying man smiled and held out a hand. "Hi, Niamh. I'm Alan Reynolds."

She smiled. She was right—it was the man she remembered. He was her boss. Wow, but he'd gotten old. She shook his hand. "It is you. I thought I recognized your name on the emails, but you'd only just started at the CPS from what I remember. I didn't think for one minute you'd be the director now. Please, come in. Can I get you some tea or coffee?"

"No, thank you. I'm fine."

She led the way down the hall and lowered herself into a chair. She leaned the crutches next to her. "So how are you? How's Morag?" *I hope she's still his wife.*

Alan sat opposite her with several case files on his lap. Sorrow flickered in his gaze as he opened his briefcase. "I'm fine. Morag's not so good. She was diagnosed with early onset Alzheimer's a few years ago. It's getting progressively worse."

"I'm so sorry. That must be hard on you both."

"It is. Now, in your email you mentioned coming

back to work in the hope it would jog your memory a little. So, I brought a couple of your most recent cases over. I can't leave them with you, obviously, but your notes and so on from your desk I can." He handed them across to her.

She set the notebooks aside and leafed through the files asking questions as they came to her. She listened as he described her job and what she did all day long. It sounded the same as what she remembered, except she was doing the job her mentor, Toby Croft, had done.

"Was I really up for a judgeship? Jared mentioned it a couple of nights ago."

"Yes. It's quite an honor at your age."

"I want to ask something. This file mentions death threats. Was this car crash related in any way?"

Consternation crossed Alan's face. "Have the police not gotten back to you yet?"

"No. I gave them what statement I could, which was nothing really, but I haven't heard anything. No one has."

"Let me look into it for you. I know for a fact SOCO were investigating."

"Thank you. What about coming back to work?"

"I, personally, don't have a problem with you coming back as soon as you feel up to it, so long as the doctor has no objections. For obvious reasons, you can't come back to exactly what you were doing before. Or to the same cases. However, Toby Croft is willing to help in any way he can."

"Wow. Is Toby still there?"

Alan smiled. "He's part of the furniture. If need be, he'll take you on as his junior for a few weeks. We'll assign you a few easy cases. Straight forward ones that won't over exert you. Get you back into the swing of things gradually."

Niamh baulked. "I'm not a child."

"I'm not saying you are, Niamh, but you have forgotten—"

She cut him off. "I was fully qualified at twenty-six. You know that. OK, I may not remember how to be a senior prosecutor, but I'm not a rookie either. And I don't need to be Toby's junior assistant again, either."

"I know that. But my concerns, and that of the bar, are that you *have* forgotten the last ten years. We just want to give you chance to relearn anything else you need to, ease back into the job. And Toby is best placed to help you with that. I know you don't like the idea, but put yourself in my place. And in the shoes of the victims you'll be getting justice for. If you were them, would you want the best prosecutor out there, or someone who can't remember last month?"

Niamh nodded. "You're right. I'm sorry. I should be grateful I still have a job at all, right?"

Alan winked. "I wouldn't go that far. And it won't be long before you're back at the helm, full steam ahead. You'll see."

She handed him the files back. "I need to get back to work, and some semblance of normality, rather than sit here and mope all day long."

"Come in on Wednesday. Have a chat with Toby and myself and we'll see where we go from there. We'll fit in with your hospital appointments, so don't worry about that."

****

Niamh spent the two days going through her

online blog, trying to glean as much information about herself and her life from it as possible. She didn't like what she read.

Am I really as mean as these entries make out, Lord? The hatred just spills from them. Even the case files Alan gave me. My notes are disparaging. I don't like who I was. Help me change. And if my memories ever do come back, don't let me become her again.

Jared picked her up just after ten on Wednesday. She wasn't going to admit it to anyone, but she'd missed his company the past couple of days. He held the door open as she climbed into the car. "There you go."

"Thank you. How's the decorating going?"

He winked. "Bit of a one person job to be honest."

"Liam still useless?" she giggled.

"And the rest." Jared laughed as he slid into the car beside her.

"He always was. Dad banned him from helping as there was always more paint on the carpet and on him than on the walls."

"Sounds about right. How have you been?"

She remained silent.

"Niamh?"

She twisted in her seat. Reaching across, she laid a hand on top of his. "If I could take back every mean word I said to you, I would. I don't know what I said, only that I hurt you very deeply. I can see that just by looking at you and hearing you speak. I'm really sorry. And yes, I know I said it before, but I still feel horrible. Reading this online journal I found, and emails I've sent, just made me feel worse. I wasn't a very nice person. And not just to you either."

He caught his breath. "There were times you were

pretty mean, I'll admit that. But you're my wife and Liam and Patrick's sister and we love you regardless."

"The thing I don't understand, is why?"

"Same reason God loves us even when we mess up."

"I guess so, yeah."

Jared parked outside the huge imposing grey and red brick offices of the CPS. "Are you sure you're going to be all right?"

Niamh raised an eyebrow. "Have you always been this much of a worry wart?"

"Yes. But worse today because you're starting over."

"Only technically. I know how to be a lawyer. I'll be fine." She smiled. "This is just a meeting to go over a few things, tell me who I'll be working with and so on."

"OK. I'll come back at lunchtime and pick you up."

"Sure, thanks. Shall I ring you?"

"No need. I'll be here at one."

"OK, thanks." Niamh shot him a smile and slowly made her way up the stone steps and into reception. It even smelled the same. Her crutches tapped on the marble floor and echoed against the high vaulted ceiling.

The guard was on his feet before she was halfway across the lobby. "Mrs. Harkin, it's lovely to see you again. How are you doing? We've all been so worried about you."

She smiled. "I'm doing OK, Duncan. I didn't expect to see you here still." He'd been the guard when she first started working here.

"I'm part of the furniture now. The place would

fall apart without me," he joked.

"True. The boss should be expecting me."

"Once you've signed in, I'll let him know you're on the way up."

"Thank you." Niamh signed her name in the huge book on the desk. "Is he still on the fourth floor?"

"He is."

"Thank you." She turned slowly and swung herself towards the elevators. She was getting quite fast on the crutches now, having mastered stairs, but there was a big difference between carpeted stairs at the house, and the stone ones she'd find here. As much as she hated elevators, it was the lesser of two evils. She pressed the button and waited.

The elevator came and she got in, pressing the button for the fourth floor. She watched the numbers change and as the elevator stopped, she exited the car and took a sharp left, straight into someone trying to get into the elevator. Papers flew everywhere and he gave out a sharp grunt. Niamh looked up, her cheeks burning. "Oh, I'm sorry—"

She broke off, staring at the tall blond man in a blue suit. His piercing lavender eyes glinted in anger. It was him, the man from her dreams, but she still couldn't remember his name.

"So you should—Niamh?" The man's firm hand gripped hers, pulling it off the crutch and pumped it several times. "How are you? I was really worried when I heard you'd been injured." His eyes raked over her, making her feel more than a little uncomfortable.

"I'm sorry. I don't…do I know you?"

"Miles. Miles Kingsman. We've worked together on several cases."

"It's nice to meet you, but I'm afraid I don't

remember you." Niamh disengaged her hand, wishing she could wipe it on the tracksuit trousers she'd worn over her cast. "I'm having a little trouble with my memory since the car crash, although the doctors say it will come back. It's just a matter of time."

He bent, gathering his papers. "That's good. Other than that, how are you? It was a nasty car crash."

"I'm OK. I'm mending slowly."

"Good, good. Maybe we could do lunch some time. Catch up, renew our friendship." His fingers ran over her arm, sending goose bumps rippling through her.

"I don't know."

"At least think about it."

Another voice echoed down the hallway. "Niamh, I'm glad you could make it. I've got tea and cakes laid on in my office. Toby is starving as always."

Niamh turned, grateful for the interruption. "Alan. You shouldn't have gone to the trouble of cakes. But it sounds wonderful." She balanced on one crutch, returning his brief hug. "I'm doing OK, a little sore, but OK."

He laughed. "Answering the question before it's asked. Come down to the office, before Toby eats all the cakes."

Niamh nodded and turned back to Miles, but he'd gone. *Hmmm, well he could have said goodbye. Especially as he appears to know me rather well, if I was reading him right.*

She turned back to Alan and walked down the hallway to his office. "I feel like the new kid on her first day at school."

"You'll be fine. It's like riding a bicycle. Once you learn you never forget. How's Jared?"

"Ummm, yeah, he's fine as far as I know. Jared's living at Liam's for a bit."

Alan stopped and turned to stare at her, his face unreadable. "Why?"

"He's helping Liam decorate, and we decided it's for the best, until my memory comes back." She paused. "Thing is, I don't know him and although we get on, it's just uncomfortable living with someone— living with a bloke that I'm not married to. And before you say I am married to him, I don't remember."

She looked away. "Don't remember him or the wedding or how we met or what it was about him that attracted me to him initially."

"So you kick him out and take off the rings? That isn't very Christian of you. Try to see it from his point of view."

"Try seeing it from mine. I don't know him. And according to everyone I've spoken to, we weren't exactly on the best of terms before the car crash." She pulled her chain from under her jumper and showed him. "Besides, I'm still wearing the ring…just not the way he and the rest of the world want right now."

Alan's expression sent shivers down her spine and he held up his left hand with the worn wedding band on. "My wife doesn't know me, either. I had to put her in a home because the dementia has reached a point where she needs twenty-four hour care. She'll never know who I am, except for maybe a brief glimpse of clarity once in a while, when all she does is apologize for being a burden. Yet I have no intention of turning my back on my vows or taking off my ring. You have a chance to start over with Jared. Don't waste it."

She nodded slowly, following him into the office.

Toby was every bit as pedantic and methodical as

she remembered. Working under him again was going to be a struggle, as she hadn't enjoyed it the first time. But if that's what it took, she'd do it.

On her way out of the building, she noticed Miles Kingsman leaning against a pillar. At her slow approach he pushed up and sauntered over to her. "Can I help you with those?" He jerked his head to her briefcase.

"No, I got it. Thank you."

"In that case how about lunch? I know this place that does the most amazing Mexican food."

"I can't. I'm being collected."

"Then another time. We could catch up. I could fill in some of the gaps you may have." His hand was warm on her arm and she shivered. He was persistent if nothing else.

"OK," she agreed. Maybe this would get him off her back. And maybe he could answer some questions. He must mean something to be in her dreams and one of the few people she remembered looking the way they did now. "But just lunch. How about next Tuesday?" That would fit in with Jared's shift pattern.

"Tuesday's good. Twelve thirty at Mancinis? Do you remember where it is?"

She nodded. "I'll find it. See you then." She signed out and headed outside to where Jared was waiting.

****

Niamh didn't see Jared for a couple of days, as he was busy decorating and working, including the Sunday, so Liam took her to church. Tuesday, she got a cab to the appointed place at the right time. Miles had offered to pick her up, but she refused, wanting to pay her own way. She arranged for the cab driver to come back for her in an hour and a half. That should be plenty long enough and avoid having to decline a lift home.

Miles was waiting at the table and rose as the maître d' showed her over to a table by the window. This place was way too classy for her, and she felt more than a little uncomfortable. A waft of aftershave washed over her as Miles moved around to pull out her chair for her. "Hey, how are you?"

"Fine, thank you." She sat and leaned her crutches against the table. "How are you?"

"I'm good." He sat down again. "I took the liberty of ordering for you."

"Oh." The uncomfortable feeling grew. "That was rather presumptive of you."

He jerked his head. "Well, I figured as I know what you like as we've been here before..." He shot her a charming smile, which reminded her of a snake. Coiled and ready to pounce. "I also ordered you a white wine."

"I don't drink."

"Since when?"

"Since the accident. I don't like the taste of it anymore. I don't drink coffee now, either." She looked up as the waiter brought their plates of food over. "Could I have some apple juice, please?"

"Of course, madam." The waiter set the plates down and left.

She looked down at the plate. Her stomach turned. "What's this?"

"Curried scallops with black olive, almond, carrot and lime puree."

Niamh looked down at the plate and closed her

eyes, saying grace silently. Then she cautiously cut the scallop and tried it. At first thought, it seemed undercooked and cold. Then she realized with horror that it was raw. Somehow she managed to force a bite down.

Miles's conversation seemed to consist mainly of his current case. Sure, that wasn't ethical, she nevertheless listened politely. The main course came. Lamb with parsnip puree, beetroot, broad beans and a spiced jus. Did she really like this food? And what was it with all the puree? That was what you gave babies when first weaning them.

She poked the lamb, to find blood spurt onto her plate. Ewww, it was rare? Didn't the chef know how to cook anything properly? She found herself longing for Jared's home cooked meat and two veg, and his quiet, unassuming manner.

A hand dropped on her shoulder. She glanced up to see Liam, his face icy. She smiled. "Hey, Li."

"What are you doing here?" His tone matched his eyes.

"Probably the same as you are. I'm having lunch."

"Can I have a word? Over here?"

Niamh put her serviette on the table. "Sure. Excuse me a minute." She pulled herself to her feet and followed Liam across the room. "What's wrong?"

He stopped four tables away and stared at her. "Does Jared know you're here?"

"No he doesn't, and so what if he did? I'm sure he wouldn't mind."

"You're married." He pointed to the ring around her neck.

"Liam, this is lunch. With a friend. I'm sure you have lunch with people other than Jacqui and she doesn't blow a gasket over it."

"Do you actually know or remember him?"

She sighed. "Look, remember the other day I asked if I were seeing someone other than Jared?" He nodded and she carried on speaking. "Right, well, I keep having flashes of a blond man with lavender eyes. He even pops into my dreams occasionally. This is him. I figured maybe over lunch he'd say something to jog my memory, but all I found out so far is I really don't like high end dining, no matter what he says. I know him from work. His name is Miles Kingsman."

"You never mentioned him before." His hand rested on her arm and the ice in his eyes and voice was replaced by deep concern.

"Yeah, well, there's probably nothing to it. If you don't mind, I'm going back to my lunch before it gets cold." She paused. "Not that it was particularly hot or cooked properly, anyway."

Liam hugged her. "There's something about him, Niamh. I don't like him."

"You don't know him. Did Jared send you here to spy on me?"

"Now you're being silly. I'm just looking out for my baby sister."

She hugged him awkwardly. "Says he who's a whole ten minutes older than me."

"Fifteen minutes, actually."

"Whatever." She kissed him. "Don't worry about me. I'm fine and the only concern is I might die of hunger."

"You really don't like the food?"

"Raw scallops and undercooked lamb? Ewww, no way. Don't tell the chef, but I'm ordering pizza soon as I get home."

Liam laughed and she waved as she made her way back over to the table.

"Is everything all right?" Miles asked.

She eased back into her seat. "Everything's fine. So where were we?"

****

Jared pulled a clean tee-shirt from his locker over his head and grabbed his mobile phone as it rang. He checked the screen and smiled. "Hey, Liam. Checking up on me now?"

"Not this time. Jared. You've got a rival for Niamh's affections. She was in that fancy place on the High Street with some bloke she insisted she knew from before the car crash."

"Did you get a name?"

"Miles Kingsman. He's someone she knows from work."

"Is he blond?" he asked hesitantly. He wasn't sure if he wanted to know or not.

"Yes."

Jared swallowed hard, nausea rising. *That would make him the bloke Niamh remembers. What's so special about him? Why does she remember him and not me?*

"She's hoping he might jog her memory, but I don't like the guy. Tried telling her, but she wasn't having it."

He sighed. "She never does listen once she decides to do something. You know that almost as well as I do."

"Well, this time you have to make her listen. Fight for her, or you're going to lose her. There is something about this guy. I've got the same feeling I did about

Vince, and you know how that ended up."

"Yeah." Jared remembered all too well how Liam almost died several times once Vince came on the scene. And the way Niamh woke screaming in pain in the middle of the night, drenched in sweat adamant someone was electrocuting her. "I'll talk to her when I get off shift tonight. And speaking of work there goes the alarm. Got to run. Bye."

****

Niamh was about to go to bed when she heard the key in the door and pulled herself up. She wasn't expecting Jared tonight, but something flared within her at the prospect of seeing him. She'd missed him. But the man who stood in front of her wasn't the one she was expecting. He was filthy. Soot in his hair and smudges on his face. "Jared?"

His hands shook as he stood there, not saying anything. He'd never come home like this before, she was sure of it.

"Are the showers at the station not working?"

Still he didn't say anything.

"Jared, you're scaring me. What's wrong?"

His tongue ran over his lips. "Bad day," he managed. "Needed to…"

She crossed over to him, and dropping one crutch, pulled him into a hug. He clung to her, the smell of smoke almost overpowering. His body convulsed as he leaned against her, huge sobs welling up and engulfing him. Tightening her grip, she held him, not sure what else she could do or say to help.

After a few minutes, he pulled back. Embarrassment flared in his cheeks. "Sorry. I didn't know who else to go to."

"It's OK. Want some coffee?"

"Please." He bent and handed her back the crutch. "Mind if I grab a quick shower?"

"Course not. It's your house as much as mine. More so as you pay the mortgage. Your towels are still in the bathroom. I'll go make the coffee."

She watched him head upstairs and then went into the kitchen. What had upset him so much? She shuddered. That smell…she knew that smell.

The smoke, thick, black, pervading everything, took away her vision. Voices echoed, someone screamed. Her hand felt along the wall, trying to find a way out. The choking blackness clung and stole the air she was trying to breathe…

"Coffee smells good."

His voice jerked her from her thoughts, and she slid the mug across to him. "Here."

"Thank you." He downed it like a drowning man gulps air and then refilled it. "It was a really bad day…afternoon. Huge fire…" His voice cracked and his eyes glistened. "We lost one firefighter, two more injured. Not from my watch, but another crew."

"I'm so sorry." She put a hand on his arm.

"It looks like arson. Just hope they catch whoever…" He covered his face with his hands, a visible struggle for control going on inside him. "And Liam rang, caught me just before I left on the shout."

"Oh."

"He told me…told me you were seeing someone else."

Niamh stood there, unsure what to say or do. Before she had chance to do either, Jared's hands gripped her arms. His face inches away from hers. Despite the anger in his eyes, she wasn't scared. His gaze searched hers intently.

"You're my wife." His voice low and with a depth of emotion she hadn't heard before.

"Jared…"

"Mine." His lips pressed hard upon hers. She'd imagined him kissing her, trying to remember what it was like, but not like this. In her mind it had been soft and gentle, but she could feel the power of his emotions coming through. A mix of rage, grief and desperation, but beneath that something else, something far more powerful and intense.

Well, two could play that game. Not to be outdone, she dropped the crutches and kissed him back fully, one hand holding him for support, the other winding through his hair. She parted her lips, and Jared deepened the kiss, possessing her, until her head spun and her heart pounded.

11

Finally, breathless, Niamh pulled back from the kiss. Intoxicating eyes, dark with desire gazed down at her, and she found herself drowning in them. Emotion such as she never dreamed possible rippled through every inch of her, and her skin flamed under his fingers. Her hand rested on his firm chest feeling his heart beat in perfect time with her own.

"Well?" Jared's voice was even lower than it had been before, almost husky.

"Not bad. Not quite what I imagined for a first kiss, but not bad."

"I'm sorry." He had the decency to go red and wiped his hand over his mouth. His lips were full and enticing and...moving. He was speaking to her again. "I shouldn't have done that."

"Well, maybe not like that, but...Jared, why are we ... I mean, can't we go out with other people as friends for lunch or whatever? I wouldn't mind if you did." Or would she? A surge of jealousy hit hard as she imagined Jared sitting across a table, sharing a glass of something sparkling and a candlelit dinner with another woman.

"Niamh, you're my wife. For better and worse, legally and under God. And unless we divorce, you'll stay that way. And a divorce isn't going to happen."

"I found emails about that. The separate rooms were a permanent thing?"

He jerked his head. "Yes. You were looking into selling the house as well."

Shock flooded her and she swallowed hard. She was going to do *what*? "Seriously? You didn't agree, I assume."

"No and I still don't. I wasn't ready to give up on us then, and I'm not now." He paused, his dark gaze never leaving hers. "Two weeks before the car crash we had a massive fight over going to marriage guidance counseling. I wanted to go and you didn't." He paused. "You came to my room to apologize and one thing led to another and we made up. I'd hoped you'd changed your mind, but it didn't seem like it, because the following morning you were back to hating me again."

"I see." Heat flooded her face. Obviously if they were married, they'd had that kind of a relationship. She shivered. Technically, they were still married, and she wasn't sure she'd be strong enough to resist if he kissed her like that again.

His hand cradled the side of her face for a moment. "I'm not saying you can't have lunch with a friend, but I don't want you dating anyone else."

"I don't want to date him. When I went into work last week, I literally bumped into him. Sent his papers flying everywhere. I recognized him as the blond haired bloke I remembered. Figured talking to him might jog my memory, but it didn't. He's seriously creepy actually."

She paused. *Papers flying everywhere...* An image of her and Miles picking up papers while wearing robes popped into her mind. She shook her head, not wanting the feeling of panic that accompanied it. "Aside from me being your wife, does me having lunch with him really bother you that much? Should I have asked you first?"

He shook his head. "No, although you used to tell me if you were having lunch with someone—whether it was a client or a fellow lawyer. Things got messed up the last couple of years, but we have a chance here. To start over."

She tilted her head. "Start over?"

His fingers traced gently over her hand. "Will you go out with me?"

"Go out?"

Jared sighed. "You're not making this easy for me, are you? You haven't forgotten dating, have you?"

"That's a silly question as we were just talking about dating. So no, I haven't forgotten. I…I'm just in shock. I've been really awful to you and you're asking me out on a date."

"I love you. I never stopped. I want to show you the man you fell in love with ten years ago. So, will you go out with me?"

"Yeah, I'd like that." She paused. "But as friends. I mean, like you said, I don't know you."

Jared smiled, the smile staying on his lips as the light died in his eyes. "Friends are fine. It's how everyone starts out. I should get back to Liam's. Thank you for earlier. You always did know how to make me feel better." He kissed her cheek.

"I'm glad I could help."

"How about Saturday? The church bonfire. We could have lunch somewhere and then go to the farm from there."

"Sounds good." She walked with him to the door.

'Friends' was her idea, but why had a surge of grief pierced her soul as if she'd lost the one friend she needed the most?

****

Jared glanced down at the bag in the well of the passenger seat. Had he remembered everything that she liked? He wanted this date to be perfect. For November, the day wasn't too cold, but whether the sun would come out from behind the dark clouds remained to be seen. He parked and took a deep breath, looking up at the house.

Help me, Lord. I want to win her back, to have her remember me. Or at least to love me again. I came so close to losing her in that car crash. And now she's changed her attitude over the fire and Dayna's death, does this mean that there is hope for us? I would like for that, but I put our relationship in Your hands. Work us to Your purpose and as You see fit.

Before he was even out of the car, Niamh had left the house and made her way down the path. He leaned across and opened the passenger door for her. "Hey."

Her smile lit the enclosed space in a way that no sunshine ever could. "Hi. It's good to see you."

He tilted his head. "You mean it? I would have thought after the other day…"

"You were upset, and I wasn't helping any. How are those friends from work?" She slid into the car and did up her belt.

"Doing OK. The funeral is next week, and I was wondering if you'd meet me for coffee or something after."

"Make it tea and sure."

He smiled. "Thank you."

Her hand touched his, her fingers brushing against

the inside of his wrist briefly. "Jared…Would you like me to go with you?"

"Would you? I mean we'll be forming a guard of honor and marching behind the fire engine…" His heart leapt at her offer. Something she used to do, work permitting. Perhaps the new Niamh was just the old one without the baggage of the last two years.

"I can save you a seat in the church…if you want me there."

"I would. Thank you." He leaned across and kissed her cheek, his lips burning from the quick touch.

"Welcome."

Rain started to pound against the windscreen, and he shook his head. "Guess it's a picnic in the car then."

To his surprise, Niamh smiled. "Oh, we used to have those all the time when we were small. I love them."

"Just as well, living in England. Mum always said we have cold rain in winter and warm rain in summer."

"Mine always said we have three types of weather in this country. It's either raining, about to rain, or just finished raining."

He laughed and drove a few miles out of town to the edge of the Chiltern Downs. Pulling into a layby, he turned off the engine, leaving the air con on to stop the windows misting up. "Not much of a view today, I'm afraid."

"It's lovely. God created the rain too, you know." She grinned at him. "So, you said something about food?"

"In the bag by your feet."

She reached down and pulled the bag onto her lap before handing it to him. "This one?"

"Unless there are any other bags down there?"

Niamh made a show of looking. "Nope. Unless they're invisible ones."

He grinned. This Niamh was definitely a pleasure to have around. Long may it continue. It was like their first few dates. They'd clicked from the get go and just never looked back. He opened the bag and pulled out two plastic plates. "Okay, have one of these."

"You brought plates?"

"Too right I did. We're doing this properly. Plate."

"Plate." She balanced it on her lap.

He handed her a cup.

"Cup?" She raised an eyebrow in amazement.

He nodded. "Something wrong?"

Shaking her head, she smiled and took it. "OK, cup."

"Now, ginger beer or lemonade?"

"Which do you want?"

"I got two of each."

"In that case, ginger beer. I haven't had that in ages. Patrick could never understand why they called it beer when it's not the least bit alcoholic."

Jared smiled and handed her the bottle. "Same reason it's called ginger ale in Canada, but not alcoholic either. By the way the drink has to go in the cup or it's not the same." He laughed as she carefully poured the liquid into the cup and sipped slowly.

"Am I doing this right or do I have to hold my little finger out at the same time?"

He snorted. "Only when you're drinking tea with the Queen."

She tilted her head and studied him. "OK. You don't have enough grey hair to be the Queen, so no sticking out little fingers as I drink, then."

He shook his head. "Now I got a choice of rolls. There's cheese salad, tuna salad, or salad salad."

"What is salad salad when it's at home?"

"What Mum always called a honeymoon sandwich. Lettuce alone."

Niamh groaned. "That is terrible. Tuna, please."

Jared handed her the roll, a scotch egg, bag of crisps, and a cake. He put a box of strawberries on the dashboard.

"Wow," she said. "Picnics were never like this when I was a child."

"Mum always used to do ours this way. It's habit. You used to love them."

"I can see why." She picked up the scotch egg a puzzled look on her face. "What's this?"

"It's called a scotch egg. It's a hardboiled egg, wrapped in sausage meat and coated with breadcrumbs before being deep fried. I introduced you to them." He watched as she bit into it. "What do you think?"

She chewed and swallowed with a confused expression on her face before she smiled. "I remember…sitting on a bench eating them. There was a huge mountain…"

"We had them on the top of Mount Snowdon." He smiled. "And it's great you remembered something."

She nodded. "Maybe other things will come back, too."

"They will. Just give it time." Jared turned his attention to his own plate, starting with the cake.

"*Cake*? You're starting with *cake*?"

"I prefer to finish with something savory, so I always eat the cake first."

"You're weird." She took a bite of her sandwich.

129

"Thank you. I think."

They sat and ate watching the rain beat down on the windscreen, the constant drumming drowning out the sound of the radio. Lightning lit the sky. "Bit late for a storm isn't it?" Niamh asked. "Is this going to affect the fireworks?"

Thunder echoed across the hillside. "No. Four years ago we went in an absolute downpour. So long as people turn up, they'll light the bonfire and set off the fireworks."

"Sounds fun."

"Oh it was. Standing huddled under an umbrella watching the fireworks explode above our heads."

"Wish I could remember that."

"Tell you what. We'll do it tonight, whether we need an umbrella or not."

****

Niamh sat in the car on Monday and looked out of the window. It had been a long, strange day. The doctor had reluctantly agreed to her going back to work. He'd wanted six weeks and it had only been four, but she'd promised to behave and not run down corridors or do anything strenuous and to rest if she got tired.

She'd gotten ready for work, and was about to ring a cab, when a car turned up. Alan had arranged a driver and car for her. She tried arguing with him, but he pointed out she couldn't drive, Jared was working and under the circumstances having work provide someone was for the best.

The day itself hadn't been too bad, despite her concerns. Toby had walked her through his current case, and she'd taken a deposition with him watching. Tomorrow she was due to take one unsupervised. Although, knowing Toby, he'd put her in the mirrored interview room and watch through the one way glass.

Miles had appeared around lunchtime and tried to insist she go and eat with him. She'd wriggled out of the invite and had spent lunch in the canteen remembering the fireworks and how good it felt being in Jared's arms watching them explode high over their heads. She was definitely falling for this man. But was it because of the bond they obviously shared or something different this time? He'd promised to cook her dinner tonight, and she was really looking forward to spending the time with him.

The driver dropped her off, promising to be back at eight fifteen in the morning. Niamh watched him go and slowly made her way up the path. The door opened as she got there.

Jared smiled. "Hey. That's one very expensive looking taxi."

"Alan's insisting on a driver." She kissed his cheek. "How was your day?"

"Full of cats stuck up trees. Better than bonfires left unattended." He returned the kiss. "Go and shower. Dinner won't be long."

"It smells wonderful. A girl could get used to this."

After her shower, Niamh looked at herself in the mirror. There was a scar just under her hairline and a deep cut on her cheek that still refused to heal. Her leg, still encased in plaster, was most likely scarred and ugly as well. She would never have described herself as pretty from photos taken before the car crash, but now? Now she was as plain as the ace of spades.

She put down the hairbrush and smoothed her hands over her dress. She headed down to the kitchen. She'd got the stairs down to a fine art.

Jared glanced up. "The sauce is done. Wow. You look pretty."

"You have a strange definition of pretty. Pretty means attractive, beautiful, pleasing. I'm none of those."

He ran his gaze over her figure, making the heat rise in her cheeks. *How can he do that with one simple look?*

"So what word would you use then?"

"Ugly, scarred, useless. I don't know. You pick one."

A thoughtful look crossed his face before he winked at her. "Nope, don't like any of those. Sorry. So, you're a little bashed up right now. You'll heal and walk and run again. You'll be better, stronger faster…"

Niamh giggled. "Just like the bionic pastor? Only I crawl more like a caterpillar right now."

Jared laughed. "Yup, but you know what they say about caterpillars?"

"They usually turn into beautiful butterflies. 'Cept this one stays ugly."

"Then you'll be the world's first ugly butterfly. You might even make the record books. So you want juice or wine with dinner?"

"Juice, please. I've gone off wine. Assuming I liked it before…"

He looked surprised. "OK. I don't drink anyway, so juice it is."

She sat as he put the plates on the table. She hadn't seen anything like this before. Meat and veg rolled up in some kind of bread. "Thank you."

Jared said grace and started eating. She looked for a knife and fork and then glanced up. He was using his hands to eat, so she tentatively did the same.

"You said you'd tell me how we met."

"What would you like to know?"

"Everything." She chewed slowly, savoring the spices in the food. She swallowed and elaborated. "How we met, where we met, what you said, what I said…"

Jared's rich baritone laugh filled the room. "Sounds like consequences."

"I haven't played that in years. I also want to know how long we dated."

He winked at her. "Do you treat your witnesses like this?"

"All the time. I think." She smiled. "This is good. What is it?"

"Fajitas. Spicy Mexican food. You fell in love with the cuisine when we went to Mexico six years ago."

"I can see why." She tilted her head. "You got some sauce on your chin."

Jared ran his finger over his chin then licked the sauce from it. "OK, to answer your questions. We met in church on a Sunday. Nine years ago. April the twenty-eighth to be precise."

"You remember the date?"

"It's a little hard to forget. You Bible bashed me."

Niamh choked on her fajita. "I did *what*?"

"You knocked your Bible over the edge of the gallery at the end of the service. It landed on my head and sent me flying to the floor. You came running down to make sure I was all right and one thing led to another, and I asked you out before you'd even helped me up."

"Let me get this right. I drop my Bible on your head, we exchange about five words and you ask me out? What did I do?"

"Said yes." Jared grinned. "I think you said yes out of guilt at first, but anyway you said yes." He chewed for a while. "I walked you to your car, told you what my job was. You told me what you did. You apologized about fifty times for hitting me with your Bible as that's not what a Bible is for. Ever since then, hitting someone with a Bible has been called Bible Bashing by our friends. Your brothers never let either of us forget."

"I see." She tried not to laugh. It shouldn't be funny, but it was.

"When we reached your car, I took your hand and did this." He raised her hand to his lips and kissed her fingers.

Tenderness instead of roughness sent ripples of pleasure through her entire body. How could one small touch cause such a seismic reaction? "What did I do?"

"Pretty much what you're doing now. Blushed, looked stunned, as if you didn't know what to say or how to react. And I thought to myself, that's the woman I'm going to marry. And I'm glad I did."

"Despite how horrid I apparently was to you the last few years."

"Yeah."

Niamh pushed up on one crutch and took her plate to the sink. "What about our first kiss? First proper kiss, that is."

Jared brought his plate over. "That was on our first date. We went to the zoo. You have this thing about penguins and giraffes. We spent ages at those enclosures. Then we had a picnic under this huge tree. I sat watching you, wondering if your lips were as soft as they looked."

Niamh's gaze settled on his lips. "Oh?"

He moved, gently pushing her against the counter. "Then I leaned forward, like this." His face was mere inches from hers, his eyes darkening as he held her gaze. "And then I did this."

Niamh closed her eyes as his lips touched hers. They were as soft as they had been on her hand. Waves of warmth flowed through and over her from her lips outwards until it encompassed her entire body. She willingly parted her lips, returning the kiss as she lost herself in it. So different to the last time he'd kissed her. If that one had been a nine, this was off the seismic scale completely.

Just before she thought she'd pass out from lack of air, Jared broke the kiss and leaned his forehead against hers. "Four kisses later, we finished lunch and went back to the penguins."

"When did you propose?"

"After our fourth date. I dug out the middle of the front lawn at your parent's house one night and planted flowers so when you opened your bedroom curtains in the morning you'd read 'Marry me Niamh' in red and yellow tulips."

Niamh laughed. "You didn't. Oh, I bet Dad blew his top. Probably a V.E.I eight."

"Oh, I did. And Dad blowing his top is putting it mildly. Krakatoa has nothing on him. He was furious. Not with me proposing, but purely because I'd ruined his lawn. I had to re-turf it."

"I bet. Dad's garden is his pride and joy. No one's allowed to touch it."

He grinned at her. "Then two weeks later I dug it up and planted pansies and marigolds that read 'She said yes'. It took all night and several torch batteries."

"Did you incur the wrath of Dad again?"

"Oh yeah. But it was worth it. I'd do it again."

Something deep within Niamh flickered. For a moment, it was almost within her reach, then it was gone. "You would?"

Jared nodded, holding her gaze. "I would. Even though he said he'd spiflicate me if I ever touched his lawn with so much as a little finger again, I would." He smiled. "I stopped by the video store on my way home and hired a film. The first one we ever went to see. I thought we could sit and watch it. I even got popcorn. The sweet one not the salted, as neither of us like that."

She smiled back. "Bring it on."

12

The next week passed quickly. Niamh easily slipped back into the routine of working. It really wasn't that different from what she remembered, and her initial qualms faded as bits and pieces of her job came back to her. Her previous case notes still puzzled her at their abruptness and outright meanness. For a Christian, she sure hadn't been acting like one. She spent time each day praying over the files, asking for forgiveness for her attitude. At least she hadn't wrongly prosecuted anyone. She had gone through every case she'd prosecuted to check.

Every evening, when Jared wasn't on nights, she spent with him. He'd come over and they'd watch TV or just sit and chat about their respective days. But they'd finish every evening in Bible study and prayer. Something he said had been missing for a while—even before Dayna died. They'd spoken of her several times. Jared had shared lots of memories with her and even borrowed all the photos of her he could in order to get copies made of them.

They'd chosen one of the three of them sitting under the Christmas tree, taken two days before Dayna died and had it enlarged. It now hung in pride of place on the wall in the lounge. Something they both decided was a good thing.

The contents of Niamh's wardrobe had been as big a shock as her journals. Full of more suits and shoes than she would ever really need and not cheap ones either. She looked at them critically and finally decided on just one suit for work. Everything else she folded and placed in five black sacks. That left her with two skirts, two pairs of jeans, the tracksuit trousers that fitted over the cast and a week's worth of shirts, nightwear and lingerie. More than enough.

Next she tackled the shoes. She kept a pair for work, a pair for best, sneakers, and sandals. The rest went in the bags.

When the driver arrived to pick her up for work, she smiled. "Hi, I have a favor to ask."

"Sure, Mrs. Harkin."

"I've got some stuff bagged up to go to the charity shop. Could we drop it off on the way? The bags are on the landing if you don't mind bringing them downstairs for me."

"Of course."

"Thank you. I'll let Mr. Reynolds know I'll be in a little later."

It took him several trips to load the car, but he did it without complaint. "Which charity shop did you want to go to?"

Niamh looked blankly at him. "There's more than one?"

He smiled. "There are five in the precinct."

"OK. Umm, pick one. I don't have a preference."

"Sure."

Once they got there, Niamh wandered around while the driver unloaded all the bags. She found a couple of skirts she immediately fell in love with and an ornament consisting of three owls. Two were the right way up, the third hanging upside down with 'It's one of those days' written along the bottom of it. She paid for them and headed into work.

****

Exhausted after her first afternoon back in court, Niamh locked up and went to bed early, Jared's voice still ringing in her ear. She'd spent an hour on the phone to him just talking about everything and nothing.

She fell asleep quickly only to jerk awake what seemed like only moments later. What had woken her?

Something had fallen. A soft but noticeable thud on the carpet, but was it in her dream or...?

No. There was harsh breathing, a footfall. Another thud and muffled curse.

Someone was in the room. A dim penlight clicked on beside her.

Her heart pounded and she reached over and flicked on the light.

A tall man, dressed in black with balaclava over his face stood next to the bed, her Filofax in his hand.

Niamh screamed as loud as she could, reaching for her phone. She caught a blur moving swiftly in the corner of her eyes, before something connected hard with the side of her head. Pain rocketed through her.

She struggled to focus on the figure beside her. Another blur as he raised his arm again.

His hand connected with her face, the blow making her see double before everything went dark.

When she opened her blurry eyes, the room was empty and she was lying face down on the floor. For a moment, she thought she'd imagined it, but the pain in her head assured her she hadn't. She reached up blindly for the phone, hoping it was where she'd left it.

It was. She dialed Liam's number.

After three rings, Jared's voice echoed down the line. "Hello, Liam's phone."

Jared? What... She had no idea why he was answering Liam's phone, but she needed him. "Jared, help..."

Concern filled his voice. "Niamh, what's wrong?"

"Please, help me..." Something dripped into her eyes and she wiped warm liquid away. Her hand was red. Was that blood?

She dropped the phone, and digging her fingers into the carpet, crawled to the bathroom, her plastered leg dragging behind her. She reached up and grabbed a towel off the rack. The tiny room spun in a haze of black and white as dizziness flooded her. She curled up on the floor, her head on the towel.

Just rest a few moments, until the pain goes away...

****

Jared fumbled his key in his haste to get into the house. As he put it in the lock, the door gave and opened. He hadn't even unlocked it. Was someone in the house with her? Exchanging a frantic glance with Liam he rattled off, "Call the police," before he ran inside. "Niamh!"

On alert, he searched for her, calling her name. Hearing a faint moan, he hurtled up the stairs. "Niamh?"

She lay slumped on the landing half out of the bathroom. Dropping to his knees, he felt for a pulse in the limp slender wrist. He cradled her cool body. "Niamh?"

Her eyes flickered then tried to focus on him.

"Jared? You're here?"

"I'm here." He took in the blood. "Liam, she's hurt," he yelled. He pulled a tissue from his pocket and clamped it over the small wound.

Footsteps pounded up the stairs, Liam appeared. He took things in at a glance and stepped over them. The water ran for a moment then Liam handed him a damp towel. "Here. The police are on their way. I'll call an ambulance, too."

Jared looked up. "Maybe run across the road and see if Nate's in." Detective Sergeant Nate Holmes, church elder, friend, lived opposite them. "He'll know what to do."

Liam nodded and left the room, already speaking on the phone.

Jared looked back down at the pale, beautiful face. He should never have moved out and left her alone. "Niamh?"

Her eyes slowly opened and struggled to focus on him. "There was a man. He hit me."

"It's OK, you're safe now." He cradled her and carried her down the stairs.

"I can walk," she protested weakly. "Well if I had the crutches, maybe…"

"Not this time." He kissed the top of her head. Her voice was a little stronger now and the fact she was complaining was a good sign.

As he reached the hall, Liam and Nate ran in. "I haven't touched anything," he said. "I found her lying bleeding on the floor upstairs."

"I'm fine, just a little shaken is all." Niamh pushed against his chest. "It's just a slight cut."

"Don't argue. You're going to hospital to get checked out, because you were out cold for a few minutes." He laid her on the couch. "Besides, Nate will only insist on a med report to back up his police report. The guy hit you, Niamh, that's assault."

Nate sat on the chair next to her. "Hi, Niamh. I'm DS Holmes. You know me as Nate."

She smiled faintly as Jared gently examined the wound on her head. "You live over the road. I've seen you with your daughter in church."

"She's my niece, but yeah. Can you tell me what happened?"

"I woke and found this man standing by the bed. He had my Filofax in his hand. I screamed, and he hit me twice. When I came too, I rang Liam. Jared answered. Then he was here."

"OK. Sit tight for a few. Can I borrow Jared to see if anything was taken?"

Niamh nodded, then raised a hand to her head. "That was silly…"

Jared glanced up, torn between wanting to help and not wanting to leave his wife. "I—"

Liam plumped down next to her. "I'll make sure she doesn't move. Go and help Nate as much as you can."

He pushed to his feet. "OK." Blue lights flashed outside the window. As he got to the door, two uniformed officers stood on the porch. "That was fast."

"We can be," Nate said dryly. He looked at one of the officers. "Ben, I want you to take Mrs. Harkin's statement. Philip, you're with me. Jared, where did you find her?"

"Collapsed on the floor half out of the bathroom. The trail of blood looks like it goes to the bedroom." He gratefully let Nate take charge and then led Nate and one of the officers up the stairs.

"I'm not sure what help I'll be." He glanced at Nate. "We've essentially been separated a while now and the past couple of weeks I've been staying at Liam's to help him redecorate." He caught the glint in Nate's eye. "I know, that makes me suspect number one, but I was with Liam all evening. Patrick also came over to help wallpaper the hall. He brought pizza with him."

They went into Niamh's room and Jared paused as he realized what a mess it was. "Besides, someone wants her dead, and that definitely isn't me."

In the mirror he caught the exchange of glances between Nate and the uniformed officer. Nate frowned. "I'm sorry? That sounded like someone wants her dead."

"She's been getting death threats at work. SOCO were investigating the car crash, but we haven't heard anything back."

"Check that out, will you?" Nate ordered.

The uniformed officer raised his radio, speaking rapidly into it.

Jared pushed a hand through his hair. "You didn't know?"

"No," Nate said. "Your address should have been flagged. Once we're done here, I need to talk to you both about the threats."

"I'll tell you what I can, but Niamh doesn't remember anything from before the car crash. That's partly why I'm not living here—though I'll tell you for nothing, that's changing from tonight."

****

Niamh glanced at Jared as he drove her into work.

143

He'd done a lot of insisting since they got home from the hospital in the early hours of the morning. He'd insisted on sleeping in the spare room, and tried to insist she take the day off work. When she'd been adamant on going in, he'd insisted on driving her himself and cancelling her car.

Now he had a contemplative look on his face that probably meant he was going to insist on something else. Despite that, it was kind of cute.

"You look serious, Jared. What are you thinking?"

"I don't want you working."

"The doctor said it was a mild concussion. He didn't say not to work. I'm not letting some goon scare me off. Something is going on, and I think it has something to do with work."

"You think?"

She twisted in her seat. "Jared, I wish that blow to my head had brought my memories back, but it didn't. But one thing I do know for sure."

"What's that?"

"I feel a lot safer having you around."

"Safer?" His voice had an edge to it.

"Not just safer." She backtracked a little. "I like having you around. I like spending time with you. I—"

He parked the car and turned his intent gaze on her. She felt the heat rise in her cheeks and her heart pounded.

Is this what falling in love means? That giddy head over heels, wow he's looking at me feeling I have right now? The intense bereft feeling when he is no longer by my side? Why did I let things between us get so bad? Will he ever take me back?

"I should go so you can get into work on time," he said slowly. "I'll come by the house later, if that's OK?"

"Of course it is." She reached for the crutches, ignoring the twinge in her heart and just going with the change of subject. "Should get rid of these tomorrow, or replace them with a cane or something. Assuming the cast comes off."

"Can you get someone to drive you back home?"

"Yeah, the usual guy will bring me home. Will you be in later? I could cook."

"I'd like that. Should be back around seven."

"Sounds good."

He leaned over and kissed her cheek. "Bye."

"Bye." She smiled and got out of the car.

Niamh made her way inside and went straight up to Alan's office. She knocked and opened the door. "Are you busy? I need to talk to you."

Alan put the phone down. "Good morning, Niamh, Likewise. Sit down. You first."

She eased into the chair. "The house was broken into last night. I got hit over the head, spent a couple of hours in the ED."

"I heard. That was DS Holmes on the phone. You shouldn't be here."

"That's what Jarrie said. But like I told him, I'm not being scared off here. There's something going on, and I'm not going to sit idly by and let it happen. God will keep me safe."

"You can take that too far. What if God decides now's the time for you to join Him in heaven? He didn't stop you being hit over the head last night."

Niamh bristled. "Maybe so, but the bloke who broke in didn't do anything other than hit me. Besides, if He wants me, I could die in my sleep at home. Or He could have let me die in that car crash."

A wry smile crossed Alan's face. "Good point. OK.

SOCO finally got back to me. It seems a certain DS Holmes got someone up in the middle of the night to chase up your case."

"He said he would. And?"

"I didn't like what I heard. Nor did he and neither will you. It confirms what the CCTV images showed. Someone tampered with your car and cut the brakes about fifteen minutes before you got into your car and left. Had I not caught you in the lift and delayed you, it's likely you'd have caught them doing it."

"I thought the only people with access to the car park were people who worked for the CPS. Everyone else has to use the public parking facility at the front of the building."

"It is. Hence this case is now in the hands of the police."

Niamh folded her arms. Why hadn't the CCTV images come up before this? Or had they just not told her about them? Either way she wasn't going to push it, so long as they were being taken into consideration now. "Fair enough. What I don't understand is why, if the Acre case was over, did someone decide to cut my brakes? Surely it'd make more sense to do it before I got him locked up?"

"You were pursuing another line of enquiry. Files were going missing, and you were making progress on finding out who was taking them. Have you remembered anything about that?"

Her brown creased in thought. "I don't think so, no. So, what happens now? I assume I'm back in the firing line."

"The police will arrange for an officer to either stay in your place or outside it. A car will continue to drive you to and from here and to the court."

"OK, but the police stay outside. Jarrie stayed in the spare room last night, and I'm going to get him to move back in. It's his home, too."

Alan smiled over the file.

"What?"

"You called him Jarrie. That's the second time since you walked in here."

"And? It's his name isn't it?"

"You're the only person to ever call him that. You came up with the name shortly after you got married."

Her heart leapt. "Really? I…no one told me that."

Alan's smile grew. "Yeah. You see there is hope for the rest of your memories yet."

"Yeah." Niamh took a deep breath. "Anyway, back to these threats."

"You also received another death threat this morning. It came to the office, addressed to me." He handed over the letter. "This is a copy. The police have the original."

You should have let things be, Mrs. Harkin. You leave this case alone or you will die. Last night was a warning We know where you live, where you work. We're watching you.

She read it and shivered. She had no idea why someone would want her dead. Thick slanting handwriting, probably a calligraphy pen she decided. Possibly a left hander from the way the letters were smudged, but that wasn't any help.

She gave it back to Alan. "Friendly person, isn't he? What kind of paper was it written on?"

"The same paper as all the others. From one of the yellow lined legal pads we use all the time."

"But why?" Her brow furrowed. "What did I ever do that was so wrong? Is it really this case or did I send his mother down for speeding and he's just out for revenge and he's using this case as a convenient excuse."

"We have no idea. They started with the Acre case—the one you won the day of the car crash. Obviously whoever is sending them, knows you're back at work and is afraid you'll catch them."

"Who knows about the letters?"

"I do and Toby does. And now the police." He held out a file. "This murder case came in late last night. Toby and I want you to take it. He's going to work with you, but you'll take the lead."

Niamh took the file. "Is that a good idea?"

"I thought you just said you weren't bothered by the death threats."

"I'm not. I was thinking more along the lines of what you said about not trusting someone who can't remember last month."

"That was five weeks ago," he winked. "Seriously, I trust you. You're the best person for this one. But Gina Luckett was found dead the day after your car crash. She'd been hung, drawn and quartered."

She shuddered. That was the traditional death reserved for criminals who committed treason against the crown, with parts of the body being sent as a warning to each of the four corners of the kingdom. But no one had died that way for over a hundred years. At least legally. "That's a nasty way to die. Who is she?"

"She was the main witness in your last case. As soon as you produced her in court, the defendant, Jonathan Acre, changed his plea. You put away a mobster for life, with no chance of parole for forty years. Miles Kingsman was the defense barrister on that case, and he's been assigned this case, too. This time the accused is Barry Jankowski. We have CCTV footage that places him outside Gina Luckett's house, DNA evidence that places him near the body at the time or just after she died."

"Are Acre and Jankowski connected?"

"So far the only link anyone can find is the same defense barrister. But something doesn't sit right with either Toby or me. This is another reason we want you to handle it. You have a nose for this sort of thing. If something smells, you track it down like a bloodhound."

She shot him a slight smile.

"Something else you should know. I had a phone call from Judge Matheson yesterday. He heard Kingsman threaten you in court after the case finished. Someone then tried to kill you. He can't be sure the two are connected, but we're not taking any chances."

The intercom buzzed. "Yes, Mary?"

"Miles Kingsman is on line three for Mrs. Harkin."

"Put it through. You take it on speaker phone," he said.

Niamh nodded and waited until the call came through. "Hi, Miles."

"Niamh, I hear they've given you the Jankowski case. Fancy meeting for lunch to discuss it?"

Alan shook his head.

"I'm busy for lunch."

"Then tomorrow?"

"Thing is, I probably shouldn't see you socially right now. Not if I'm your opposition on this case."

"It never stopped you in the past."

"I'm not the same person as I was then." 'Coffee?' she mouthed. As Alan nodded, she spoke aloud. "I could make coffee the day after tomorrow. Give me time to read the files and so on."

"Sure. Usual place?"

"Ummm, how about..." She read the piece of paper Alan slid across the desk. "...my office, say about eleven?"

"Sounds good, I'll see you then."

"Sure. Bye." Niamh hung up and looked at Alan. "And the fact my office will probably have moved to an interview room with a one way mirror, or the office across the hall with the glass walls, is beside the point?"

Alan laughed. "You read my mind, lassie. Read my mind." He paused, his face hardening. "And if you do remember anything about those files, anything, no matter how small a detail it may seem, I need to know immediately. Or tell Toby and he'll let me know."

****

Back in her office, Niamh pulled out her mobile and rang Jared at work. Surprised he answered the phone, she wasn't going to question why he was at the reception desk. "Hi, Jared. I've got a favor to ask."

"For you, anything."

She put the file on her desk and lowered herself into the chair. "I was wondering if you'd be willing to move back in permanently. In separate rooms, of course."

"I wouldn't have it any other way, hon." His smile echoed down the phone.

"Hon?" She pulled a face at the phone. "I thought I said don't call me that. For now at least."

"Sorry."

She yanked open the drawer, pulling out a yellow

legal pad and her pencil. "It's fine, Jarrie, just don't make a habit of it."

"I'm not a priest. No wait, they don't wear habits. Nun's do."

She laughed. "You're silly."

"Thanks. Uh, did you call me Jarrie?"

"Yes. That is your name, right?" She opened the file and angled the paper on the desk to write on.

"Yeah it is. I love you."

"I'm glad you do. Now go do some work. I'll see you tonight. Bye."

He laughed. "Bye."

****

After dinner that night, Niamh knew without a doubt she had started to fall in love with Jared and that scared her more than she wanted to admit. It terrified her because she didn't remember how she'd behaved with him before. What if she was too changed for him now? Or did things differently? What if he didn't like the new her? Either way, she had to know.

She took a deep breath as he closed his Bible and looked up. "Jarrie, what if I've changed too much?"

"What do you mean?"

"I'm not the same person as I was before the car crash. I've read my diaries and so on. I don't like who I was, and I don't want to be her anymore. What if you don't like the new me?"

"I like the new you just fine."

"Are you sure?"

"Yes." He wrapped his arm around her and she leaned against his chest, listening to his heart beating. "I like the way we talk now, listen to each other, read and pray and just be with each other without the nastiness and sniping. It's like when we first met."

"And that's a good thing?" she asked.

"It's a very good thing."

****

Seven hours later she woke suddenly to find Jared standing over the bed. "Jarrie, what time is it?"

"Early. Are you awake?"

"I am now. What's up?"

He picked her up and carried her from the room. "Something to show you."

"Fair enough." She snuggled into him, listening to his heart beating.

They reached the hall. "Grab your coat."

Confused she did so, and then shivered as Jared carried her from the house. "You're one crazy man. Did you know that?"

"Course I am. That's why you love me."

"Hmmm that's kind of presumptuous don't you think, Mr. Harkin?" She tightened her grip on him. "I said I like you, didn't say anything about loving you. And after this? I mean you come in at the crack of dawn, wake me up, grab me from my bed…" she broke off trying not to smile.

"I didn't hear you complaining at the time." He carried her across the patio and sat down on one of the chairs, holding her firmly on his lap. "This will be worth it I promise."

She shivered again, leaning into him. "It had better be."

Jared wrapped her coat around her. "Or what?"

"Or you make your own dinner tonight."

"Sounds like a pretty safe bet to me."

Slowly the light of the sun peeped over the horizon. Jared nodded to the rose bush next to him. "Look."

She turned her head. The dew caught the light of the rising sun, giving the plain white roses an almost jeweled appearance. "Wow. That is so pretty."

"Isn't it? You used to love coming out here, just sitting watching them."

"I can see why."

"And just like the sun rises every morning, no matter what, so my love for you never ends, no matter what."

The sequined winter roses sparkled. She reached out a hand but was unable to touch it. Just like her memories, fragmented and shining with promise but unreachable. But perhaps one day they would come back. Until then she had the roses and the dew and the promises each new day would bring. Most importantly, she had the love of the man holding her.

"What are you thinking?"

"Aside from how pretty it is? Thinking that the dew on the roses is a lot like my memories. There, sparkling like treasure, but I can't reach them."

"Maybe look at it as if that's a good thing—it gives us a fresh start with no hang-ups from the past."

"But some things I'd like to remember. Dayna's first word, silly things she'd say or do. Anything about her basically. Remembering why someone's trying to kill me would also be good. And other important things from the past ten years."

"Such as?"

"Oh, I don't know. Ummm, you perhaps. Know what you like, don't like. What turns you on, where you're ticklish…"

He kissed her cheek. "You can relearn that very easily, my love, when you're ready. Just know I still love you. Did you find someone to take you to the clinic this morning?"

"Patrick's doing it. I'm hoping the doc'll say I can lose the cast today. He should do."

Jared ran a finger slowly down her face, a trail of fire following it. "That would be great. So there should be less of you when I get home tonight?"

"Are you implying I need to go on a diet?" she asked in mock shock.

"Nope. Well, just your left leg, that's all."

His finger brushed over her lips, and she held his gaze. His head inched towards hers, and she eagerly raised hers to meet it. The kiss was long, slow and tender, his hands moving through her hair.

Finally, he broke off. "I should go."

"Yes, you should." She paused. "You say that an awful lot. If this were a book, the editor would have her red pen all over it."

He chuckled. "Perhaps we could continue this conversation tonight. Don't worry, I'm not asking more than you're prepared to give."

She smiled. "OK. We'll continue later."

After he left, Niamh ate a leisurely breakfast and read the morning paper. Then she puttered around the house for a while, dusting and rearranging the ornaments on the sideboard. She could still feel his lips on hers, and her body resonated with his touches.

She glanced at the clock. *Just before ten. Patrick should be here any min—*

Boom!

The entire house rocked. A deafening explosion

thundered. Niamh hung onto the sideboard, trying to keep her balance.

What was that? Where was it? Had someone targeted the office or court expecting her to be there today?

She glanced out of the window. A huge fireball billowed in the air, followed by a mushroom cloud. Thick black smoke expanded outwards. Not the direction of the court or the office. Or the fire station.

A swift chill settled over her and she shuddered. *Lord, keep Jared and the rest of the firefighters who respond to this major incident, safe out there today. Protect them, give them the courage to do their jobs.*

****

Jared gazed out of the window of the fire engine at the massive conflagration in front of him. The phone call—petrol tanker hits petrol station—hadn't done it justice. The fire encompassed not just the petrol station, but the resulting explosion had taken out five of the surrounding houses and commercial properties. So far it covered half the block. Pumps twenty, persons reported. It was going to be a long, hard day.

Flames hissed and crackled. Over one hundred firefighters from the twenty pump and ladder vehicles that had responded, plus an aerial platform ran large volume hoses from the edge of the cordon that had been set up. A few firefighters advanced on the flames, behind hoses, towards the buildings.

Lord, help us get control of this fire quickly. Keep us safe and if there is anyone trapped, let us reach them. Or if it's Your will to take them, do so swiftly.

He leapt down, the heat hitting him full on. He

strapped on his breathing apparatus as Brad barked instructions. 'Persons reported' was never a good thing in a fire. But with the speed this one was spreading, it wasn't surprising that people were trapped inside the buildings. He handed his tally in at the BA board.

"Bravo two, with Skippy."

Jared nodded.

A hysterical woman grabbed him and pointed to a house on the edge of the cordon. Flames were shooting high into the sky from the roof and one of the upper windows. "My babies are in there. Upstairs in the front room."

"We'll get them out." He turned to Skippy. "Get the ladder positioned by that window. And get some water cover on it."

"You can't go in there."

"Watch me."

Half way to the house, an explosion behind him rocked the area. The blast wave sent him flying to the ground.

Pushing upright, he ran over to one of the houses spurting flames.

As soon as the ladder was in position, Jared ran up it, pole in his hand. Flames leapt from the building, the intense heat making him sweat under his layers of fireproof clothing. Making sure his mask was secure, he inserted the pole through the window, checking the floor. He really didn't want to climb through if the floor had gone. Assuring himself it was there, he climbed over the window sill and into the room.

The entire room was blazing. "Anyone here?"

Whimpering came from his right. One hand in front of him, he edged over to the sound. "Hello? Where are you?"

The whimpering came from under the bed. Kneeling down, he raised the burning cover. A small face, grimy, streaked with tears peered out at him. "Hey, little one. Let's get you out of here."

"Mummy...."

"Yeah, we'll go and find mummy." He gently pulled her out and wrapped protective arms around her. Five steps took him to the window, and he passed her through to the waiting firefighter on the other side.

"Guv wants you out."

"No. There's still another child in here. Going to check the crib."

"Jared..."

He turned and headed back into the inferno. The floor shifted beneath his feet. Moving as fast as he could, he reached the crib and grabbed the baby. "I got you."

He returned to the window and handed the baby out.

"Got him. Now get out of there."

Not needing to be told again, Jared grasped the window sill. At that instant, the floor beneath him vanished. He tightened his grip, his legs dangling in the hole opening under his feet. Glancing up he could see Skippy backing down the ladder carrying the baby.

His hand slipped.

"Niamh."

He fell into the raging inferno below him.

13

Throughout the drive to the hospital, Niamh kept a worried eye on the sky. Even in the car with the windows closed, she and Patrick could smell burning. She got out of the car as Patrick finished parking.

Thick black smoke hung over the town and the entire northern sky was orange. She wrinkled her nose as a waft of fuel blew across on the wind. Maybe it was a pile up on the motorway.

Patrick locked the car and smiled at her. "Good job we're not going to the ED. They're going to be busy." To emphasize his point, several ambulances shot past the car park.

"Yeah."

"Ready to go in?"

"No. I hate hospitals. Always have, but the clinic is the worst. Hours of sitting and waiting to spend three whole minutes with the doctor."

"But if you lose the cast it'll be worth it. Right?"

"Guess so." She walked slowly down the hallways to the fracture clinic. She smiled at the receptionist. "Niamh Harkin to see Mr. Smyth."

"Take a seat."

As they walked to the only spare seats, Patrick nudged her. "Where shall we take the seats? Maybe they'd fancy a coffee?"

Niamh giggled. "You're silly."

"I do my best. Is he on time?"

"Sometimes. Not always."

"Can I get you a coffee?"

"I don't drink coffee anymore. I prefer tea, but no thank you. I'm fine."

Twenty minutes later they were still there.

Patrick's phone rang. He shot the receptionist an apologetic look and pulled it from his pocket. "I meant to turn this off."

"I turned mine off before we left the house. I'm a good girl."

"Yeah, right. Wonder what Liam wants?" He flipped the phone up. "Hey, bro. What's up? Can't chat. I'm in the fracture clinic with Niamh. Receptionist is giving me the evils…" The color drained from his face and the joviality vanished from his voice. "That's why her phone's off." He handed Niamh the phone. "It's for you."

Niamh took the phone. "Liam?"

"Niamh, I just had a call from the ED." His voice was quiet and laden with emotion. "They rang me because they couldn't get hold of you."

Niamh's entire body went numb. Her heart fell into her shoes and her stomach twisted into a hard knot before plunging after her heart. "The…the fire? What happened? Is Jared hurt? Why'd they ring you?"

"Jared named me as his second next of kin if no one could reach you. They rang me when you weren't home or answering your phone. They didn't give me any details. I think you should get over to the ED. I'm on my way, and I'll see you there."

"Kay." The phone dropped from her hand. "Jared's in the ED. He was hurt in that fire. He's in the ED." Bile rose and for a horrible moment she thought she was going to be sick. "I have to get down there."

Patrick stood. "Let me cancel your appointment and we'll go."

****

The ED was heaving when they arrived. Niamh made her way to the desk. "I'm looking for my husband—Jared Harkin. He's a firefighter. He was brought here from the fire."

"Take a seat. I'll get someone to come and see you."

Niamh nodded and turned. There wasn't an empty seat, as it was so busy, but that didn't matter. A voice called her name and she looked around. The man standing there was in firefighter uniform, coat undone and covered in soot, his arm in a sling. He looked familiar but she couldn't put a name to his face.

He held out his unbandaged hand. "Phil Rodgers. I'm Jared's watch manager."

"What happened? Is Jared all right?"

"I don't know. He wasn't conscious when they brought him in."

"Was he burned?"

Phil didn't answer.

"Please…no one is telling me anything. Did he get hurt in the fire?"

"Yeah, he was on fire when we pulled him out. That's how I did this." He moved his injured arm. "We got to the shout to find several houses as well as the petrol station on fire. Jared went up the ladder into one of the houses, searching for the children trapped inside. He found the little girl, passed her through the window and went back to look for the baby. The heat and ferocity of the flames were like nothing we've seen in a while. He handed the child out and then the floor collapsed."

Flames shot out from every window in the burning house. Glass shattered, the fire roared and crackled, destroying everything in its path. A sickening crashing came from inside, then two screams—one high-pitched and childlike, the other the cry of a man she knew so well.

"Daddyyyy…Mummmyyy…"

"Dayna…Nooooooo…"

Terror and shock flooded her. The cry of *mummy* she heard in her dreams was the dying scream of her daughter. The last thing Dayna ever said was Mummy. Everything spun. Her stomach turned and plummeted. The blood rushed from her head and she closed her eyes.

Strong hands gripped her and guided her to a seat. Someone pushed her head between her knees. "Deep breaths, Niamh." The voice belonged to Patrick. "Can we get a doctor over here?"

Niamh tried to take the deep breath, spots flickering in front of her eyes. Voices echoed around her. She opened her eyes to find a pair of black shiny shoes poking out from navy blue trousers.

Footsteps…footsteps, blue trouser legs, black shoes. Always the bringer of bad news.

****

The soil was soft under her fingers as she dug out spaces for the new flowers. Pansies and marigolds sat in trays next to her. A splash of color to chase away the late winter gloom. She'd already planted white alyssum and red tulip bulbs which would bloom with the daffodils a little later on.

A car drove slowly down the road and pulled up. Car doors closed far quieter than they normally did. Footsteps echoed up the path. Two pairs. She wasn't expecting anyone. It's probably the sales people again. They never could take no for an answer.

She put down the trowel. Then she saw the two polished shoes and navy blue trouser legs standing next to her. Her stomach plummeted. An official visit by uniformed officers could mean only one thing. She looked up, time slowing. 'Please, no,' she whispered silently, recognizing them.

A fire engine carrying a coffin decked in a Union Flag. A hat rested on top of it, with several hundred men in dress uniform walking behind as the procession wound its way through the streets, pausing outside the warehouse where the six men had lost their lives.

Six coffins.

Six funerals.

Six men dead in the line of duty. Giving their lives selflessly to save those of others.

****

"Niamh?"

"Mrs. Harkin?"

Niamh opened her eyes. "Why am I lying down?" She struggled to sit.

"Lie still for me." A man in a white coat took gentle hold of her wrist. "You passed out in the waiting area. I'm Dr. Price."

"I'm fine. I came here to see my husband." She pushed up, taking a deep breath. "How is he? Can I see him?"

"He's in Resus being treated right now. He has a couple of burns, lots of scrapes and bruises. He's also got smoke inhalation."

"They said he was unconscious."

"He came around briefly, but we want to keep an eye on him for a while."

"I have to see him."

"In a few. Have you ever fainted before?"

"Not that I can remember. I lost my memory in a car crash a few weeks back."

He smiled. "I remember you from when you came in. How are you doing?"

She sat up slowly. "Remember bits and pieces. Like just now when I heard Jared was hurt. It just took me by surprise. Really, doctor, I'm fine."

"Well your pulse is normal, and your color is a lot better. You can wait here or in the relative's room."

"I don't want to take up one of your beds when someone else needs it."

Patrick helped her to the relative's room, where Liam was already waiting. She fell into her twin's arms, barely keeping the tears in. "Been here before," she sobbed. "I remember black shoes, navy trousers. I was gardening and they came for me. There were a lot of coffins, several funerals."

Liam rubbed her back. "The warehouse fire. They came to tell you that Jared had been seriously injured before you heard about it on the radio or the television."

"And I remember the fire that killed Dayna. But I didn't come here then." She looked up. "I really hated Jarrie, didn't I?"

Her brothers nodded and she cast her gaze downwards.

"I was a fool to ever let him go. I love him."

Liam looked at her. "So tell him that. I know you

are dating as friends, but if you want more then go for it."

"What about the divorce? I know he didn't want it, but I found papers saying I'd filed regardless."

"Stop it," Patrick said firmly. "Before it goes any further."

"It's too late."

"It's never too late. Not as long as there is breath in the both of you." He pulled out his phone and pressed it into her hand. "Ring your lawyer and stop it."

Niamh took the phone. "OK."

****

Jared opened his eyes, pushed up on the bed and pulled off the mask with a bandaged hand. He didn't need to be here. The slight movement set off a coughing fit, wracking his body with one paroxysm after another. The taste of smoke, ash and fuel made him retch and cough again.

A nurse appeared at his side. "Why do all firefighters think they are superheroes? Lie down and put that mask back on."

"Because we are superheroes," Jared protested, grateful to be pushed back down on the bed. "I just prefer to wear my pants inside my trousers."

"And you need to recharge your batteries before you take your next flight. Your cape needs washing."

"I need to go home."

"You *need* to wait for the doctor to come and see you. OK? You also need to wait until the IV has finished. We have to replace all those fluids you lost."

"OK." Jared leaned against the pillows. It hurt

rather more than he was going to admit but the pain meds would take care of that. As soon as they gave him some. He'd already had both hands examined and x-rayed and wrapped. Now he just wanted to go home so as not to worry Niamh by not being there when she got back from the clinic.

Had she heard the explosion and seen the smoke? It was certainly the biggest shout he'd attended in a long time. Since the warehouse fire earlier in the year which had claimed the lives of several of his friends. Had this one done the same? He closed his eyes and prayed that everyone was safe and accounted for.

"Just going to give you the pain meds into the IV. They'll kick in pretty quickly."

He coughed as he tried to remember actually rescuing the kids, but he couldn't. He just remembered climbing into the building, and then waking on the grass with two paramedics and his fire crew standing around him.

He coughed harder, tasting the foul residue of the fire in his mouth. He waved off the nurse, insisting he was fine and just wanted to go home. But the coughing got worse and finally unable to catch his breath, he didn't argue when he was pushed back onto the bed and the oxygen mask slipped back over his face. He closed his eyes feeling the pain meds start to kick in.

****

Niamh slowly swung herself across the room. Her eyes were fixed on the figure lying on the bed. His hands were bandaged and he wore an oxygen mask. She moved over to him, barely hearing the nurse next to her. "Jared?"

He opened his eyes and pulled off the mask. He pushed himself off the bed and into her arms, wrapping himself tightly around her.

She didn't say anymore, there was no need. He was here and safe. That was all that mattered. She held him tightly, tears in her eyes. She'd almost lost him. She knew without a doubt that she was in love with this man. She had no idea what she had felt for him in her past life, but here and now, she loved him. She held him as another coughing fit wracked his body.

"I hear you're quite the hero." She knew they'd just sedated him, and he wouldn't be awake for long.

He coughed. "No, just did my job." He slowly let go of her, struggling to keep his eyes open.

She laid him down and kissed his cheek. "Sleep, Jarrie. Let us protect you for a little while, huh?"

He nodded, his eyes closing as the meds took effect and knocked him out.

Niamh looked up at the doctor as he came over. "Is he going to be all right?"

Doctor Price nodded. "He'll be fine. I want him to stay in for observation for a couple of days as he inhaled a lot of smoke and fumes out there. The burns are first degree and should heal, with little or no scarring within a few days. It won't affect his career or his ability to work in any way."

Niamh nodded then turned her attention back to Jared. She'd sit here until he woke and stay with him as long as she could. How would she cope if she lost him? Not now she finally realized and admitted to herself how she felt.

She loved him. But he loved her too. It didn't matter to him that she was scarred. He loved her and she loved him. Her heart, which had gone through the wringer of so many emotions was now singing and dancing within her. She'd wait until she had written confirmation from the lawyer before saying anything to him about the divorce. Or rather, the lack thereof.

****

During the two days Jared was in the hospital, Niamh had spent most of her time at his bedside. They talked non-stop. The more time she spent with him, the more she loved him. She just wished she could remember more about him. But, she decided, stuff the old. Time to make new memories.

She walked with him to the car, Patrick having driven her in to collect him. She needed to talk to him and Patrick had promised to put the radio on to give them some privacy.

As Patrick drove them home, she glanced at Jared. She was ridiculously giddy in his presence, just like she'd been as a teenager every time Simon Jansen had looked her way in math class. "Jared," she began.

He smiled at her. "Out with it," he said lightly.

"Huh?" she asked.

"That's your 'I have something to tell you and you're not going to like it voice'." He paused. "So just out with it and get it over with."

Niamh took a deep breath. "This is weird," she said. "You know me better than I know myself."

He shot her a quick grin. "It's called an unfair advantage."

"Very unfair, I'd say."

Patrick shot her a wicked grin and wink via the driving mirror.

She scrunched up her nose at him. "You all have—

you, Li and Pi."

"But just think of the ammo you have on your brothers. Stuff that they've forgotten about, you remember as if it were yesterday."

"Very true. Hadn't thought of it like that."

Jared grinned. "See, every cloud has its silver lining. But what did you want to say?"

Patrick put the radio on and turned it up loud.

Niamh leant close to Jared. "I rang my lawyer when you were admitted to hospital." She took a deep breath, trying to calm her racing heart.

Jared's eyes clouded over. "Oh."

"No, no, nothing bad. I stopped the divorce."

There was an audible sharp intake of breath. His eyes widened and he blinked several times. "You...you did?"

Niamh nodded. "Yeah. I kind of like having you around."

"I see."

"That's not a very good way of putting it. I suddenly realized that I, whoever I was before the car crash, was a fool to let you go. I like having you around the house, talking with you, being with you. When I heard you were hurt, something..." She pushed a hand through her hair. "I remembered a fire before and lots of firefighters in uniform and coffins draped in flags. I don't want that to be you."

"What are you saying?" He frowned. "You want me back but under certain conditions? Do you want me to quit my job?"

"No, I don't want you to quit your job. I'm making a mess of this. I don't want you to move out. I want to date you properly. Have you live in the house, after all it's your house too, and it's big enough for the both of us."

Jared put a bandaged hand onto hers. "I'd like that."

She looked down at their hands for a moment and then raised her gaze to hold his. "I know things are different now, but," she paused. Color rushed to her cheeks.

"Hon, I'm not asking you to sleep with me until you're ready. If that means waiting years or never, that's fine." He looked at her. "I can wait, I promise."

"Thank you," she whispered, a huge burden falling from her mind. It wasn't just that she didn't remember the wedding, it was more she didn't feel married. She was dating this guy nothing more. At least not yet. They'd just have to wait and see what happened, if anything did come of it at all.

"I put dinner in the oven before we left to get you. It should be done when we get back. It's nothing special, just shepherd's pie, but…"

"It sounds wonderful." His eyes creased for a moment, then cleared. "No crutches or splint?"

She shook her head. "Got rid of them yesterday. You mean you only just noticed?"

"Well, you kind of side-winded me with the 'I've cancelled the divorce' thing."

"That was afterwards…"

"And I had this really gorgeous woman come and pick me up."

She smiled. "Flattery will get you nowhere."

Jared leaned forward and kissed her gently. "Made you smile though. And I happen to like your smile."

"Like yours too."

She left her hand in his and rested her head on his

shoulder for the rest of the drive home.

****

By the time they got home, dinner was ready. Jared somehow managed to balance the fork and eat despite his bandaged hands. He was grateful Niamh had made something easy to eat. Had she done it on purpose? Either way, shepherd's pie was one of his favorites. "This is amazing. Even better than mum's."

"Seriously? The amount of time you spend raving about your mum's cooking, I didn't think anyone could hold a candle to it."

"You'd be surprised."

"Do your hands hurt very much?"

"A little, but I've been here before. It's just minor burns. Keep them wrapped for a week, keep them moving to keep the skin supple and back at work in no time. We're off the next four days anyway, so don't need any more time off sick."

Her smile lit her eyes. "Just glad you're home and OK. Well, relatively OK." She hesitated for a moment. "Jarrie, I…"

He set his plate down and took her hands in his. "What's wrong?"

"Nothing's wrong. Everything's right. At least I hope it is. I love you." Her eyes glistened with hope and the fear of rejection.

His heart filled and exploded within him. Wrapping his arms around her, he hugged her tightly. "I love you, too."

Jared smiled. He could hardly believe he was blessed enough to have her fall in love with him twice. Now he just had to romance her before proposing again. Because he would. Then he would remarry her and they could start over. Just the two of them, the way it should be.

14

Niamh glanced up as Alan came into the office. Glass walled, it had a one way mirror on what looked like a book case in the far corner. Despite the fact it left her on public display, it was bigger than her previous office, and she grudgingly admitted she liked the spacious feeling the room had.

The coffee, or to be more accurate as neither of them had drunk coffee, tea meeting with Miles had left her hackles raised and her sixth sense reeling.

"Hi, Alan. I assume you listened in."

He nodded. "I heard most of it. I missed the first ten minutes or so because I was on the phone. Duncan from security is making sure Mr. Kingsman signs out and leaves the building."

"Good." She looked down at the file in front of her. "Something's not right. I was expecting him to plea bargain; they always do, but this? There is no way we'll just drop the charges and he knows it. Add to that the fact he wasn't happy about delaying the meeting."

"You had other priorities with Jared in hospital."

"Yeah, but try telling him that. He's convinced himself this is a huge miscarriage of justice, and we're out on a vendetta against anyone connected to Acre."

Alan raised an eyebrow. "I'm sorry."

"That's what I thought. And those are his words, not mine. That just tells me there is a definite link between Acre and Jankowski, and I'm not going to rest until I find it." She paused. "Question. Is it illegal to investigate the defense barrister during an ongoing case?"

"You personally can't do it."

"Can I ask someone to?"

Alan nodded slowly. "Quietly. If it comes back to bite you, it'll get messy really fast. Who were you thinking of asking?"

"I have a contact in the security services. I've used him before, a long time ago."

A wry smile crossed Alan's lips. "It'd have to be if you remember it."

She tossed a wad of scrunched up paper at him. "Pffttt. I get enough of that from Jarrie and my brothers, thank you very much. I come to work for a respite."

He perched on her desk. "No, you come here to work." He held her gaze for a while, making her squirm and glad she wasn't a witness in the box being cross-examined by him. Intimidating wasn't the word. "OK. You can make discreet inquiries. Nothing that can be traced back to us, however. We can't afford to stuff this up."

"Stuff this up?"

He threw the wad of paper back at her. "I can do street talk with the best of them, lassie. But I'm being serious."

"He'll be discreet. He has to be in his line of work."

"OK then. Keep me informed. And keep it out of the office. What you do in your own time is your business." He pushed up and headed to the door. "Oh, while I think of it, move the rest of your things in here.

This is your new office."

"Sure." She scrunched her nose at his retreating back. "Just chuck me some fish flakes and call me Nemo."

Alan laughed as he shut the door, his voice floating through the crack. "But I know where you are, lassie."

Niamh threw her pen at the closing door and slid her phone from her pocket. She pulled up Patrick's name then hesitated. What if someone was the other side of the one way mirror, listening to her every word? Changing her mind, she cancelled the call and sent him a text instead. She'd have this conversation out of the office, just to be on the safe side.

****

Niamh sat opposite Jared, menu in hand, trying to decide what she wanted.

Patrick slid into the seat next to her. "Hey, sis. What gives? You said it was urgent, and it looks as if you're having a cozy lunch with your husband."

"He's my cover." She grinned at him. "I need your professional services on the quiet. It's in the menu."

Patrick picked up the menu. "I see." He opened it and read the cover sheet quickly. "The steak looks good, but I'm kind of snowed under right now. I don't have much free time."

"Nor do we. This is important, Pi."

"Is it?"

Jared set his glass down with a thump. "It could be related to the death threats." His low, urgent tone startled her. As did the incredible depth of emotion contained in the husky voice. "Just in case you need an additional incentive."

The two men exchanged a long hard look, before Patrick turned his piercing gaze on his sister. He slid the paper from the menu, expertly folding and sliding it into his pocket virtually unseen. "Consider it done. What's your time frame?"

"Soon as. It's an active case. Nate, one of the elders from church is the other interested party."

He nodded and turned back to the menu for a moment. "Egg and chips. With a mug of tea."

Niamh smiled. "That sounds good to me."

"Ditto." Jared got up. "I'll go order."

"Thanks, Jarrie." Niamh grinned as he blew her a kiss before hooking his thumbs in his belt hooks and easing his way across to the counter.

Her heart did its usual pounding, her breath caught. He was all man and he was hers anytime she wanted. But what made him all the more special was the fact he was prepared to wait for her. Either until she remembered him or until she was ready. But until then, she had his hand in hers and kisses that drove her wild.

"Earth to Niamh. Come in Niamh, your time is up."

Jerked out of her thoughts, she looked at her brother. "I'm sorry, I was miles away."

"I noticed." He winked. "You haven't looked at him like that in a long time."

"I was a fool. But at least I have a second chance. The car crash gave me that."

"Yeah, and speaking of car crashes? You need to be careful."

She turned her coaster over and over. "I am. I have a police escort and everything."

"You do?" Patrick raised an eyebrow and glanced around the room. "Where? I can normally spot them a mile off."

She jerked her head to the left. "Over there. The blonde supermodel and the stud who looks like a movie star."

"I bet Jared loves that."

"Actually he hasn't said anything."

"I haven't said anything about what?" Jared slid back into his seat and playfully trod on her foot as he did. "Unless you're talking about Tweedledum and Tweedledummer over there."

Patrick coughed. "That's not a nice thing to say. Are you tarring us all with the same brush?"

"You're not a cop. You're a spook. There's a difference."

Niamh laughed. "Yeah, spooks are scary."

Patrick pulled a face at her. "Oh, ha, ha, ha."

"Food's just coming." Jared winked. "Now play nice, children."

"We always do. I was just saying to Ni how nice it is to see you two getting along again."

Jared smiled, his smile sending a blaze of joy through her. "Yeah, it is. Things are going to be different this time."

She nodded. "Different in a good way."

Jared took her hand and kissed it, her skin warming under his lips. His gaze held hers. "This time we make it work and don't give up."

****

Later that week, Niamh stood in the grand hall of the mayor's chambers, a glass of juice in her hand.

She'd declined the champagne as she was driving for the first time since the car crash. Never mind the fact that the mere smell of alcohol made her queasy and had ever since the accident.

Jared had received the Queen's Gallantry medal, for saving the life of two of his colleagues in the warehouse fire. He was doing the rounds, talking politely with the brass that had come down for the occasion. A sense of awe filled her that this incredibly good looking, courageous man wanted her, loved her.

Had she felt like this the first time? That sounded so strange. The *first* time.

Somehow she thought love would only come once in a lifetime, if you were graced enough to find it at all. But she seemed to have found it twice.

Not that she remembered the first time. Her life with Jared began when she woke up in hospital after the car crash she didn't remember either. Before then she didn't exist. At least not as she was now which was scarred and broken. OK, the doctor's had fixed her, and put her back together again as best they could, but some things would remain broken. She just had to accept that now and move on. So long as Jared was there, she could do that.

"Hey, Niamh," a voice said, startling her out of her thoughts.

She glanced up and smiled. "Hi, Phil. That was a lovely ceremony. I wondered if Jared's smile could possibly get any wider."

"Knowing him, it probably could." He jerked his head in Jared's direction. "You've got a very brave husband there."

Niamh glanced over at him, bursting with pride. "Yeah, just wish his job didn't terrify me so much at times. I don't resent him doing it. It's just the thought of what might happen every time he goes out on a call." She paused. "Shame it's not all cats up trees."

Phil smiled wryly. "That would get boring after a while. Seriously, Niamh, Jared is one of the most capable firefighters on the watch. He's methodical, careful, and resilient. Sure he's a risk taker, but we all are to some extent."

"Not sure what I ever did to deserve someone like him. If half of what I've been told about the past couple of years is true, even *I'd* have left me."

"He loves you," Phil told her. "He stuck by you. Even when it didn't look like you'd make it, he was there, holding your hand, begging you to come back."

She looked at him. "That's the first thing I remember. Waking up in ITU, with this totally drop dead gorgeous bloke holding my hand." Then she blushed. "Sorry, you're his commanding officer I shouldn't talk about him like this."

Phil smiled. "It's fine. I'm also his friend. My wife says the same thing about him. In fact, most of the single women I know are jealous of you."

"Me? Why? I'm no one special."

He nodded. "Yes you are, and not simply because the best looking firefighter at the station comes home to you every night." He looked at her. "Probably shouldn't say as much, but he never lost hope, never strayed."

Niamh looked surprised. "Never?"

"No. He's never once looked at another woman since I've known him. He's a one-woman man and totally devoted to you."

She smiled slightly. "Thank you."

Jared came back over to her and she slid her free

hand into his. "Hey."

"I think this is my cue to go find the wife. Nice talking to you, Niamh."

"And you, Phil." As he left, she turned to Jared. "My hero."

His eyes twinkled and the dimple in his cheek shone as he smiled. "Why, thank you."

Holding her glass steady, she extended her index finger to slowly trace the medal on his chest. "You take too many risks, but it's who you are. I wouldn't change it or you for anything."

He kissed her cheek. "I could say the same about you."

"Being a lawyer isn't dangerous. OK, maybe it is when someone wants me dead, but so long as you love me and are here for me, even that doesn't seem so frightening."

"Speak for yourself. The thought of someone wanting to hurt you scares the living daylights out of me."

She tilted her head and winked at him. "Maybe I should try scaring the dead nightlights out of you instead then?"

His deep chuckle thrilled her. "I'd like to see you try."

****

The following evening she sat in the kitchen with Liam, talking about a dozen different things at once. Jared was working the night shift and didn't want her to be alone. According to him, two cops parked out the front of the house didn't count. He wanted someone in the house with her.

"It just feels, oh I don't know, wrong to wear the ring," she finished. "And wrong not to, if that makes any sense at all."

"So why not just wear the ring and be done with it?"

She shook her head, pulling the chain out from around her neck. "But that would imply too much." She ran her fingers over the ring. "To wear his wedding ring would be an invitation back into my bed, and I'm not ready for that."

She paused. "I can't believe I just told you that. You're my brother and here I am discussing whether or not to sleep with a guy."

"You're my twin. I know what you're thinking before you do. Besides, we always have talked about everything. You know that."

She nodded.

Liam sipped his coffee, studying her over the cup. "Anyway, back to the subject of sex."

Niamh blushed, hiding her face as Liam roared with laughter.

"You started it. Look, I'm sure he wouldn't assume you wanted to sleep with him if you wore his ring. Why are you so worried about it, though?"

"Because we're not married," she said slowly. "I love the guy so much, my heart beats faster or just plain skips a beat every time I see him. The sound of his voice fills me with butterflies and to be in the same room with him is more than I could ever hope for. But I put his ring on my finger and that changes everything."

"But you *are* married."

"According to him, and you, and the photos, and the marriage books in church, yes but..."

"But what?"

"I don't remember it," she whispered. "Or feel it. It'd be like living in sin, and I can't do that. And before you say God thinks we're married as well, it's my conscience that's getting in the way here. I'm trying so hard to make things right…with God and with Jarrie. I don't want to do anything that would jeopardize that. Am I making any sense at all here? Or spouting utter nonsense? Again."

Liam nodded. "You're making perfect sense. I feel the same way and so does Jacqui. Sex is for marriage only. Sometimes saying goodnight and leaving, or even breaking off a heated kiss before we go beyond the point of being able to stop is almost too much to bear. But we do it, because it's the right thing to do. Which is why Jacqui and I aren't living together."

"Yeah."

"Jared's a good guy; he won't push you into doing anything you don't want to."

"I know. Just not sure this is fair on him. He's been through so much."

"You both have. Thing is you've come out the other side. Just give it as much time as you need. He'll wait."

"It's just, his touch is familiar somehow. I feel safe and secure when he's around, but is that enough? I'm trying so hard to remember, but don't."

"You're over thinking things."

"I am?"

He nodded. "Just accept the way you feel for each other and go with it. What's in the past is over. You have a clean slate with him. Take it as a gift and make new memories."

"I will." She yawned. "I'm tired."

"Then go to bed. I'll clear up down here."

Niamh nodded. She kissed his cheek and got up. "Night."

Locking up as she went, she made her way upstairs to her room. The light bathed it in a soft pink glow. Sitting on the bed, she picked up the photo of Jared in uniform. "Keep him safe out there tonight, Lord. Bring him back to me. Thank you for this second chance we have. Please, let it work out this time."

15

A tap on the door distracted Niamh from the pile of files on her desk. She smiled seeing Patrick standing there. A friendly face was a welcome relief after the morning she'd had. She beckoned him in. "Hello. What brings you to this neck of the woods?"

He fiddled with his visitors ID badge. "It's kind of awkward actually."

"Oh?" She swiveled her chair and stood. She walked around the desk. "What's up?"

"I tried texting, and you didn't answer."

"Sorry. I was in court this morning, so the phone's been turned off. I can check it now."

Patrick shook his head. "Can we go for a walk?"

"Sure." She closed the file on her desk and picked it up. "Let me lock this away."

"Do you lock all your files away?"

"Yes. Though it doesn't stop them going missing. Another reason I'm now working in a goldfish bowl. That and so they can watch me the whole time. See that mirror?"

"It's very you, sis," he said, his stance indicating that he knew what she meant. "I'm surprised you haven't put fairy lights around it. The same way you did with the mirror in your bedroom when you were ten."

She clicked her fingers. "That's what's missing. Maybe you could fit some." She shut the filing cabinet and locked it, sliding the key into her jacket pocket. "OK, let's walk."

Patrick nodded, not saying another word until they were out on the cold, damp street.

"So, what gives?"

"We have a file…a pretty thick one as it happens. I'm going to turn a copy of it over to Nate Holmes as he's handling the Gina Luckett murder. A copy will also be going to your department."

She raised an eyebrow. "And you're telling me this because?"

"Common courtesy seeing as how you put me onto it."

"Our mutual friend?" She didn't want to name him, just in case someone was close enough to overhear.

"There are definite ties between him and one former client, and possibly a current one. And I don't mean a client/lawyer thing either." He glanced at her. "But you are going to have to watch your step. If he wanted you out the way before, he definitely will now. Do you remember why?"

She pulled off her glove and rubbed the back of her neck. "All I know is it had something to do with the recent death. A missing file and…and she gave me…"

"And," Patrick prompted. "Who's she?"

"Give me a minute." Niamh rubbed her neck harder then looked up. "Gina Luckett."

"OK, good. Now, think, sis. What did she give you?"

"A letter. She gave me a letter. She stopped me on my way out of court…"

"Mrs. Harkin, please wait."

Niamh turned around at the running footsteps, to see Gina Luckett tearing after her.

"Mrs. Harkin, could you take a look at this? I received it this morning and I don't know what to do. I was going to hand it to the police, but now the case is over I thought maybe you should have it instead."

She stopped, clutching the briefcase tightly in her hand. Still unnerved from the encounter with Miles, she wanted nothing more than to reach the safety of the robing room. She managed a smile. "Calm down, Gina. The danger is over now, everything's fine. What can I do for you?"

"I wanted to thank you for all you did. I can't tell you what a relief it is, knowing Acre will be off the streets now. And I also wanted to give you this."

"I can't accept gifts…" She shifted the papers in her arms and took a step away.

"Oh…no it's not a gift. Uh…it came this morning. It's why I was late. I very nearly didn't come at all."

Niamh paused mid-step. "Oh?"

Mrs. Luckett pressed the letter into her hand. "Please, do with it what you need to." Panic filled her eyes and she backed away. "I have to go."

Stumped, Niamh just stood there for a moment, before realizing that Miles was at the end of the corridor watching them. Shifting the pile of papers, she slid the letter into them and hurried towards the robing room. She'd read it when she got back to the office.

"And did you?"

She shook her head. "Did I? Oh, no. No. I don't think so. I don't remember doing it, but then I might have done."

"I need you to check."

"Now?"

"Now is as good a time as any."

"OK, but you can't really be in the office when I look. I'll text you if I find anything and show you later."

"I could always hide in your bookshelf."

"You will not. Let me do this. I'll call you later."

He hugged her. "Then I shall go catch some bad guys of my own."

"You do that." She returned the hug. "I'm sure the country has far bigger problems than me."

"You'd be surprised." He paused. "You know what with Li and his terrorists and you and your death threats, the country has enough troubles right here in Headley Cross."

She playfully thumped his arm. "In that case, you can walk me back to my office. But first we stop off at the takeaway on the corner and buy hotdogs. That way it looks like you took me for lunch."

****

Taking her half eaten hotdog into the office, Niamh wondered where she'd have put the papers. She knew where she'd put them now, but that didn't mean she'd have done the same thing before the car crash.

She turned around and saw Alan passing. "Alan?" she called.

He opened the door. "Hey."

"Got a question. Where would the papers from the Acre case be? I remembered something while I was at lunch and I want to see if I was right."

"Past cases are filed down in the basement. Active ones in the filing cabinets up here."

"Cool. In that case, my lunch and I are going to the

basement."

"Fancy some company?"

"Sure. You can save me hours of searching for it on my own."

They headed towards the elevators. Alan pressed the button. "So what did you remember?"

"Gina Luckett gave me a letter. It's probably nothing, but it was the day the case ended, the day I crashed. I just wondered what it said."

"Did you not read it at the time?"

"No, I was too busy escaping Miles for some reason."

"He accosted you in court. Remember, I told you about that."

"Yeah, right, you did." She slid into the elevator and pressed the button for the basement. "I shoved the letter into the files and meant to read it later. Whether I did or not is anyone's guess. So figured I'd look for it while it was fresh in my mind."

Despite the basement being dark and dingy and lit by a single bulb, it didn't take long at all. Niamh took the file over to the desk and flipped on the light. As she opened it, a sinking feeling came over her. "You didn't bring this one to the house?"

"No, lassie. Toby thought it best not to."

She flipped through the pages. "Is this all there is?"

"What were you expecting to find?"

"I had a load of papers loose in my hand. They fell to the floor, and I picked them up...no that was in the courtroom. She gave it to me afterwards."

"Who gave you what afterwards?" A fresh voice from the door made her glance up.

"Oh...Toby."

He pushed away from the doorframe. "They said you were down here. Alan, there's a phone call for you."

"Thanks. Come see me when you're done down here, Niamh."

"Sure." She went back to the file, flipping through it. "I'm sure it would have been here."

"What are you looking for?"

"I remember running into Gina Luckett just after leaving court. I was flustered after the brush with Miles and wanted to get out of there."

"You remember that?" His tone meandered between passing interest and something deeper.

"Bits and pieces. It's irritating. Anyway, she called after me and I stopped. She gave me a letter, and I shoved it in with the papers. I don't remember any more but can't find it."

"I'll give you a hand. Sometimes the files get separated."

Twenty minutes later Toby found the other box of files. "Here. Under Z."

"Well that makes sense. Not." Niamh pulled the lid off. "Not filed in a folder." She picked them up. An envelope wafted gently to the floor. She picked it up, her heart beating erratically. Her palms grew damp. "This is it."

Toby sat on the desk next to her. "Open it."

She slid one finger under the back and carefully opened it, not wanting to disturb the contents too much. "Should I have gloves or something on?"

He shook his head. "So long as it's only you—your fingerprints will be on file."

Niamh drew out the letter and unfolded it. Dark bold lettering stared up at her. She gasped and dropped the letter onto the desk. She'd seen that writing before.

"Niamh?"

She put a shaking hand into her pocket and laid a creased piece of paper on the desk alongside the letter. "This came via internal mail this morning. The font is the same."

She looked down at the letters. Aside from the name on the top, the words were identical. And internal mail could only mean one thing. Miles wasn't working alone.

Back off now or you die.

****

The driver dropped Niamh off at home. She walked up the drive, aware of both him and the cops watching her. She was early, but knew Jared would be home, even if he was sleeping. Right now, she needed him. Just to see him, to be held by him, told that everything would be all right, and that the police would catch this guy before he tried to kill her again.

Dropping her bag and coat to the floor, she went up the stairs to his room. His strong, muscular frame lay across the bed, his scarred back in full view. Not wanting to wake him, she tiptoed across the room and sat on the edge of the bed.

The shaking started in her fingers and gradually worked up her arms and across her shoulders until it encompassed her whole frame. Tears followed, slowly at first, then a torrent and finally a flood.

Hands pushed through her hair, a calm voice spoke her name and she found herself leaning against Jared's bare chest. She clung to him, taking the comfort he so willingly offered. After a while she looked up at him, her cheeks wet. "Sorry…"

"Don't be, my love."

"I didn't mean to wake you."

"I had to get up anyway." He kissed her gently. "What's upset you so?"

"I got another letter. It looks like it's from the same guy who killed that woman."

His gaze searched hers. "Seriously? Are the police upping your protection?"

"They want me to go away," she whispered. "But I don't want to do that."

A flash of lightning split the room, followed a few seconds later by a crash of thunder. Rain poured against the window, the wind howling. She pushed tighter against his chest, his heart beat soothing her.

"What do you want?" His voice whispered in her ear.

"You," she said. She flicked her gaze up. His eyes, dark with passion and need looked at her. "But I'll settle for a kiss for now."

As the storm intensified, Jared nodded, his lips covering hers. He pushed her back against the headboard, his hands moving through her hair.

Niamh kissed him back, heat consuming her. She clung to him, not wanting him to stop and whimpering slightly as he drew away. "Jarrie…"

His fingers ran down her cheek, fire following in their wake. "If I don't stop now, I won't be able to." His eyes had darkened to ebony. "I want this to be right. OK?"

She didn't answer, couldn't answer. Her whole body ached for his touch.

"OK?" he repeated.

"OK," she whispered.

He kissed her forehead. "I'll go take a shower and you put the kettle on."

As she nodded, Jared grabbed a pile of clothes and left the room. She sucked in a long breath, her fingers resting on her lips. She could still feel him, taste him.

Is it so wrong to want him? Everyone keeps telling me I'm married, but would it still be classed as a sin because I don't remember marrying him? Is that why he stopped? What if he no longer wants me?

She took a deep breath and went downstairs, trying not to imagine Jared standing naked in the shower. Then she shook her head. He was hardly going to shower with his clothes on, now, was he?

After she put the kettle on to boil, she rummaged in the freezer and pulled out cheese and onion pasties and chips. Not the most exciting of dinners, but it would do. The storm finally ended and Niamh crossed to the window, drawn by the huge rainbow hanging in the sky.

Jared's arms slid around her, pulling her against his hard frame. "Pretty, isn't it?"

"Yeah it is."

"I have something to show you."

"Oh?"

"Slip some shoes on and come outside a minute."

"But dinner…"

"Won't burn if you just leave it for a couple of minutes."

"OK." She went to get her shoes, then followed him outside. The rainbow, even more brilliant and now double, still hung overhead, the calm following the violent storm.

"So…what did you want to show me?"

"Little Miss Impatient." Jared laughed.

"That's me."

He grinned and knelt on the wet ground in front of her.

"What are you doing?" *Surely he's not doing what I think he is?*

He pulled a small box from his pocket. "Niamh, I love you, more now than I did all those years ago when I first met you." He opened the box and held it out to her. "My life just isn't complete without you in it. I came so close to losing you, and it just about tore me apart. I don't want to spend another minute without you beside me all the time. Niamh, hon, will you marry me?"

Her gaze shifted from the ring to him and back again. It wasn't the same one she'd thrown at him several weeks ago. "But you and everyone else say that we are married…"

"You don't remember that. I want you to remember marrying me."

"That's not the ring I gave you back…"

He smiled. "No. It's a new one. This is a new start for the both of us. A new start deserves a new engagement ring, though I'd like to reuse the wedding rings, if that's all right with you."

Niamh dropped to her knees beside him, tears pouring down her face. "Yes. Yes to both. I'll marry you," she whispered. "I love you so much."

He slid the ring onto her finger, and wrapping his arms around her, kissed her.

Niamh closed her eyes as he deepened the kiss, totally oblivious to the rain that cascaded down onto them as the storm returned full force.

Only the sound of the smoke detector going off

inside the house broke Jared's steamy embrace. His eyes widened, and Niamh doubled over with laughter as he raced into the house to try and save the dinner from complete destruction.

16

"Are you sure you want to talk about the wedding, now?" Jared asked, amazed at the way Niamh had paper everywhere as she worked on the files in front of her and talked to him at the same time. She hadn't lost focus on either task. If only he had the ability to multi-task like that. "You just look so busy."

"Yes, I'm sure." Her face lit up as she smiled at him. "This is just catch up stuff. Look, I've put the pencil down."

"OK. Well, I was thinking…if you wanted, we could have a really big wedding with long white dresses—"

"Dresses plural? Are you planning on wearing one as well?"

He scrunched up his nose at her. "Oh, behave, will you? A long white dress, singular for you, an arch of axes, your mum can cry, your dad can give you away, Liam can object at the relevant section, your great aunt can come over from Nevada, and your cousin Elfic can come over from New Zealand. Then there's Adric and Rhiannon, Idris, Iestyn and Ivor from Neath in Wales. Oh, and the Irish contingent."

"No, I don't want that. Not a big wedding. Just you and me." She glanced down at the files. "They'll have done it once and flights are expensive at the best of times." She shoved the file closed and winked at him. "'Sides, I don't want to wait too long."

He rolled his eyes. "We might need a couple of witnesses. And a church—unless you're thinking we elope and get married on a beach. Or we could drive to Gretna Green and get married tomorrow."

"Yeah, like that would help. Seriously, I don't want a huge wedding. Just immediate family and anyone from the church who wants to come, is fine."

"Are you sure?" Amazement gave way to surprise. The first time around, she'd insisted on the biggest, most expensive wedding possible. He thought she wanted to get married and yet she didn't seem bothered one way or the other now. Maybe she wasn't multi-tasking quite as well as he first assumed.

"Quite sure. Dad will give me away. I've asked Jacqui to be my bridesmaid. You just need to pick a best man and book the church."

"What about a honeymoon?"

She shook her head, opening the file again. "No. We can have a holiday anytime."

"OK." Jared nodded, masking his disappointment. He wanted to do this right for her and her mixed signals were confusing him to put it mildly. She didn't remember the first one, she'd made that abundantly clear, and here he was offering to repeat it for her and she didn't want it. Was she doing this for his benefit or was this part of the change in her? She was much softer and more money conscious than ever before. The weekly shopping bills showed him that much.

And she hadn't so much as bought a single pair of shoes since the car crash. In fact she hadn't bought any clothes in weeks. Not even to replace the horrendously expensive suit that they had to cut her out of in the ED. Actually, now he came to think about it, he had only seen her in one suit since she returned to work.

"I'll give Pastor Jack a ring. See if I can arrange a date. Any day in particular?"

"A Saturday. That way no one has to take the day off work. Unless it's you. Fit it in with your off duty. Actually…" She smiled and reached behind her, pulling the calendar off the wall. She handed it to him. "I marked your shifts on here in green, since your green watch."

"I like it." He ran his finger down the dates. "You know I could just take the day off. Or fit it in with night duty." A cushion flew across the room, hitting him in the face. He pushed it aside. "What was that for?"

"So you marry me at three and then go to work at six. Great, nice one. Thank you." She concentrated on her notes, scribbling rapidly on them.

"OK, maybe not."

"The first day off of your set of four would be ideal."

"Let me see when the church is available, and we'll go from there." He picked up the phone and dialed. He smiled as Pastor Jack answered on the second ring and immediately put the call on speaker. "Hey, Pastor, it's Jared."

"Hello. How are you?"

"I'm well, thank you. I was wondering if you had a free Saturday at some point in the next few weeks. I know it's busy in the run up to Christmas, so if you haven't its fine. Niamh and I want to get married."

"I thought you already were married."

"Renewal of vows, then. Thing is she doesn't remember the wedding and neither of us want to live together as man and wife without that."

Pastor Jack chuckled. "Fair enough." Paper rustled

as he flipped through his diary. "Well as you don't need to post the banns, you don't need to wait. I can do this weekend, although that probably isn't enough notice for everyone."

Niamh grinned and waved at the phone. "Not really. Hey, Pastor."

"He can't see you wave," Jared laughed.

"Hi, Niamh. Jared's right. I can't see you wave, but I'm waving back anyway. How are you doing?"

"Getting there. I'll need a couple of weeks at least, in order to find something to wear."

"OK. How about three weeks? That would make it December the sixth?"

Niamh nodded and shot Jared a thumbs up.

"Sounds perfect, and it fits in nicely with my off duty." Jared blew her a kiss. He grinned as she mimed catching it, before sending a kiss back. "How does midday sound?"

"I've written you in."

"Thanks, Pastor. See you on Sunday. I'll give you all the details and so on then." Jared hung up and grinned at Niamh. "So now we just need to find you a dress."

"Should be simple enough. I mean, how hard can buying a dress be?"

"Pfft." Jared crossed the room in three strides and plumped down next to her. "You've not been clothes shopping since the car crash. You are the most finickity person ever."

"Finickity isn't a word. It's pernickety or persnickety. Or finicky. Depending whether you're using English or American English."

He kissed her nose. "Whatever the pronunciation, or language, you are the most overly fussy woman imaginable to go shopping with. There's a reason I never used to go with you."

She set the papers aside and snuggled into him. "Overly fussy, am I now? We'll see about that. I shall go tomorrow afternoon and come home with a dress."

"Are you going to show me?" He rubbed his arm as she playfully thumped him. "That's a no then."

"You'll see it on the day and not a minute before hand."

"Fair enough. But just so you know, if you can't find a dress you like, I'll marry you barefoot, in a shift dress and pregnant."

"Pregnant? That will go down well in a church."

"OK, maybe not pregnant. But barefoot and in a shift dress."

"OK." She leaned her head on his shoulder. "Did you really never go shopping with me?"

"Nope." He kissed her forehead.

"Am I that bad?"

"You used to be." He paused half wondering if now really was the time to push it.

She twisted her head and gazed at him. "What is it?"

"At one point, you had a suit for every day of the week and a pair of shoes to go with every single outfit. Yet, now you wear one suit to work and barely change your shoes."

Her finger traced the pattern on his shirt, sending ripples of heat that settled low in his belly. "I gave most of them to charity. I mean, who needs ten suits and twenty-seven pairs of shoes. Most of which would could cripple a person the heels are so high. One suit is fine. As are two pairs of shoes, a pair of sneakers and a pair of sandals for the summer. As for the rest of my clothes…honestly some of them just aren't me. I can't believe they ever were. So I packed them all up too."

"I didn't like half of them, but wasn't going to say. I prefer your new simpler tastes." His hand rested on the long, flowing skirt she wore. "Like this one."

She laid her hand on top of his. "Three pounds fifty in the secondhand shop in the precinct."

Jared jerked his head up in amazement. "You're kidding?"

"No. Perfectly serious. Why?"

He lowered his face to hers and kissed her. "Because you told me on several occasions you wouldn't be seen dead in a charity shop."

Her lips caught his. "Then I was a fool." Her arms went around him and all conscious thought left him.

****

Bad morning in court just didn't cut it. Having been wound up beyond anyone's limits by the defense, and ignoring her two escorts, Niamh left the court in a foul mood and headed to the High Street for some retail therapy. She parked the car and headed to the only bridal shop in town, convinced she'd find a dress in less than an hour. But shopping for her dream gown, soon turned into a nightmare.

She had very specific ideas as to what she wanted, but despite having tried on almost every dress in the shop in her size, nothing came even close to resembling the picture in her mind. For some reason her usual size didn't fit. This didn't help her bad mood, only serving to sink her further into the mire.

Every single dress the assistant brought out either reminded her of a meringue, or was too plain, too straight or made her look fat. Especially the ones with ruffles across her mid-section. That wasn't attractive even on a good day. Good job Jared *hadn't* come with her.

"How about this one? It's the last one we have in your size." the assistant asked, bringing out a long ivory dress.

Not bothering to say it wasn't her size, Niamh shook her head. "It's massive," she whispered. Disappointment resonated through her and she blinked hard. "Thank you, but I think I'll leave it."

Leaving the shop and plodded along the pavement. Rain drizzled through her hair, streaking her mascara and hiding the tears.

Is Jarrie right? Am I just too fussy? And why doesn't anything fit anymore? I know what size I am, even if things are a little tight now. Did I use to work out in the gym?

She rubbed a hand over her face and went straight into the café. Ordering hot chocolate with cream, marshmallows, a flake and sprinkles, she eyed the cakes up before adding an apple Danish pastry and a chocolate slice to her order.

Sitting by the window, she ate slowly, watching the rain hit the window. The sweet treat turned her stomach, but then most foods did that right now. She sipped the chocolate. *What do I do? If I can't find a dress, what do I wear? Did he mean it about marrying me barefoot and in a shift dress?*

After the café, she crossed the road and went into the clothes shop. Not even bothering to look at dresses, she found leggings in various sizes and tried them on. To her horror, she realized the girl in the bridal shop was right about her size.

A wave of nausea flooded her and she sat down.

She pulled a tissue from her sleeve and wiped her face. It was hot in here. She took a couple of deep, shuddering breaths. Maybe she just gave this up as a bad job and went home.

On the way to the checkout, she saw a pair of white shoes she liked, but without a dress, they were useless. She hesitated for a moment then left them. By the time she got home, she was tired, distraught, and more than a little nauseous.

Jared came into the hall as the front door closed. He reached her side in four quick steps and immediately wrapped his arms around her. "Honey, what's wrong?"

Niamh collapsed into his arms, sobbing. Her knees gave way, tiredness sweeping over her and everything too much.

"Baby?" Concern flooded his voice. He gathered her into his arms and carried her into the lounge. He sat down and cradled her on his lap, rubbing her back until she calmed down.

As the nausea subsided and the sobs eased, she raised her tear soaked face to him. "I can't find it," she managed.

"Find what, hon?"

"A wedding dress. I know what I want but I can't find it." Tears started to fall again.

"Oh, hon." He pulled her snug against his chest, his warm lips pressing kisses on her forehead. "It's okay. The wedding's three weeks away yet, you've got time. You can always get married in what you're wearing now."

"Noooo," she sobbed. "This isn't a renewal of vows or a civil service. It's the only wedding I'm likely to get and I want…need it to be perfect."

"Then barefoot and in a shift," he whispered. "So long as you meet me at the top of the aisle I'll be a happy man."

****

Saturday morning Niamh sat in bed, drawing pictures of her ideal dress then scribbling over them. Jared had left for work at half past eight as usual. She'd stayed in bed as long as she could, hoping the nausea would pass. She was obviously working too hard, so a lazy day was called for.

When the doorbell rang, she was tempted to just ignore it. After the fourth ring, she got up and pulled on her robe, before heading down to answer the door. She opened it. "Yes?"

Jacqui smiled at her. "Come on you."

"Hmmm?"

"We're going shopping."

"What for?"

"I need a dress for your wedding. Unless you wanted the bridesmaid to wear jeans."

"If you want. Don't care, wear whatever you want."

"Niamh? What's wrong?"

"Nothing. You better come in while I throw on some clothes." She rubbed a hand over her eyes. "And then we can go and find you some new jeans."

Jacqui stood in the hall, her critical gaze making Niamh squirm. "You look awful."

"Don't feel that great. And I'm having the most crazy nightmares about being chased."

"Too much stress at work, maybe? Liam told me about your police escort."

Niamh heaved a sigh. "Wherever I go, they go. It's all getting too much. Part of me wishes this guy would make his move and kill me already."

"Niamh!" Jacqui managed to sound outraged, shocked, and sad all in the one word. "That's an awful thing to say."

"At least this mess would be over. The police have all the evidence, even Patrick is convinced he knows who it is, yet no one's arrested him. And I have to face him, day after day in court…"

She broke off, her hand flying up to cover her mouth. "Forget I said that."

"Said what? Come on, you need some fresh air."

"OK. I'll get dressed. Then we go find you something to wear to the wedding."

"What about you?"

She thought a moment. "Something black maybe."

"Oh don't be silly."

"I'm not!" Niamh snapped. "That way I can wear it more than once."

"Oh, for crying out loud. Will you listen to yourself? This is your wedding day. It doesn't have to be long and white if you don't want that. I don't even have to wear a dress."

Niamh rubbed her hands slowly through her hair. "I'm sorry. I don't know what's wrong with me. I feel sick, and I'm on edge the whole time. I'm sure it's just stress. If Jarrie knew, he'd insist I go back to the doctors. I don't want that."

"Then we don't tell him." Jacqui hugged her. "Don't worry about it. Let's go buy jeans for me and a short black thing for you."

"Or I borrow your jeans. That way it's old, borrowed and blue in one foul swoop."

Jacqui smiled. "Or we just throw caution to the wind and buy the first thing we see. Ohhhh. How about we go for matching jeans? You know the ones with precut holes and ladders in."

"That sounds good. Jared would be horrified." She paused. "OK, let's go and look, see if we can find some."

17

Niamh followed Jacqui around the shops, trying to summon up enthusiasm. She had looked in all these places yesterday and found nothing. Nothing that fitted and nothing she liked. Not even jeans. And if she were being truthful, she felt too sick to do anything. Maybe she was coming down with stomach flu.

They did however find a red dress for Jacqui. With long sleeves and made of silk, it curved around her body perfectly. Best of all it came from a high street store and wasn't your typical bridesmaid's dress. It was something that could be worn again and again. Jacqui looked radiant in it. "Now to find something for you."

Niamh looked at her. "What I have on is fine," she whispered.

"Rubbish," Jacqui said, winking at her. "You can't have the bridesmaid outshining the bride."

"Sure we can. It's my wedding." She took a deep breath. "I just wanted it to be perfect. But it's not going to happen."

"Oh, ye of little faith." Jacqui pulled a couple more dresses off the rail. "This is pretty."

"Yeah it is." She ran her fingers along the material. "It's gorgeous."

"What size?"

"Normally a twelve. Today I seem to be a fourteen."

"They have every size but that."

Niamh sighed. "That figures."

"How about I just put it back on the rack and we go look someplace else? I think there is one store we haven't tried yet. They might have something similar."

"It's not worth it. Let's just buy your dress and call it a day."

"OK."

Niamh nodded. She led Jacqui to the cashier's desk and paid for the dress. "Liam will like you in that dress. Not that he doesn't like you anyway. He told me how you guys met."

Jacqui laughed. "Yes, the 'say it with flowers incident.' Not exactly getting it off on the right foot. And then I ended up in floods of tears the first time he took me to dinner. Kyle came over and threatened to deck him for it."

Niamh raised an eyebrow. "Really?"

"Fortunately, Liam had gone to the bathroom at that point. He was drinking again then and it may well have turned into a fight."

"He doesn't drink now though." Niamh tried to think.

"No. He's back on the wagon and going to the AA fairly regularly. He's staying dry for himself, rather than someone else now. That makes all the difference."

"Yeah, it does." Niamh opened the door, her mind going back to the dress issue. "Jarrie's no help with this wedding outfit, though."

Jacqui laughed as they left the store. "He's a bloke. They have no idea when it comes to dresses."

"He told me barefoot and in a shift would do fine." Niamh walked slowly down the high street trying not to cry. "Least one of us will look a million dollars."

Jacqui looked at her and then down. "Yeah."

"Let's just go home," Niamh whispered. "I'm sorry, I really don't feel well."

"You look awfully pale again."

Niamh swallowed hard. "Probably stomach flu or something I ate. A lie down and I'll be fine. At home I won't be followed everywhere by those two. I know there's a reason, but I'm tired of it."

****

Jared came in from work to find Niamh curled up on the couch. "Hey, hon."

She glanced up. "Don't ask."

He nodded. "OK." He flopped down on the couch beside her, wrapping his arms around her. "Does that mean you still haven't found anything to wear?"

"I said, don't ask. The bridal shops are hopeless, and the one ball gown I did like they didn't have in my size. Not that it was white. It was pale peach, but it was so pretty and even Jacqui like it, and it wouldn't have clashed with her dress. But I'm too fat and ugly right now to wear anything pretty."

He held up a hand. "OK, I won't ask or mention it again, tonight. I just want to marry you. I don't care what you wear. And you're not fat or ugly, hon. Just tired, stressed and overwrought."

She hugged him back and looked down at her jeans and sweater. "Is what I have on all right, then?"

"What you have on is perfect, hon," he said kissing her.

She kissed him back. "OK. Jeans it is."

He smiled. "You know, we can always postpone

the wedding. Till some of the work pressure and so on is over."

"No. I want to marry you in two weeks. They might never arrest him."

"They will." He kissed her again. "I'll go put dinner on."

"OK. Nothing too heavy, not feeling so good today."

Hiding his concern, Jared got up and headed into the kitchen. Shutting the door, he moved swiftly to the phone and dialed the manse. At the same time, he rummaged through the freezer looking for something to eat.

"Hello."

"Hey, Pastor, it's Jared. Is Cassie there?"

"Sure, one second."

The phone went quiet for a moment before Cassie answered. "Hey, Jared. How are you?"

"A little frustrated actually. Niamh can't find a dress she likes. None of the wedding dresses she's seen will do. Jacqui even tried getting her a ball gown, but the only one she liked they didn't have in her size. I know you don't make dresses as a rule, but could you do me a huge, huge favor? Talk to her, see if she'll let you make one."

"Sure. Send her to the store on Monday and I'll see what I can do."

"Thanks. Bye." He hung up just as Niamh came into the room. "Fish fingers and chips do you?"

"Yeah, that's fine. Who was on the phone?"

"That was Cassie."

"Pastor Jack's wife?"

"Yeah. She makes the occasional wedding dress. I rang her. She's willing to help if you want."

"Wedding dresses?"

"She actually made the royal wedding dress."

"Seriously? The *royal* wedding dress?"

"Yeah. Long story. But there was a massive fire in London that resulted in Princess Rebekah needing a dress the day she and Prince Edwin were visiting Headley Cross. This was like three days before the wedding. They saw the one Cassie had made for the window display and the rest as they say is history. The only other one she's made was her own, but she's willing to make you one. If you want."

Niamh paused. "I don't know."

"At least go talk to her. If need be she can glam up your jeans for you. Or Lara can bedazzle them."

Niamh smiled faintly. "OK. Bedazzled jeans it is."

****

Monday morning, Niamh sat in her office, listlessly pushing the papers from one side to the other. She glanced up at the tap on the door. "Hey, come in."

Alan came in, a pile of folders in his hands. "You look terrible. Go home."

"I'm fine, it's just stomach flu. It's been hanging around for a few days now. It'll go."

"Have you seen a doctor?"

"Not since my last hospital appointment. I'll be fine."

"You don't look fine. Go home."

"I have an appointment with a dressmaker at lunch time."

"Then curl up on the couch until then. Seriously, Niamh, you are no good to me like this."

Not needing to be told twice, Niamh walked

unsteadily to the couch. She curled up on it and closed her eyes. After a moment, she opened them again. "Are you just going to stand there and watch me sleep?"

Alan chuckled. "How did you know I was still here?"

"I hadn't heard you leave. Are those files for me?"

"Yes, but they can wait. Rest and go home once you're done with your appointment."

Niamh pulled a face.

"I mean it. I'm telling the driver now, so there's no excuse to come back to work." He dropped the files onto her desk and headed to the door.

Niamh slowly got up and picked up the files. Taking them over to the filing cabinet, she locked them away. Then she went back to the couch, curled up and shut her eyes again.

Going home and going to bed would be nice. I don't know what's wrong, wish I did. Feel so sick the whole time. Maybe it's just stress. Should I go to the doctor? Or assume it'll go away.

She clutched her stomach, wishing it would stop turning for a few minutes. Her phone beeped. She groaned and pulled it from her pocket. Pulling up the text, she smiled. Jared seemed to know instinctively when she was down or sick.

'Hey, thinking of you. You feeling better?'

Typing quickly, she replied. *'No. Alan made me lie down. He's sending me home in a bit.'*

The reply came instantly. *'What's wrong?'*

'Still feel sick. But like I told him it'll go away.'

'You've been sick for a week. Time to see the doc.'

She sighed. *'Not you as well. Alan said the same.'*

'Then make the appt. I'll take you on Friday. They owe me four hours so I'll take them.'

'OK. If I'm not better by then.'

'Sounds good. Alarms going. Got to go. See you tonight. Love you.'

'Love you too.' She put the phone down and closed her eyes.

What only seemed minutes later, she jerked them open as a hand fell on her shoulder. "What's wrong?"

Alan smiled. "Nothing. It's almost noon. What time's your appointment?"

Niamh sat, pushing a hand through her hair. "Oh. I didn't mean to sleep. I'm sorry."

"Don't worry about it. I don't want to see you in this afternoon. Or tomorrow if you feel like this."

"I'll be fine. Not going to let this stop me doing anything." She grabbed her bag and phone. "I'll see you in the morning." Her gaze landed on a fresh set of files on her desk. "So what are those?"

"I'll walk you to the lift and tell you on the way."

****

The shop bell tinkled as Niamh pushed open the door. She wasn't really sure why she was here. She made her way over to the counter. "Hi, Cassie."

Cassie smiled at her. "Hi. How are you doing?"

"I've felt better, but not as bad as I have been."

"That's good. Jared said you've been having problems finding a dress."

Niamh nodded. "Nothing looks right or fits. I don't think I'm a meringue person and the straight ones look awful." She sighed. "I don't want to put you out though. Jared said you don't really make dresses."

"For you I will. Come through the back, and we'll see what we can come up with."

"Don't I choose the fabric first?"

Cassie smiled. "Design first, then fabric to fit that."

"How fancy does it have to be?" Niamh asked following her.

Cassie led her into the small back room. She filled the kettle and set it to boil. "That's up to you. It's your dress. Have a seat. Do you want some coffee?"

"Thanks. I'd rather tea. Coffee makes me sick these days." She perched on the edge of the chair. "Jared said you did the royal wedding dress."

"Yeah. That one was originally what I'd intended to get married in, if I ever got married. I ended up designing something different when it came to my wedding. Every bride wants something individual, right?"

"I guess so."

Cassie brought the tea across, sat down and pulled over her sketch pad. "So, what did you have in mind?"

"Floor length, flattering, pretty, long sleeves with buttons on. Although right now I'd settle for something white, that fits. Although white seems hypocritical somehow."

"Ivory then. Or go for a color. A pale green or blue. What color are your bridesmaids?"

"Christmas red. Jacqui looks really pretty in it. We bought that dress on Saturday."

"OK."

Niamh rubbed the back of her neck. "Jared said he'd marry me in a shift." She caught the glint in Cassie's eye. Had they both had the same thought at once?

Cassie's pencil flew over the paper.

Niamh's smile finally grew as she saw the dress come to life. "That is perfect."

"Now all you have to do is decide on a color and accessories."

"Is that all?" Niamh put the tea down as another wave of nausea swept over her. "I'm sorry. Can we leave that for another day? The accessories that is. I'm not feeling too good."

"Sure. What about color?"

"Ivory. It really doesn't matter what fabric. Something simple, but warm. Not too much beadwork or lace." She closed her eyes and took several deep breaths. "I'm sorry."

"Do you need a lift home?" Cassie asked, concern filling her voice.

"No, I have a car and driver out the front." She pushed to her feet, more unsteady than she'd have liked. "I'll be fine, thank you."

"Let me see you to the car."

Niamh took the offered arm. She'd go home and go to bed and sleep off whatever this was. Perhaps Alan was right about taking a day off sick.

In the end, Niamh took two days off sick. She knew she was worrying Jared from the comments he kept giving her, and she reluctantly agreed to the doctor's appointment if the over the counter stuff he'd bought her didn't do the trick.

****

Thursday morning, Jared loitered on the landing waiting for Niamh to finish in the bathroom. As the door opened, concern flooded him. She didn't look any better. If anything, she looked worse. Huge bags under her eyes made her look gaunt. "This is silly," he said. "I'm making you that doctor's appointment."

Niamh wiped a hand over her mouth. "It's just stress."

"Rubbish," he told her bluntly. "It's gone way beyond stress and being back at work. You've been sick every morning for almost two weeks now."

A sudden thought struck him and he dismissed it just as quickly. She hadn't gotten morning sickness the last time. In fact, she'd breezed through the entire pregnancy with never a twinge.

"Jared…"

"Don't argue." He took in her suit. "You're not seriously going into work today?"

"It's the opening day of the Jankowski case. I have to be in court."

"Alan won't let you." If the situation weren't so serious, he'd find the resoluteness in her face amusing.

"Alan won't have a choice." Her voice wavered for a moment. "Look, it's not like I have to drive anywhere. And if I didn't have court today then, yes, I'd stay home. Get the work faxed over or whatever. But you know how much a trial costs, and if we delay because I'm not feeling so good, it could be months before we get another date."

"You got this one quickly enough."

"Pre-trial stuff. Show we have the evidence and so on. See if he wants to plea bargain." The color drained from her face. "Ohhh…"

Jared wrapped his arms around her. "I'm sure the others can handle it. You need to rest."

"I'll be fine." She pulled out of his arms. "You worry too much."

"I don't want anything happening to you. That's all."

Her hand touched his face and he tried to quell the

shards of heat, and longing. "Nothing will."

"OK. I'm not in the station today. Doing inspections of schools and old people's homes. Checking the smoke alarms work and so on."

"That sounds exciting."

"Oh, yeah, it is. Hundreds of kids and lots of little old ladies on zimmer frames. It's not just you who has a thing for the uniform," he teased trying to lighten the mood.

Niamh smiled at him. "Just tell them you're taken and to go chase some other hunk in uniform. I'm sure you can't be the only good looking man on green watch."

He laughed. "They won't listen."

She tilted her head. "Maybe I should come check them out."

"You'll do no such thing." He kissed her cheek. "Are you sure you're going to be all right?"

"Yes. Now go."

"I'm making that doctor's appointment the first chance I get." He held her gaze. "I mean it. You've got me really worried."

Her expression softened. "I'm sorry. Since the car crash, everything's been so weird. Maybe I should get checked out. Just to put your mind at rest if nothing else."

Relief filled him, in part at least. "Thank you."

"You're welcome." She looked at the clock. "Jarrie, you need to run or you're going to be late."

He smiled and kissed her. "I'm gone."

****

Niamh pulled open the door of the locker and

reached in for her wig box. She pulled it out and wrinkled her nose. It was now more grey than white. She really ought to get it cleaned.

"That's seen better days," Toby joked. "Maybe it's time for a new one."

"Nah. I'll get it cleaned."

"I wouldn't stick it in the washing machine. Wife did that to mine and it shrunk," a voice chimed in from the other side of the robing room. "I ended up buying a new one, cost an arm and a leg. But then if you get this judgeship, you'll need a new one anyway."

"If," she said doing up her tie. "It's by no means certain I'll even interview for it."

"I thought it was all cut and dried," Toby said. He adjusted his robes. "You wanted it, they wanted you. The interview is just a formality, surely."

"That was before the car crash. Now, I'm not sure what I want." She pulled out her robes, something white fluttering to the ground. She bent to pick up the folded piece of paper.

A wave of dizziness swept over her as she read the front. Her hands, suddenly numb and cold, dropped the paper and she fell into the locker.

"Hey…" Toby's voice came from a long way off. Hands guided her to a seat and shoved her head between her knees. "Deep breaths. Someone see if there's a doctor around. And find Judge Matheson."

"I don't need a doctor. Or the judge. I'm fine."

"Stop arguing and just breathe." Toby's tone was harsher than she'd ever heard. Paper rustled, and she heard his sharp intake of breath. "And get Alan Reynolds from the CPS over here."

Footsteps ran from the room.

Toby's voice whispered in her ear. "That was

another death threat, but I think you knew that. That ups the stakes if they are threatening you in here. We need to discuss with Alan and the judge where we go from here."

"Closed court," she whispered. "I'm sorry."

"Not your fault."

Deep, heavy footsteps echoed in the room, swiftly followed by Judge Matheson's booming voice. "Philip Forrester said you needed me. Is something wrong?"

Niamh raised her head. Did she look as bad as she felt? She took the note from Toby and glanced at it, before offering it to the judge. "It was in my robes, in my locker. It's not the first."

Judge Matheson read it, his expression darkening. "Is Alan Reynolds on his way?"

Toby nodded. "Yes, My Lord."

"Right. I want you both in my chambers now. Once Alan arrives, he can join us." He turned to the security officer behind him. "The case in court number five. Keep the defendant in the cells until I say otherwise. And tell his barrister there is a four hour delay. If he wants a reason, tell him..." He broke off as the doctor came in.

Niamh shook her head. "I'm fine, really. I don't need to see a doctor."

"Well I'm here now," the doctor said. He took her wrist.

She looked at Judge Matheson. "Just don't tell the defense I'm sick."

The judge grinned. "Tell Mr. Kingsman I've been unavoidably detained on a personal matter. I'm seeing to a sick friend. The case will be heard at two p.m."

"Yes, Your Honor." The security guard left.

"A sick friend?" Niamh asked. Maybe she really

wasn't well. Normally she kept up with the conversation much better.

He nodded. "You. You're a friend and right now you're not feeling so good."

"Well, your pulse is fine, Mrs. Harkin. You look a little pale though."

"Stomach flu. I'll be fine."

"Just take it easy for a bit."

Judge Matheson's voice boomed again. "No worries there, Doctor. She'll be sat in my chambers for the next four hours drinking sweet tea and engaging in harmless chit chat."

Niamh sat still as the doctor left. She took several deep breaths. "Is there anything else in my locker that shouldn't be there?"

Toby checked. "No. Do you want me to ring Jared?"

"No," she said quickly. "I'll tell him tonight. No sense worrying him, too." She stood and brushed her hands over her skirt. "I wouldn't mind some of that tea actually, Your Honor."

"Then let's go find it. Alan will find us once I open the chocolate biscuits."

18

Jared let himself into the house. "Hi, I'm home."

Silence greeted him.

"Niamh?" He hung his coat on the wall hook and went into the kitchen. A tall male figure stood by the worktop, peeling potatoes. "Patrick, what's going on? Where's Niamh?"

"She's sleeping." Patrick glanced over his shoulder. "There was an incident in court this morning."

Jared's heart flip-flopped and stopped. "What? Is she hurt? Why didn't anyone ring me?"

Patrick turned and held up a hand. "Take a deep breath before you hyperventilate. She's fine. She's not hurt. She's sleeping because she's sick, has been for a while according to Liam."

"Yeah, stomach flu. I'm taking her to the doctor's in the morning."

"Good. She got another death threat this morning. This one was in her robes, in her locker at the Crown Court."

Jared froze. "In the court building itself?"

"Yes. Needless to say, we've upped the protection. Hope you don't mind a houseguest for a while."

"You?"

"Yeah. And yes, I'm armed before you ask. I'm not going to let anything happen to her, Jared. I promise."

"What about in court? You can hardly sit beside

her."

"She'll be wearing Kevlar under her robes at all times. I'll be in court, as will more court officers than usual. We've made the judges in charge of her cases aware of this and they're on board with what we're doing."

"Good." He let out a deep breath. "Is she all right?"

"Shaken, but you know Niamh."

"She hides things, Patrick. She may not look bothered by this, but she is. I've heard her crying at night when she thinks I'm sleeping. I've gone in a couple of times, but she just clams up."

"Then push it," Patrick said bluntly. "Wait a minute. You guys still sleep in separate rooms?"

Jared nodded. "Yes, we—"

Niamh cut him off. "We are until the wedding." She moved into the kitchen, sitting on Jared's lap and sliding an arm around his neck. "Hey, you."

Jared hugged her tightly. "Patrick told me about your day."

"Horrible. Majorly horrible. How was your day?"

"Oh, full of adoring little old ladies on zimmer frames and kids all wanting to be firefighters."

She nestled against him. "How many of the kids called you Sam?"

"Most of them." He kissed her cheek. "You sure you're all right, baby?"

"Now you're here," she whispered, closing her eyes, humming Fireman Sam quietly to herself.

Jared held her, listening to her breathing slow. He looked at Patrick.

"She's been dozing on and off since she came home. That doctor's appointment is a good idea. What time is it?"

"Ten o'clock tomorrow morning. I've got the morning off to take her." He slid a hand through her hair. "It's not like her to be sick. Even when she was pregnant with Dayna, she wasn't sick at all. She was the envy of every woman in the ante-natal class. I'm hoping it's just stress and nothing more serious."

"Want to pray about it?"

"Please."

Patrick sat beside him. Placing one hand on Jared and the other on his sister, he started to pray, handing the entire situation into the Lord's hands.

****

Niamh came out of the ladies and crossed the doctor's waiting room. She slumped back onto her seat between Jared and Patrick. "They didn't call me, did they?"

"No." Jared frowned, concern plastered all over him. "Look, maybe we ask for a home visit instead."

"No, I'm here now."

"Here in spirit perhaps," he muttered. "You've spent more time in the loo than here in the waiting room with us."

"On the floor next to the loo, not in it," Niamh corrected.

He snorted. "You had to do that, didn't you?"

She leaned her head on his shoulder. "Yeah, because you were expecting it, and I didn't want to disappoint you."

He kissed the top of her head. "I love you."

"Love you back." She paused. "And your front and your side and..." She broke off as the buzzer sounded. Her name flashed up on the screen. "That's me."

"Want me to come with you?"

Niamh shook her head. "I'm a big girl now. I won't be long."

"But—"

"No buts. You and Patrick can sit and talk while I'm gone." She stood and headed through the door to the consulting rooms. She read the numbers on the doors and knocked on the one labeled six.

"Come in."

Niamh opened the door and smiled. "Hello."

Dr. Brown smiled at her. "Hello, Niamh. How are you doing?"

"Not great." Niamh sat down and put her bag on the floor.

"You don't look so good. How can I help?"

"I'm assuming its stomach flu, but it's been going on for two weeks. I'm tired all the time, can't keep anything down and my sense of smell is so heightened it's untrue."

"I see." Dr. Brown reached out and took Niamh's pulse. "How's work going?"

"Stressful. Can't say much, but yeah, lots and lots of stress." She rolled up her sleeve and took a deep breath as the doctor did her blood pressure. "I haven't eaten or drunk anything I'm allergic too. At least, I don't think I have as Jared's pretty good at stopping me."

"Your blood pressure is up slightly, but if you're stressed that would explain it. Let me run some blood tests. When was your last period?"

Niamh shrugged, wincing as the needle went into her arm. "Things haven't been right since the car crash.

Surgery, stuff going on at work, and I couldn't tell you when the one before the car crash was."

"Is there any chance you're pregnant?"

Niamh shook her head. "No. I'm not married. Well, I am, but we're not, we're not sleeping together. And according to Jared, I wasn't sick the last time."

"OK. The blood tests should come back in about a week. I'll ring you if there's anything to be concerned about."

"In the meantime what do I do? I can't work like this, and I'm in the middle of a really big case."

The doctor wrote a prescription. "This should help with the nausea. Rest as much as you can."

Niamh took it and stood. "I will. Thanks." She went back into the waiting room, stifling a smile as both men almost leapt from their seats. She waved the prescription. "He gave me something to help with the sickness, and I have to rest as much as I can."

"But what's wrong?" Jared asked.

"He's running tests. Find out end of next week. Let's go find a chemist."

"I'll buy you a coffee while we wait for it," Jared said.

Niamh swallowed hard. "I thought I was the one with the dodgy memory. I don't drink coffee anymore Thanks anyway, but I'm due at work."

Jared nodded, sliding a hand into hers. His skin was warm and her nerve endings started tingling.

Outside a fine rain began to fall and she leaned into him as they walked. Patrick walked in front and the two other officers behind her.

"Niamh, when's your interview?" Jared asked.

"For the judgeship?"

Jared nodded.

"I decided not to go for it. I don't know half of what I should any more, and I'm happy where I am. Well, most of the time."

"Are you sure? You were so keen to start with and so happy when you got selected."

"I'm sure." Niamh looked at him. "Sides, I don't think I'm cut out to make decisions like they have to every day. Can we go now? I have a pile of stuff to do at the office. Then I have a meeting at four."

"I'll take you," Patrick said.

"I'm coming with," Jared said at the same time.

"Actually neither of you," she said firmly. "The two cops behind me are coming. You two are food shopping and cooking tonight. And don't argue with me. I'm a lawyer so way better at it than either of you."

****

Four o'clock on the dot, the CPS driver dropped her at the door of the haberdashery. The bell tinkled as Niamh opened the door.

Cassie beamed at her from behind the counter. "Hey, glad you made it. Can you manage alone for a bit, Danny?"

Danny grinned. "You're hardly here anymore, and we're not exactly busy. I'll be fine."

"Thanks, bro. Come out the back, Niamh. Danny will keep watch in case Jared or one of your brothers decides to drop by."

Niamh followed Cassie into the small storeroom at the back of the shop.

Cassie reached up, pulling back the curtain revealing a dress cover. She unzipped it. "There you go."

"Wow," Niamh whispered. Tears stung her eyes. She'd never seen anything like that. Completely overwhelmed she just stood there.

Based on the shift dress Jared had said would do fine, Cassie had added sleeves and a slight train at the back. Understated beading lay around the square neck and around the high waist.

"Is it all right?" Cassie asked after a few minutes.

"It's beautiful," Niamh whispered. "It's even prettier than it looks on paper."

"Would you like to try it on?"

"Can I?"

"Of course."

She took off her dress and let Cassie slide the dress over her head. She stood in front of the mirror as Cassie fastened it. "Wow."

She turned first one way and then the other. The dress was a perfect fit, but given Cassie's apparent expertise in this, she wasn't surprised. "What do you think? Will Jarrie like it?"

"I'm biased. Do you want Danny's opinion?"

"OK."

Cassie smiled and stuck her head around the door. "Danny, we need a bloke's opinion."

"Nah, Jack's just walked in. He'll be better than me."

Niamh shook her head. "He's marrying us, so he can't see it either."

Cassie smiled at her. "Nope, she wants yours."

After a moment, Danny's head appeared around the door. His eyes widened and a huge smile lit his face. "That is amazing. Niamh, you look fantastic."

"You think he'll like it?"

"Yeah, I do. You look beautiful. He'll be stoked. "

Niamh stood there while Cassie added a headdress and veil. "That's incredible," she whispered. "It's much better than I imagined."

Cassie smiled. "I'm glad you like it."

"I love it, thank you." She changed out of it and let Cassie hang it back in the bag. "What do I owe you?"

"Just what we agreed at the beginning."

"Are you sure?"

"Yes. And I promise, not a word to Jared. Do you want to leave it here while you go shoe shopping?"

Niamh shook her head. "I've got my footwear sorted," she said.

Once she got home, she hung the dress in the wardrobe hiding it right at the back. The boxes containing veil and headdress went under the bed. She shut the door and by the time Jared got home, she sat innocently watching the TV.

Jared leaned over the back of the sofa and kissed her. "Hey, hon. How was your meeting?"

"OK. How was the shopping?"

"Busy." He flopped beside her. "Patrick's unpacking it now. Did you find anything to wear yet?"

Niamh leaned against him. "I don't want to talk wedding dresses anymore. I found something to wear. Something old, new, borrowed and blue."

"Fair enough." He ran his fingers through her hair, sending ripples running through her. "Old blue jeans, Liam's shirt and new socks?"

Niamh smiled. "Got it in one."

"OK. I thought I might wear my uniform, the dress blues. If that's all right with you?"

She nodded. "You can wear what you like, hon. It's your wedding, too." She saw the flicker of disappointment in his eyes and for a moment was tempted to tell him the truth. "But you know what I think about men in uniform."

He grinned. "You always did have a thing for them. Blue uniform it is. With the hat."

She kissed his cheek. "Or just the white shirt and the hat."

He looked at her, his eyes sparkling.

"What did I say?" she asked.

"The honeymoon," he winked. "That's what you asked me to wear."

She closed her eyes, a sudden flash of memory hitting her. She grinned as she looked at him. "But I bet I look better in it than you do."

His lips caught hers. "Definitely."

19

Niamh walked down the halls with Toby, their footsteps echoing in the high vaulted chambers of the Crown Court. "Can we do that?"

"Alan seems to thinks so."

"But if the judge rules it as inadmissible, then where does it leave us?"

"We've still got enough on DNA evidence alone."

"So why risk using the note at all? Surely proving he was paid to do this is only going to play into the defense's hands?"

"Not if we do it right. It makes him a coldblooded killer. Not a heat of the moment thing."

Niamh tucked her hair behind her ears. "Killing someone like this could hardly be described as an impulse murder."

"Exactly. If you were told to take someone out what's the easiest way?"

"I don't know." She shifted the files in her arms. "Bullet between the eyes, or run them over." *Or cut their brake line perhaps.*

"And if you were told to do this to someone?"

Niamh stopped and lowered her voice. "What if they then turn around and say he didn't have a choice? That Acre had something on him or he'd kill his wife or kids or dog if he didn't comply?"

"Then why didn't he come to us? Niamh, think about it. They've got to you, they got to your files, and they got to your witnesses all throughout the Acre trial. And now the same things are happening again. Not so much the files since we moved your office to the goldfish bowl, but..."

"Other stuff," Niamh finished.

Toby held her gaze. "The notes are the same. Same writing, same pen. Just don't bring the ones you've received into the equation. Just mention the one Mrs. Luckett got."

"All right."

He smiled and held open the courtroom door for her. "Then let's go bag us another bad guy."

Twenty minutes into the pre-trial evidence, Niamh got exactly the reaction she was expecting.

Miles Kingsman rose to his feet. "Objection, My Lord. We all get letters through the post. The fact Mrs. Luckett did isn't at all relevant to this case."

"Mrs. Harkin?" Judge Matheson peered at her over the top of his glasses.

"It is very relevant, My Lord. If this letter can prove that Mr. Jankowski received instructions from a convicted criminal to murder Mrs. Luckett, then it is very relevant indeed."

Miles sneered at her. "*If* you can prove he was on the take? Is that really the best you can come up with?"

She shot him back a withering glare of her own. "My starter for ten."

"I'll allow it for now. Go on, Mrs. Harkin. Present your evidence."

Niamh nodded. She glanced up at the public gallery, making sure Patrick was there. The judge was playing his part to perfection. All she needed to do was play hers and soon this whole thing would be over. One slip up and it would be her neck on the line rather than that of the guilty party.

She picked up the file and opened it. "Mrs. Luckett was the primary witness in the case of Jonathan Acre. My Lord will remember the case from a couple of months back. She'd originally agreed to testify, and then changed her mind. Mrs. Luckett was concerned for her safety and with good reason. I managed to persuade her to give evidence. As soon as she appeared in court, Mr. Acre changed his plea to guilty. On her way out of court, Mrs. Luckett gave me a note, a death threat."

Miles was on his feet again. "And just when did this snippet of information come your way? Begging Your Honor's pardon, but my learned friend was in a very nasty car crash and doesn't remember the case to which she keeps referring. Hence the case-file on the desk in front of her."

"Mr. Kingsman, could you remember every single detail of every case you've worked on over the last say six months?" Judge Matheson asked.

"That's different."

"No, it isn't. You would brush up on your notes, refer to documents, just as you are doing right now. Just as every lawyer I have ever come across does during every single case to ensure the defendant gets a fair trial. Please continue, Mrs. Harkin."

Niamh pulled the letter from the file. "Exhibit A, My Lord. A letter given to Mrs. Luckett stating that if she gave evidence against Mr. Acre, she would die." She handed the letter in its protective covering to the court official. He in turn handed it to Judge Matheson. Niamh continued speaking. "A murder we know was carried out by Mr. Jankowski."

Judge Matheson glanced over the letter.

"That proves nothing," Miles objected.

"It proves your client knows the defendant in the trial Mrs. Luckett testified in," Niamh responded quickly.

"I'll allow it."

"Thank you, My Lord." Niamh glanced across at the defense bench, in time to see Miles sit and write something on the file in front of him. Her breathing caught, and her stomach twisted at the sight of the slanted letters, and the calligraphy pen.

It can't be. Even though the evidence was mounting and was past the point of suspicion, to suddenly see the same handwriting appearing in front of her, worried and disappointed her.

Miles raised his head and met her gaze. His smirk sent shivers of terror down her spine. He stood and started speaking.

Niamh gripped the desk in front of her as his voice faded.

She sat at her desk, the letter Gina Luckett had received in her hand. The slant was exactly the same. Precise penmanship, care taken to ensure every single letter was perfect. If only she could remember where she'd seen it before. And it wasn't the ones addressed to her either.

A slow knock on the door frame brought her back to reality. She glanced up to see Toby Croft standing there watching her. "Hey, Toby."

"Problems?" He uncurled his long frame and moved towards her.

Niamh smiled and shoved the letter into a file, closing it. "No. Just checking through a couple of things before filing this."

"Congratulations on winning the Acre case this morning. One really bad guy off the streets."

"Thanks."

"Oh, this came through for you. Depositions from Miles Kingsman's next client. I'm beginning to think he only chooses your cases. Either that or he likes losing."

"That wouldn't surprise me." She opened the file. Miles's perfect copperplate handwriting adorned the page. Slanted, black, calligraphy. An exact match for the death threats in the file on her desk.

Every nerve in her body tightened. She straightened, sucking in a deep breath as if it were her last. Everything made sense now.

"Is Alan in?"

"No. Why?"

"I know who's sending the letters. And I know why." She gathered her papers. *"I'll go lock these away and see him first thing in the morning."*

"I'll give you a hand."

"—and I'm sure you'll agree that would be a grave miscarriage of justice," Miles concluded.

Niamh raised her eyes to Patrick, bile rising in her throat. Toby knew as much as she did before the car crash. She picked up the glass of water and sipped it before replacing it on the other side of her files. A sign that she needed a break. Fortunately, the judge was paying attention.

"Mr. Kingsman, do you have anything more to add?"

"No, My Lord."

"Then you may present your evidence tomorrow. The last thing we want is a grave miscarriage of justice. We'll reconvene here at ten o'clock." He stood and picked up his files.

"All rise," intoned the court clerk.

Niamh rose with everyone else as Judge Matheson

left the court. Miles gathered his papers and hurried from the room. Niamh made to follow him, but Toby caught her arm.

"Wait a minute." He let go of her arm. "Nice one. I doubt I could have pulled it off so well."

"Sure you could." She gathered her papers and shoved them in her briefcase.

"Are you all right? You seem a little on edge."

"I'm fine. Patrick will want me out of here quickly." A glance up at the public gallery showed her brother had already left.

"I'll see you later."

Niamh made her way swiftly to the robing room. She opened her locker, for an instant glad only Miles was in there. "That's an interesting pen you have."

"Oh?"

"Calligraphy, isn't it? A little unusual for everyday use."

"Ah, yes. I always use one. My English professor insisted good penmanship would open doors to high places. Why the interest?"

"I was just wondering."

Miles was in her face in less than five seconds. "You need to be careful what you see and wonder about, Niamh. Sometimes it's better to be like one of the three wise monkeys. See nothing, hear nothing, and say nothing. Sometimes you should just drop things and walk away."

It was as if an arctic blast issued from his mouth. Every hair on her arms and the back of her neck stood on end. Inside her inner voice was screaming, *get out, raise the alarm*, but she was frozen to the spot. "Are you threatening me?"

"Haven't we had this conversation? Only it was

the other way around? I don't make threats, I make promises. And besides, why would I do that? And here would be a little stupid wouldn't it? In a building full of lawyers."

He leaned away as the door opened and Toby came in. "So I hear you're getting remarried on Saturday?"

Niamh found herself able to move and shoved her robe and wig into the locker. "Yes, we are."

"Well, all the best. Perhaps you'll be a better wife than lawyer." Miles walked away, leaving a frigid atmosphere behind him.

Toby opened his locker. "What was that all about?"

"Just Miles being, well, Miles."

"Don't lie to me. He was giving you grief over something."

Niamh pulled on her coat. "It's him. Same writing, same pen. And he warned me to drop it and walk away."

Toby stiffened. "Go home. I'll sort things from here."

"It's not your problem, Toby. It's mine."

"Go home, Niamh." His voice hardened and his eyes glinted. "I'll talk to Alan. This will all be over tomorrow."

Can I trust him, Lord? Do I have any other options? I don't think I do.

"OK. I'll see you in the morning."

****

Jared came home and tossed his jacket over the banisters. "Niamh?" There was no answer. The air was filled with the smell of cooking. He moved through the hallway and pushed open the kitchen door. "Hon?" She wasn't there but the table had been laid for two and there were candles on it. He wandered over to the oven and peeked inside. Dinner was almost done by the looks of it and the two pans on the stove were simmering gently.

Niamh came up behind him and wrapped her arms around him. "Hey, handsome."

He turned in her arms and kissed her with as much passion as he could find. "*Hey, good looking. What are you cooking?*" His singing was flat, off key, and he knew he'd gotten the words wrong, but he didn't care.

She kissed him back. "Dinner. Roast beef and Yorkshire puddings, and all the accompanying vegetables, including cauliflower cheese."

"Roast dinner on a week night? You're spoiling me."

"Well, you're moving into Liam's tomorrow until the wedding, so I'm not going to see you. I'm going to miss you. Although as it's technically a remarriage, maybe that bit doesn't count and you can stay here."

Jared kissed her. "Niamh, this does count. You still don't remember the first wedding or the first eight years of our marriage. But if you'd rather I didn't sleep at Liam's its fine. It's not like we share a room or anything." He winked at her. "Yet."

"It's OK. Patrick has no plans to move out for the foreseeable future so I'm not alone. Just wish this work thing was over. But it should be by tomorrow."

His interest piqued. "Oh? You got a lead?"

"Concrete proof. So tomorrow, one way or the other."

Jared hugged her. "That's great, hon." He glanced

around the room. "Speaking of Patrick, where is he?"

"He's gone over to Liam's. He said we have two hours and not a minute longer. We do however have an armed cop in a car on the driveway. I'm also wearing a panic button."

"That's better than nothing." He paused. "Hang on, wearing a panic button? Where can't I touch you?"

Niamh laughed. "You're quite safe I assure you."

He nuzzled her neck. "I'm never safe with you around. You're the blue touch paper to my heart."

She arched her neck a little, giving him more access. "How did I cope with this before?"

"Me kissing your neck?" He pulled back and looked at her. "You'd usually reciprocate."

"Work, silly, not you."

"Oh, right. Well, you'd hide behind that nasty manner of yours."

"I must have been horrible."

Jared kissed her. "You could be. I loved you then, and I love you even more now."

"Glad about that."

"Me, too." He took a deep breath. "Dinner smells wonderful."

"Hopefully it tastes wonderful and you like it."

"I like everything you cook."

"Flattery will get you everywhere. Go shower and let me start to dish up. You have ten minutes."

"Ten whole minutes?" he teased.

"Nine and a half now," she said, laughing at him.

He headed back into the hall and took the stairs two at a time. He showered quickly and went back downstairs to find the candles lit and two plates on the table.

Niamh looked up from pouring the sparkling

grape juice. "That was fast."

"I can be," he said sitting down. "This looks wonderful." He paused. "This was the first thing you ever cooked for me."

She looked over at him as she sat. "Really?"

"Yeah. It's always been one of my favorites." He watched the way her eyes sparkled in the candlelight, then took her hands and said grace. He took a mouthful of the juice, and then put the glass down picking up his knife and fork. "I thought I was going to lose you. That shout shattered my world."

She looked at him. "I'm sorry."

"Don't be. Hon, you didn't ask for that car to hit you or for your brakes not to work. I just wasn't expecting to find you in that RTC."

"But you did lose me. Well, you lost the woman you married, the one you spent eight years with."

He shook his head, chewing slowly. "She's right here still. Oh, things are a little different now tis true. For example, she sleeps in a different room, but at least I don't hear her snoring."

"You beast." she said poking her tongue out at him. "I do not snore."

Jared laughed. "You see. That is your normal retort for me insulting you. Which incidentally makes you a beast's wife."

"Surely it should make me Beauty if you're the Beast."

"Ha, ha, ha. In that case, you'd better not make me angry, because you wouldn't like me when I'm angry."

"Uh huh. Really? You turn green or something?"

"Yeah really or something like that. You're still there, still the woman I married and am planning on remarrying the day after tomorrow."

"Sounds good to me." Niamh ate silently for a moment. "It's been a rough time since the car crash. But I made it."

He nodded. "Yes hon, just like I said you would."

He picked up the glass again. "To us. To the happily ever after we both deserve."

Niamh touched her glass to his. "To us."

20

Judge Matheson peered over his glasses at Miles Kingsman. "Is that it, Mr. Kingsman?"

"Yes, My Lord. We believe that our witnesses will provide enough evidence that my client did not, in fact, kill Mrs. Luckett because he was nowhere near Headley Cross at the time."

Niamh stood. "Can my learned friend prove this? Does he have a bus or train ticket? CCTV pictures from a petrol station? A boarding pass for a plane? Perhaps he wrote the threatening letter to Mrs. Luckett himself."

"As I tried to explain yesterday, my client did not write that letter."

"Mrs. Harkin and Mr. Kingsman," Judge Matheson said. "This is not a tennis match to score points off each other with. There is a simple enough way to prove one way or the other if Mr. Jankowski wrote the letter, Mr. Kingsman. If your client is willing to do a handwriting test?"

"Anything to prove his innocence in this matter."

Judge Matheson nodded. "And we'll need a control to compare it with. Perhaps you'd oblige, Mr. Kingsman? I'll read a line from the letter in front of me and you both write it down."

Miles hesitated.

"You have a problem with that?"

"Am I being accused of something, Your Honor?

Surely in the interest of fairness, Mrs. Harkin and Mr. Croft should write it out as well?"

"Sounds good. Mrs. Harkin, Mr. Croft, if that's all right with you. I'd like you all to use identical pens. The clerk will give you one. Along with a sheet of paper."

Niamh nodded. "I have no objection to this, at all." She took the pen and paper from the clerk, seeing Toby do the same out of the corner of her eye.

Miles muttered under his breath as he pulled the lid off the pen. "What do you want us to write?"

"Tell anyone what you saw and you will die," Judge Matheson said. "And then sign your names at the bottom."

Niamh did as she was told. She stood quietly as Miles and Toby wrote the same thing. She shivered as the all too familiar slanted words appeared on the sheet of paper. She glanced up, catching his eye. Fear struck her to the core.

She raised her eyes to Patrick in the gallery, trying to silently communicate with him. The room closed around her as her throat tightened, making breathing hard. She reached for her glass of water, but Toby's hand covered hers, stopping the movement.

"Mrs. Harkin? Your paper, please?"

"Sure." Her hand shook as she held out the paper to the clerk who collected all of them before crossing over to the dock and took a matching sheet from the defendant. The clerk gave them to the judge.

Toby reached over and touched her arm. "I'm going to ask for a recess," he whispered. "We need to discuss this away from the courtroom."

"There's nothing to discuss." She pulled her arm away, not meeting his gaze, and then straightened.

"Can you smell smoke?"

Toby nodded.

Niamh glanced up. "It's coming from the vent."

The fire alarm went off.

Judge Matheson stood. "If you're in the public gallery, please follow the court official to the nearest exit. Court officers, please escort the defendant from the building following evacuation protocol delta."

Niamh grabbed the files in front of her and shoved them into the briefcase. Then she headed to the door.

Toby ran beside her. "Take the north fire exit," he yelled, raising his voice over the clanging alarms.

"Why?"

"Because the smoke is coming from the south."

Niamh stopped running and looked at him. "You seem pretty certain about that."

"No time to talk," Miles said from behind her. "Toby is right. The north exit is better."

"Then I'm going the other way." Niamh dodged past them and ran back the way she had come. Footsteps and voices echoed behind her. She dodged into a side corridor and ran towards the east exit, the one that lead to the car park.

The smoke seemed thicker the further down the corridor she ran. She reached the fire exit and put a hand on the metal bar. Crying out, she pulled it away. "It's hot."

"Of course it's hot, you stupid woman." Hatred resounded in the familiar voice. She slowly turned around to see a gun pointed unwaveringly in her direction. "Now I suggest you come this way. Or you'll die sooner than intended."

I never dreamed of this scenario when I imagined how it would play out. Lord, please, work this for Your good. If there is any good to come from this.

"Why?" She struggled to get the words past the lump of betrayal in her throat.

"Because you wouldn't leave things alone. You had to keep pushing and investigating."

"That's my job. I thought it was yours. Or did you get a better offer?"

Smoke shot out from under the door, swirling around her feet then retreated as quickly as it appeared.

"The door behind you is going to blow any second. I suggest we move. Now." He grabbed her arm, forcing her to run with him, back the way they had come.

****

Jared sighed as the alarms echoed across the fire station. He'd just got the engine clean enough to see his refection in, and now it was going to go and get dirty again.

"Fire at the Crown Court. Both pump and ladder to go. Make pumps twenty-five. Persons reported."

The call sent a cold wash of fear over him, and he caught his breath.

Oh God, no. Niamh's there all day today. And twenty-five pumps make it a massive fire.

His fingers shook as he climbed into his gear. He glanced up as Brad touched his shoulder. "I know what you're going to say, Guv. My wife is there. There is no way I'm staying behind."

"Then you follow orders. We're not the only unit responding, and I don't want you risking anyone. And that includes yourself."

He jerked his head in response, climbing on board. The sirens rose and fell in their two tone wail as they raced across town.

"Time for more prayers," Skippy told him.

"I haven't stopped."

****

The blast blew Niamh to the floor. She pulled her arms up to protect herself as a wave of intense heat flashed over the ceiling. A whistling sound accompanied the roar and crackling. Foul smelling smoke clogged the air, replacing what oxygen there was. Once it lessened, she scrambled upright and pushed open the door to her right. She didn't care what room it was, perhaps she could climb out of the window and get away.

She shut the door behind her, fumbling with the latch, trying to lock it. She had to put distance between her and them.

Thick, choking smoke surrounded her, seeping under the door and pouring through the vents. It was so dark she could hardly see, never mind breathe. *Forget the door. Just get out of here.*

Falling to her knees, she crawled along the floor, the air slightly better there. Tears blinded her, her throat constricting, coughs wracking her body.

The door behind her opened, allowing more smoke into the enclosed space. "Niamh?"

She tried not to cough, but the smoke filled her lungs, and she had no choice.

"I know you're in here." Shuffling steps came up behind her. "Come on, Niamh. Let's talk about this."

"Nothing to say, Miles." She kept crawling. Surely

the window was in front of her, but she was so lightheaded she was no longer sure.

"Niamh, I found a way out. Where are you?"

"Where's Toby?"

"Saving his own skin. We need to get out of here. Come and give me a hand trying to get this door open."

Why is he doing this when he wants me dead? "Why should I believe you? You're in this as deep as he is."

Groping fingers found a wall and door frame.

His voice was husky. "You believe me because you know Toby wrote those notes as well as I do, Niamh. How else could you receive them in the internal mail? And now the judge knows. Toby cut your brakes. He took the files and gave them to me. He set the fires in here. We can send him down."

"While you plead insanity? Or turn Queen's evidence?"

Miles's hand gripped her wrist and hauled her to her feet. "Do you want to get out of here or not? Just help me with this door."

After a couple of shoves from both of them, the door gave enough for them to roll through. She shut the door behind her. Pushing upright, she staggered to the window. It had bars across it. She looked around for a chair. She was back in the courtroom.

Flames crackled from the bench and around the doors. She was trapped. Picking up the fire extinguisher, she raised it and aimed it at the window. It just fitted between the bars.

Nothing happened. *Of course, reinforced glass. It won't break and besides I'm on the fifth floor. Far too high to jump.*

She jumped as a hand grabbed her, pulling her

away.

"No, you don't." Miles dragged her to the center of the room, pushing her against the central pillar. Yanking her hands behind her back, tying her securely.

"Miles…" Terror filled her. Tears blinded her as the heat from the acrid smell seared her throat. "What…?"

"You've heard of Joan of Arc?" he whispered in her ear. "This is Niamh of Headley Cross. Different story. Same end."

21

Flames issued from every window of the court building as Jared's fire engine reached the shout. Thick smoke rose high into the sky. The hissing, crackling sound Jared knew all too well, filled the air. Dozens of other fire engines had already arrived. Hoses ran across the courtyard and well over one hundred firefighters stood kitted up in breathing apparatus.

Water streamed from high volume hoses, making little impact on the immense fire.

He resisted the temptation to look around for Niamh. Every building had standard evacuation procedures, the judiciary even more stringent ones, and the court officers would make sure everyone got out. Until told otherwise he would assume she was safe. He had to. Otherwise, he couldn't focus on his job.

Jared pulled his BA onto his back and fastened it. He checked his air and gave his tally to Phil who stood with the breathing apparatus entry control board.

"You're Alpha One team," Phil remarked as he checked Jared's details.

Skippy handed over his tally.

"Alpha One with Jared."

Brad looked at him. "Jared, I want you manning the BA board."

He shook his head. "I want in there, Guv, please."

Toby ran over to him. "Niamh's still in there.

Miles has her."

"What?" Terror gripped him. "But he wants her dead." He spun around to face his commanding officer. "Please, Guv. This guy's been after her for weeks. If he set the fire, if he kills her now after everything she's been through…"

"Fine, but you don't take any risks. Skippy, go with him."

"Thanks. Toby, where is she?"

"We were in court five, towards the back of the building. It's on the fifth floor. Miles, Niamh, and I left together. There was an explosion in the fire exit stairwell, we got separated as we headed back the way we'd come. I got out through another exit. I don't know what happened to them."

"Skippy, let's go." Pulling his mask on and rushing the pre-entry check, Jared ran towards the burning building.

Lord, if I am to die here, help me get at least one person out. Let me save Niamh. I couldn't save our daughter two years ago, allow me to redeem myself now. And let Patrick be safe. I don't have time to check he got out.

The heat was intense, almost pushing him backwards. The building crackled and shimmied around him. He hadn't been this scared in a fire since the one that claimed Dayna's life.

Keeping close to Skippy, he dodged the dancing angels of fire coming at them from every wall and vent.

He pointed towards the fifth floor and Skippy nodded. Once the ladder was secure, Jared took the lead, running up the ladder with the hose. He checked the floor before clambering over the window sill. Fire raged inside, but spraying water on the fire as they moved, the two men made their way up to the corridor.

The radio crackled in his ear. "Alpha one withdraw! The front of the building shifted. It's unsafe."

Skippy pulled his arm. "We have to go."

Jared shook his head. "You go. I'm not leaving Niamh."

Boom!

An explosion to the left sent both men to the floor, a shower of debris covering them. Jared quickly pushed it off and scrambled to his feet, hauling Skippy up with him. "I'm staying," he repeated.

"Then so am I."

Jared let go of him and turned the hose on what had become an inferno. If he ever imagined hell, this is what it would look like. Thick black smoke assailed him from every angle. Hissing and blistering flames impeded his path, sizzling under the impact of the water. Sweat dripped down inside his mask, pooling inside his collar. Deep inside, the persistent fear he was too late, tried to get out. But if he let it, he was doomed.

****

Niamh watched helplessly as Miles sloshed petrol around the floor, the clanking can mixing with the sound of the fire.

"Why pour fuel on a fire?"

"Setting up a flashover. Toby will send that fool of a husband in to find you. This will deal with him. The explosion puts out the fire by the door so I can get out."

She twisted her hands. A futile gesture as the rope

was too tight. "Please, let me go. We can both get out of here."

Miles set a trail of petrol from her feet to the door. Then he tossed the can away. It landed by the bench, the last dregs of petrol eking towards the flames.

Niamh struggled harder. "Help!"

Miles pulled the gun from his belt and pointed it at her. "Oh be quiet."

She looked at him defiantly. "Help!"

Miles held the gun in the air and fired.

****

"What's that?" Jared turned hearing something. "Sounded like a gunshot."

"In there," Skippy said. "Court five. Isn't that what he said?"

Jared nodded. "Niamh, are you in there?"

"Jared." Her voice was muffled behind the door, but he knew it was her.

"Here." He shouldered the door.

"Check the door for heat, Jared."

Skippy's call came too late. The door blew open, sending a backdraft of light and heat and fire hurling towards them. Jared dived, pushing Skippy out of the way.

Heat and light barreled over him.

He automatically held his breath, forgetting his air tank would still supply his oxygen.

Once the heat passed, he stood and hauled Skippy to his feet. "Are you all right?"

"Fine. You?"

"I will be once we find Niamh." He turned his attention to the door. The fire had lessened. "Niamh?"

"Jared, in here."

Taking a deep breath, he reacquired the hose and aimed the water onto the fire and into the room beyond.

****

To Niamh it looked like a scene from a film, with the firefighters standing silhouetted against a fire filled doorway. Her heart leapt. He'd come for her.

The floor creaked beneath her. Miles stood beside her, gun aimed at her head. Tears streamed down her face. Her chest heaved with the effort to breathe as she twisted her hands against her bonds.

Water sprayed from the hose, clearing a path towards her. She twisted her hands, feeling the rope loosen a little. "Jared," she called, the one word sending her into a paroxysm of coughing.

"Let her go." Jared's voice was muffled behind the mask, his coat scorched. He held out a hand. "Just let her go and we can all get out of here. Hon, take my hand."

Niamh twisted her head as the floor at the corner of the room buckled. "I can't move. Please, Miles, untie me. Don't do this."

Jared's voice took on a stronger tone. "We have to go now." His hand stretched through the flames.

His image shimmered in the heat, and she blinked hard. "I can't move."

Was this how Dayna felt in those last few moments of her life? Heat searing her body, unable to breathe or see.

She moved her hands again, the rope finally giving and slipping from her wrists.

Jared took a step towards her. She reached out, trying to grasp his hand.

The gun clicked. The hose moved, the jet of water hitting Miles and sending him across the room.

The floor creaked and gave way beneath her. She screamed as she fell.

Her arm jerked as something grasped her hand. She glanced up and saw Jared leaning over the hole, his gloved hand folded around her wrist.

"Give me your other hand."

She stretched up. Something heavy grabbed her leg. She glanced down to see Miles leering up at her. He looked dark against the brightness of the flames beneath them. She squirmed, trying to free herself. Was this was like to be roasted on a spit? The intense heat felt like it melted the soles of her shoes.

Jared grunted with effort. His grip faltered and her hand slipped.

"Don't drop me," she screamed. *Please, God, don't let him drop me.*

"Give me your other hand."

She stretched as far as she could, but not far enough. Her fingers grazed his, not able to grasp them. She slipped a little further. The weight on her leg dragging her down.

Just as she was about to fall, another gloved hand grasped hers. She glanced up as both Jared and his partner heaved, pulling her to safety.

The hand on her ankle loosened, and a scream echoed as Miles fell into the inferno below. Then she was tossed over Jared's shoulder as he and the other firefighter made their way from the room.

The floor beneath them creaked, and the walls buckled. Jared broke into a run. No sooner had they rounded a corner than the corridor behind them fell into oblivion.

Niamh raised her head. Through blurred eyes, she glimpsed the two firefighters point. Their muffled words made no sense over the roar of the flames.

She closed her eyes praying hard. She had no idea how they were going to get out. There was no human way they could get out. The stairs were gone, the floor behind them gone.

Only God could save them now.

Then Jared began moving again with a greater sense of urgency. The whole building began to move.

She raised a hand to protect her head as masonry began to fall around them.

22

Niamh sat on the stretcher inside the ambulance, a blanket around her shoulders, and an oxygen mask over her face. She smiled at Jared as he stood outside the doors. He was hopping from one foot to the other as the paramedics checked her over. She smiled, trying to ease his nerves. "I'm OK."

"No talking," the paramedic chided. "We're taking you to hospital. You inhaled a lot of smoke."

"Then I'll come with," Jared said, climbing in beside her. "I don't want to let you out of my sight."

Brad came over to him. "I need you here, I'm afraid."

"Guv?"

"Niamh isn't in any danger. Unlike the building behind me. If we don't get a handle on this fire soon, we'll lose it and the one next to it."

Niamh could see the indecision play on his face. Torn between love and duty. "I'm fine, Jarrie." She pulled the mask off and kissed his soot covered cheek. He smelled of fire and smoke. She probably did as well. "They need you here. I'll get Liam to come and sit with me. And if you should see Patrick anywhere, tell him where I am."

Jared held her gaze, and then pulled her in for a gentle kiss. "OK."

She ran her hand down his face. "Just stay safe. No more heroics tonight. I intend to marry you in the morning."

"I promise. And I'll find out about Patrick if I can."

"Thank you. I love you."

"I love you, too." He leapt down from the ambulance and did his jacket up as he headed back towards the fire with the other firefighters.

Thank you, Lord, for getting us out of there. Keep him safe. Keep them all safe.

Darkness had fallen and the sky was lit with an eerie orange glow. Soot and ash rained down from the sky. A loud crash sent embers high as the back of the building fell inwards.

"We've got to go. They're pulling everyone back."

Just as the door closed, a voice she recognized spoke. "Wait a second. That's my sister."

She pulled the mask off again. "Patrick."

The door opened slightly and, in the next instant, she was in his arms. "I thought I'd lost you," she cried.

"I thought the same." He sat down and pushed her to lie down. "We can talk on the way."

The paramedic strapped her down and the ambulance pulled away, sirens blaring.

"Patrick, Toby…"

"Toby is safe. He went back to the office once he'd been checked over."

She shook her head. "Toby is the inside leak. It's his handwriting. Judge Matheson has the papers. Or he did. He'll know."

Patrick's eyes grew wide, and he pulled out his phone. "He'll be after the judge." He dialed rapidly. "Nate, its Patrick. You need to arrest Toby Croft. And get someone over to Judge Matheson's immediately. Croft's the inside man and he'll try to take out the judge next. I know. No, Niamh's safe. I'm with her now on the way to Headley General. Sure, we'll meet you there."

Niamh closed her eyes and let Patrick's voice fade into the background. All that mattered was Jared and the fire he was fighting. Her mind played back the images from inside the court. He'd put his own life on the line to save her. He was doing the same thing now, to put out the fire before it spread. That made him one very special man. And he was hers.

****

The fire finally under control and his shift over, Jared strode across the ED reception. "Jared Harkin. My wife, Niamh was brought in by ambulance from the fire at the Crown Court."

"Take a seat. Someone will be with you shortly."

He nodded and crossed over to where Patrick sat. "How is she? Why aren't you with her?"

Patrick held up a hand. "Take it easy. She's in with the doctor. They'll let us know when we can go in. She wanted me to wait here for you. Fill you in."

"First of all, you should know we pulled Miles Kingsman out. He's alive, but going to wish he wasn't. They airlifted him to the burns unit at Dirham."

"OK, good. The police will want to speak with him. It wasn't just him. Toby Croft was involved as well."

"Wait a minute. *The* Toby Croft, the CFS guy Niamh was working with?"

"Yeah. Nate Holmes was going to arrest him. He wrote the letters, cut her brakes, stole the files…"

Jared rubbed his hands over his face, sinking into the chair beside his brother-in-law. "I don't believe it.

She trusted him."

"A lot of people did."

He glanced up as Liam joined him. "Been here before," Jared joked wryly. He got to his feet and exchanged a manly hug with his brother-in-law. Niamh always called them that because she claimed men never hugged properly, in case the hug got taken the wrong way.

"At least this time she's awake and not in any danger," Liam told him. "Thanks to you."

"I was doing my job." He sank back into the chair. "But it's a lot easier when it's not Niamh I'm rescuing."

"I bet it is. Has the doctor said anything?"

"Not yet."

Liam sat beside him. "Shame we don't get paid to sit here."

Jared scrunched his nose up at him. "Yeah, really." He sighed. "What's taking them so long?"

"You know doctors. And she inhaled a lot of smoke."

Jared started pacing again.

"Jared."

He spun as someone called his name. Nate and a uniformed officer strode over to him. "Hi, Nate. She's in with the doctor. They haven't said anything yet."

Nate nodded. "We picked up Toby Croft. He's in a holding cell for now. I'm here to talk to Niamh."

"So she's safe?"

Nate nodded. "As far as we know. PC Williams is going to stand outside her cubicle for now. I'll be back in a few." He moved over to the reception desk and flashed his ID. Then he and the uniformed officer vanished through the doors.

Jared sighed. "How come he can do that and I

can't?"

"His ID is better than yours," Liam told him.

"Evidently so." Jared stretched out his booted feet in front of him and folded his arms over his chest. He closed his eyes. "Tell me when I can go in."

"You're going to sleep?" Liam sounded horrified.

"Like you said, she's not in any danger. And I'm not sleeping. Just resting my eyes."

Fifteen minutes later a nurse came over to him. "Mr. Harkin? You can go in now."

Jared stood, instantly awake. "How is she?"

"She's doing OK. The doctor wants her to stay in, but she's refusing."

"Sounds like her." Jared followed the nurse, relief filling him. If she was well enough to argue, then she wasn't too badly hurt.

"Then I'll sign a disclaimer." He could hear her voice as he approached the cubicle. "I'm getting married tomorrow. I want to go home and start getting ready."

Jared pushed aside the curtain. "You really are stubborn, woman."

"Jarrie…"

He covered the floor to the bed in three swift strides and folded his arms tightly around her.

She clung to him tightly. "I'm OK."

He looked over the top of her head at the doctor. "How is she?"

"Her lungs are clear, but I really would rather she stayed in overnight."

"Is she in any danger if she went home? She isn't going to be on her own."

The doctor shook his head. "No."

Niamh sat upright. "Then I want to go home. It's

been a really long day. All I want is a bath and my bed."

"I'll get the paperwork."

Jared pulled Niamh back into his arms and kissed her soundly. "When I knew you were still in there..." he whispered.

"It's over," she told him. "I was terrified, but then I saw you silhouetted against those flames, hose in hand. A real hero."

Her fingers trailed down his face. He caught her hand in his in a vain attempt to quench the rivers of fire and desire caused by her touch. "It's my job."

She nodded. "They caught them both. It's over."

"Good. I assume you won't be prosecuting either of them when the case gets to court?"

"No. I'll be a witness." She sucked in a deep breath. "Toby pleaded guilty to murder, attempted murder, and arson. They'll charge Miles with the same. Assuming he survives."

"He was pretty badly burned."

"That could have been me, should have been me." Sobs shook her body, and Jared cradled her tightly, rocking her gently.

"It's all right," he whispered. He closed his eyes and began to pray, thanking God for delivering them both safe from the fire.

****

Jared sat on the edge of the bed and smiled at Niamh. He chinked his mug of cocoa against hers. "To the night before the morning after."

"Shouldn't that the morning after the night before?"

"I said what I meant," he told her. "Tomorrow is the first day of the rest of our lives. This is the last night of what has to be one of the longest years ever. So we're drinking to tonight—the night before the morning after."

"The night before the morning after, and a happily ever after to boot." She touched her cup to his and sipped it, before leaning back on the pillows. She put the cup down and coughed violently.

"Are you sure you're all right?"

"Yes. Just tired, that's all."

They drank in silence, not needing to say anything. He finished his cocoa and kissed her cheek. "I should let you sleep. I still need to iron my shirt for tomorrow. And polish my boots."

"Jarrie, would you sleep here tonight?" Color touched her cheeks. "I mean, the spare room, not here, here."

"I can't."

"Why not?"

"It's not the done thing for the groom to sleep over the night before the wedding. Besides, my uniform is over at Liam's."

"Don't care. I don't want to be alone."

"You're not. You've got Patrick in my room, and your parents staying in the other room. Liam and I are on the other end of the phone. You'll be fine." He gathered her into his arms and gave her a lingering kiss. "See you in church."

"You bet you will." Tiredness was evident in her voice, and she looked almost as pale as the sheets. "Top drawer in the dresser. There's something for you."

Jared got up and opened the drawer. He pulled

out a small box with a gold bow on it. "This one?"

"It's a wedding present. Want you to have it now."

"I don't have yours with me." He felt bad for not thinking. "I can come back with it."

"Tomorrow's fine." She yawned, her eyes closing. "Tired..."

"Thank you, hon." He opened the box, tears filling his eyes as he gazed down at the gold cufflinks with a tiny diamond and his initials. "Oh, hon..." He glanced up, to find her fast asleep.

23

Niamh looked at herself in the mirror as her mum and Jacqui fussed around her, smoothing the skirt of her dress. It looked even more amazing this morning. Butterflies tossed and turned and she placed a hand cautiously over her stomach, glad her secret was still a secret. Despite what the doctor had said the previous evening, she hadn't let herself believe until an hour ago when she'd finally plucked up the courage to do the test she had bought when the doctor first suggested pregnancy the previous week.

Just hope Jarrie will be pleased, Lord. After all he did say barefoot, pregnant and in a shift. Although it's kind of weird being a pregnant bride—although we're still married, I just don't remember. I assumed my missed periods were down to stress or just recovering from the car crash. A baby never crossed my mind. But what I don't understand is if things were so bad between us before the car crash, why did we make love anyway? Old time's sake maybe? A last ditch attempt at trying to patch things up? Whatever the reason, thank You. Keep the child safe within me. I'll tell Jarrie later. And the others when we get home.

She took a deep breath. *I love him, there's not a single doubt on that score. Just wish I could remember everything.* Sure the odd conversation had come back to her, usually in flash backs, but it wasn't the same. For Jared this would be a simple reaffirmation of their vows. But she would be committing her life to him for the first time.

Jacqui looked at her. "You look beautiful, Niamh."

Niamh felt and saw the color rise in her cheeks in the mirror. "So long as Jarrie likes it, that's all that matters. He still thinks I'm wearing jeans." She winced and rubbed her temple.

"Are you all right?"

"I've got a really bad headache. I woke with it and it's getting worse."

"Do you want something for it??"

"No, it's just nerves. Or the after effects of the fire yesterday. It'll go." She glanced at the clock. "It's time, isn't it?"

Just then, her father's voice echoed up the stairs. "The cars are here. We need to go if we're going to be on time."

****

Jared straightened his dress uniform and glanced in the mirror at Liam. "Does it look all right?"

Liam smiled. "It's fine. You could have gone for a tux this time, you know."

"Yeah, I know, but I wanted to wear this, like I did before. This may be a renewal of vows for me, but for Niamh it's her first wedding. Even if she is going to turn up in jeans."

"Jeans?" Liam said surprised.

Jared nodded. "She couldn't find a dress, got really upset over it. So I told her she could wear what she had on if she wanted. She looked down at herself and agreed. Jeans and a T-shirt. And when I pushed it, she told me she'd got the old, new, borrowed and blue. Jeans, a shirt and socks."

Liam shook his head. "I doubt it. She'd never wear that to church on a Sunday, never mind to a wedding. She'll find a dress of some description."

"Maybe, but so long as she turns up, I'm not bothered what she wears." Jared looked at himself in the mirror and pulled his cap on. "OK, let's go do this."

****

Niamh arrived at the church to find Pastor Jack waiting for her. "You look beautiful," Pastor Jack told her. "I'll go tell him you're here."

"Thank you." She tugged at her dress, convinced it was tight across her stomach, but it probably wasn't.

Her father smiled at her. "Ready?"

"More than ready." She closed her eyes for a moment, the headache surging. "Maybe I should have taken something for the headache. Too late now."

The music started as Niamh toed off her old shoes and stood barefoot on the carpet. She slowly made her way into the church and up the aisle. She kept her eyes fixed on Jared. He was standing facing forwards, not daring to turn around.

Please turn around. I can't do this without seeing your face.

Jared turned around and his eyes widened as he took in what she was wearing. Shock then delight crossed his face. He beamed at her, love filling his eyes and spilling from every pore. When she reached him, he grabbed her hand. "Wow," he whispered. "You look amazing. You bought a dress."

"Thank you," she whispered. "So do you. And of course, I did. Cassie designed and made it. How could I refuse the royal dressmaker? Besides, you did say you'd marry me barefoot and in a shift. We just fancied up the shift." She lifted her skirt slightly. "See."

Jared grinned at the sight of her toes. "I wasn't serious."

"Well, Cassie and I figured, why not. Not often a girl gets to do this twice."

The service began and after the first hymn and introductory speeches, Pastor Jack began the wedding proper. Jared and Niamh both answered the legal declarations before Niamh's dad made a joke about giving her away again, which even Niamh found funny.

Then they turned to face each other, holding hands tightly.

Pastor Jack turned Jared. "Will you, Jared, take Niamh to be your lawful wedded wife? Will you love her, comfort her, honor and keep her, and forsaking all others keep only unto her as long as you both shall live?"

Jared grinned at Niamh. "I will."

Pastor Jack smiled at him and turned to Niamh. "Will you, Niamh, take Jared to be your lawful wedded husband? Will you love him, comfort him, honor and keep him, and forsaking all others keep only unto him as long as you both shall live?"

Niamh took a deep breath and looked straight at Jared. "I will." She blinked slightly, her head hurting more now than when she had left home.

For a moment, there were two Jared's.

Don't let me faint. Please, let me just get through this.

Jared looked at Niamh and took her hand, repeating his vows after Pastor Jack. "I, Jared Jason, take thee, Niamh Frances, to be my wedded wife. To have and to hold, from this day forward. For better, for worse, for richer, for poorer. In sickness or in health, to love and to cherish till death do us part. And hereto I pledge thee my faithfulness."

Niamh looked at him. The headache peaked, and she staggered slightly. Tears poured down her face as a sudden influx of memories filled her. She'd done this before. She remembered standing here, exchanging vows with him, different vows, but she remembered. She glanced around the church, her whole body trembling now. She knew the faces in the congregation, really knew them. And she knew without a doubt just how she'd gotten pregnant—making up after the fight two weeks before the crash.

Pastor Jack's voice echoed. "Niamh, if you repeat after me. I, Niamh Frances, take thee, Jared Jason…"

Everything spun as she remembered their honeymoon in Guernsey, being pregnant before, walks in the park and teasing Jared over dinner. Her hand rose to her head, the pain and sudden influx of too many memories, making her dizzy.

Jared looked at her worriedly as her whole body went cold and numb. "Hon?" he said. "What's wrong?"

A quiet murmur broke out amongst the congregation.

Niamh looked at him, tears falling uncontrollably. Everything spun and went dark and she fell.

****

Jared pulled her into his arms, holding her gently. He knelt and laid her on the floor, his fingers automatically going to find a pulse.

Pastor Jack looked over the congregation. "Is there

a doctor here?"

Footsteps ran down the aisle and a suited figure knelt beside him. Jared looked up. "Derek…"

Dr. Derek Clay smiled at him. "Did she eat this morning?" he asked starting to check Niamh over.

Her mum nodded. "She wasn't hungry, but she ate. She's been complaining of a headache. It's a bad one. She refused pain meds, but wouldn't say why."

Dr. Clay nodded. "I want to check her over completely. May we use the vestry, Pastor?"

"Of course."

Niamh groaned and opened her eyes, blinking hard.

Jared immediately leaned over her. "Hon?" He gently sat her up, his arm around her. "Let's get you into the vestry, so Derek can check you over."

Niamh shook her head. "No, I'm OK."

"Please, just come and sit down for a minute. Get away from everyone looking at you."

"OK."

"Then let's take you through," Dr. Clay said. He helped Jared move her over to the vestry.

As they left the chapel, Pastor Jack announced a hymn and the organ started playing. Jared helped Niamh into the chair and sat next to her.

Dr. Clay took her wrist again. "How's your head? Your mum said you have a headache?"

"Really bad one," she whispered. "Just need a minute."

"Then let me give you something for it."

"No." The word came out hard and fast and surprised Jared.

He sat quietly, giving the doctor room to work.

What's wrong? She's shaking like a leaf. Did I push her

into this? Is this an after effect of yesterday? Maybe I should have cancelled or postponed the service.

He took a deep breath and took her hand. "What is it? Hon, if you can't do this, if you don't want to marry me..." His voice trailed off, a sick, devastated feeling welling up inside him. He was all too aware of his family, Niamh's family, and their friends standing in the chapel, singing, probably wondering if there was actually going to be a wedding.

Just like he was.

He took a deep breath and continued. "If you can't marry me, then we can stop now. It's fine."

Niamh looked up at him. "No, I want to marry you." She drew in a deep, sharp breath. "The headache just got a bit much for a moment."

"Then maybe you should take the meds Derek offered."

"I can't. I'll explain later, I promise." Her gaze held his, her eyes glistening. "I love you. I want to marry you. Now."

"I'm glad. I love you, too. Are you sure you're all right? You want some water or something?"

She shook her head. "No, I'm fine. Have you got a tissue?"

He nodded. He pulled one from his pocket and handed it to her. "Don't want it back though," he teased as she used it.

"Just as well," she answered, tucking it up her sleeve. "I'm fine now."

Dr. Clay looked at her. "As soon as the service is over, I want you back in here so I can check you over again. Is there a reason you're refusing pain meds?"

"That's fine and yes, but I'll tell you later. Please don't make me keep refusing them. Right now, I just want to get married."

Jared offered her a hand up and led her back into the church and over to where Pastor Jack stood.

He stopped singing and smiled hesitantly at them. "Is everything OK?"

"Everything's fine. I'm sorry," Niamh apologized. "I have this really bad headache, that's all."

"Are you all right to continue?"

Niamh nodded. She took a deep breath and looked at Jared taking his hands again. The hymn finished and the congregation sat down.

Pastor Jack looked at them. "We're going to continue as Niamh is feeling better and wishes to carry on with the wedding."

Liam dropped a hand on Jared's shoulder as he stood next to him again. "Is she really OK?"

"Other than having a headache and being stubborn, she's fine."

"I am here, you know," Niamh told them. She rolled her eyes. "This is meant to be a wedding, not a circus."

Jared snorted. "Too late for that."

Pastor Jack looked at Niamh. "Repeat after me. I, Niamh Frances, take thee, Jared Jason, to be my wedded husband."

Niamh looked at him and then at Jared. A small smile started at the corners of her mouth and spread over her entire face. Her eyes sparkled and then lit up like Christmas tree lights. "I, Niamh Frances, take you, Jared Jason, to be my husband, my partner in life and my one true love. I will cherish our friendship and love you today, tomorrow, and forever. I will trust you and honor you. I will laugh with you and cry with you. I will love you faithfully through the best and the worst, through the difficult and the easy. What may come I will always be there. As I have given you my hand to hold so I give you my life to keep."

As she spoke Jared's eyes filled with tears and his heart welled up within him, until he thought it might burst with joy. Those were the vows she had originally used when she first married him eight years ago. He let the tears fall, not bothering to wipe them away.

She finished speaking and looked at Pastor Jack, smiled slightly and then looked at Jared. She reached up on tiptoe and whispered into his ear so only he could hear. "I remember. Everything."

He pulled her into a hug. "Oh, hon," he whispered. "That's the best wedding present a man could ask for."

She hugged him. "I love you Jarrie Jace," she told him.

He looked at her and kissed her soundly.

Pastor Jack gave them a moment and then coughed slightly. "We haven't got to that part yet," he said gently.

Jared smiled awkwardly at him. "Sorry. She just got her memory back. All of it."

At that, the whole church erupted into rapturous applause.

Niamh blushed hard and buried her face in Jared's jacket while he just hugged her, a huge grin on his face.

Once things had calmed down, Pastor Jack nodded to Liam who placed the rings on the Bible. Pastor Jack then offered them to Jared.

Jared took the smaller of the two and placing it half way down Niamh's finger said, "With this ring I thee wed, with my body I thee honor and with all my worldly goods I thee endow. Again." He slid the ring the rest of the way down and raised her hand to his lips, kissing it.

Niamh took the other ring and put it onto his finger. "I give thee this ring as the token of the covenant made between us this day and the pledge of our mutual love." She slid the ring on completely and kissed his fingers.

Pastor Jack smiled at them. He spoke a few more words and then smiled again. "I now pronounce you husband and wife. You may now kiss the bride. Again..."

Jared grinned and pulled Niamh into his arms, kissing her.

Pastor Jack turned to the congregation. "I give you Mr. and Mrs. Harkin."

As rapturous applause broke out again, Niamh looked at him, a huge grin on her face. She kept her voice low enough for only him to hear. "I have a question for you, Mr. Harkin."

"What's that, Mrs. Harkin?"

"You know this separate bedroom thing we had going on..."

Jared raised an eyebrow. Where was she going with this? And was now the time? *She sure knows how to pick her moments, Lord.* "Uh, yes, but I actually have every intention of sharing your room tonight."

"I didn't mean that. I meant, could we redecorate what was your room?"

He scrunched his nose. "Is this the time to talk about this?"

Her grin widened. "I have a wedding present for you...Daddy."

His heart leapt within him, tears filled his eyes. *Lord, does she mean? Are you not only giving her back to me whole, but a child as well?* "Daddy? Niamh, are you pregnant?"

Niamh nodded, tears glistening in her eyes. "Yeah. Two weeks before the car crash, when we made up the fight. 'Sides you did say barefoot, in a shift and pregnant. I'm just fulfilling the obey part of the vows." She kissed him. "I love you."

He lowered his face to hers, kissing her, not caring they were the center of attention. Everything was all right. God willing, they'd get their happily ever after.